SONS OF PRIVILEGE

BIKER

#2

MIKE BARON

WOLFPACK
PUBLISHING
— EST 2013 —

SONS OF PRIVILEGE

STAN

AS TEN THOUSAND UNIVERSITY OF WISCONSIN students prepared for commencement, three friends gathered in the Brat Haus on State Street, a Madison institution for over fifty years. Stan Newton, Luke Askew and Morris Silverstein were members of the Delta Tau fraternity housed in a three-story brick Federalist revival up Langdon. Six feet, blond and buff, Stan closed his phone, turned to his friends and hoisted his fifth mug of Mutiny IPA.

"That was my dad. I just got a tryout with the Broncos," he said, grinning.

"No way!" Luke said.

Morris punched him on the shoulder. "Dude!" Morris turned to the buzzing room, which held three dozen. "Hey! Listen up! My man Stan *Newton* just got a tryout with the Broncos!"

Boozy cheers and applause.

"Way to go!"

"What's wrong with the Pack?"

"Traitor!"

Stan upended his mug and glugged, slamming it on the wood bar top. "What the fuck was I thinking majoring in poli sci?"

"You want fries with that?" Morris said.

"But you minored in queer theory," Luke said, ducking as Stan threw a fake punch.

"Morris is so stupid he signed up for queer theory to meet chicks!" Luke said.

"But seriously, when's the tryout?" Morris said. He was a short, wiry Jew with curly black hair in profusion and a dorsal fin nose.

"They're flying me out at the end of June. They're paying for two, so I'm gonna ask Ellie." Ellie was Stan's girlfriend, a business major who also played varsity volleyball.

"What about the Packers?" Morris said.

"They looked but they didn't buy," Stan said. "They already got their white running back." He took out his phone. "Hang on. I gotta tell Ellie." He dialed her number and walked out of the buzzing building to State Street, still popping at eleven thirty on a Friday night. Ellie belonged to the Tri Gammas and didn't pick up.

"Babes! I got a tryout with the Broncos at the end of June! Want to go to Denver?" Ellie's social calendar was even crazier than his. Just finishing her junior year, Ellie had a 4.0 grade-point average and a room stuffed with trophies for gymnastics, volleyball and skiing.

Next he phoned his sister, Fig. Another overachiever! She didn't answer, so he left the same message.

When Stan returned to the bar there was a full mug waiting. He eyed it dubiously. "Jeez I don't know."

Luke nudged him. "Don't be a pussy. You're not driving anywhere."

What the hell. Stan had been a good boy throughout the year, only getting shit-faced once or twice. With his heavy schedule it couldn't be otherwise. In addition to carrying sixteen credits, he'd had football practice and games through December and regularly played handball throughout the winter to stay in shape. Now that it was spring, he was back to running five miles a day or riding his bicycle around Lake Mendota.

Stan stared at the mug. The garnet in his class ring caught the bar light and gleamed like a ruby.

"Do it!" Luke said.

"Do it!" Morris said.

"Do it, do it, do it!" Luke and Morris yelled. The crowd picked up the chant.

"DO IT, DO IT, DO IT!"

To cheers and applause, Stan picked up the mug and chugged it. When he finished, he set the mug on the bar, wiped his mouth with the back of his hand and belched like a buffalo.

"That's it, fellas!" Stan declared, heading for the door. "I'm gonna crash."

Morris turned to Luke. "Maybe we should go with him."

"Nah," Luke said. "Let that pussy go. The night is young."

Stan exited to the State Street transit mall, weaving around cyclists and bar hoppers down Lake Street toward Langdon, a street lined with fraternities and university buildings, bookended by the towering redbrick Roman towers of the Science Building on one end and the Edgewater on the other.

Stan had to piss. In his inebriated state he let propriety slide, walked through the Student Union parking lot onto the pier that extended into Lake Mendota. He stood on the end of the pier gazing up at the full moon and splattering of stars, pissing into the lake while hearing faint shouts and music from the Union.

"Hey!" a girl shouted in outrage. Stan quickly zipped and headed back, feeling a vague sense of guilt. He walked down the lakefront past Lowell Hall. He had gone perhaps a hundred yards, wending through frat house backyards, when someone called to him from the shadows.

"Yo dude." Stan paused and looked around. Was someone calling him? The guy had a Latino accent.

"Yo dude, over here!" the voice hissed with urgency. "I got something for choo!"

"What?" Stan said. Was someone playing with him? Frat brothers? "I'm fuckin' drunk, dude! Don't mess with me."

There was a rush from the undergrowth, the sound of twigs breaking and powerful hands seized Stan by the arms and shoulders and propelled him toward the water.

THE INSANE ASSHOLES

CRAZY JACK'S WAS A BIKER ROADHOUSE OUTSIDE Waunakee on State Highway BB. At ten thirty on a Saturday night in the first week of June, three Insane Assholes out of the Quad Cities roared into the gravel parking lot and parked their choppers on the strip in front of the porch. A sign said, MOTORCYCLE PARKING ONLY.

Josh Pratt watched them enter from his perch at the bar near the front door. Pratt, a licensed private investigator, worked club security when he couldn't get detective work. He was a bouncer. The Assholes looked like trouble. First, their name. Second, their colors: a hand flipping the bird with FUCK YOU tatted on the knuckles. And their size and demeanor—big guys with shaved skulls, two with beards, eyes and nostrils rimmed red. Josh exchanged a glance with Clarence Peet, Crazy Jack's owner and bartender.

Crazy Jack's had been cited twice the previous year, once for serving a minor and once for permitting a motorcycle race inside the bar. Clarence had removed all the chairs and tables surrounding the rectangular bar during Bike Week, as choppers struggled for traction on the hardwood and sawdust floor.

It was a miracle they still had their liquor license.

The Spencer Davis Group's "Gimme Some Lovin'" was blasting on the juke as the three Assholes commandeered a booth as soon as the couple sitting there got up to play pool. Josh kept an eye out to see if the couple complained. It was his third week on the job and thus far he'd had to eject only five patrons, none of whom had put up much of a fight. Josh was a solid five-ten with a buzz cut and the tail end of a dragon tat peeking up over his collar. He had a scarred brow and fighter's eyes. His tank top revealed blue-tatted sleeves. He picked up his ginger ale and took a sip.

The middle-aged couple looked at where the Assholes had taken their booth and left. The tavern was near its 150 capacity, patrons standing three deep at the bar. Bourgeois Bohemians rubbed shoulders with rednecks and bikers. Josh caught a whiff of marijuana but it was beneath his notice. He was there for the rough stuff. He watched the waitress, Cassandra, who would have fit right in at Hooter's, take the Assholes' orders. A hand reached up to touch her and she stepped back.

It was dim in the bar, lit primarily by strings of Christmas lights surrounding the mirror and by track lights along the ceiling, most of them focused on paintings by local artists, each with a little tag showing provenance and price. Most of the paintings were of Wisconsin landscapes. Several were of cows. Clarence filled wicker baskets on the bar with peanuts, which he scooped out of a wooden barrel. Peanut shells crunched underfoot. A few minutes later Cassandra approached Josh with a worried expression.

"Josh, they're laying out lines on the table."

"Who? The Insane Assholes?"

She gave a tight little nod and Josh sighed. He didn't relish confronting outlaws pumped on meth or blow or whatever they were snorting. Maybe it was animal tranquilizer, which had the opposite of its intended effect. The fact that they were jammed in a booth worked in Josh's favor. They couldn't all jump him at once, not until they got outside. The last thing Clarence wanted was a police visit.

Josh headed over. It took him a few minutes to negotiate the SRO crowd but at last he stood at the end of the dark booth looking down at the Insane Assholes. They stank of body odor and were passing a copy of *The Horse*, on which lay several white lines trailing off into smears.

"Gentlemen, I'm going to have to ask you to put that shit away."

The Asshole nearest him looked up. He had prominent cheekbones, a spade jaw and a pointed skull that gave his head a diamond shape, a nose stud and pierced ears. His eyes were feral creatures peeking out from subterranean dens. His denim vest was covered with flash, including

IIWWII,the diamond One Percent patch and his name, BUDDHA, over his rank, PRESIDENT.

"Fuck off!" he said.

"Gentlemen, I'm going to have to ask you to leave."

Buddha erupted like Mt. St. Helens, standing and using his bulk to bull Josh back. Josh stuck out his right hand as if to shake. Buddha stared at it and automatically responded, squeezing with all his might. Josh let his hand relax and used his left hand to seize Buddha's index and middle finger, which he bent sharply back, using his right hand to pop the elbow up so that Buddha's arm was straight. Applying minute but painful pressure, Josh used his leverage to walk Buddha toward the front door.

"You're dead, motherfucker, dead!" Buddha snarled, but there was nothing he could do to escape Josh's grip.

It took the other Assholes a minute for it to register, by which time there were patrons between them and Josh. They boiled out of the booth and bull-rushed the front door, knocking people down. Just inside the door, Josh used his leverage to turn Buddha between him and the Assholes.

Clarence opened the front door and Josh pulled Buddha out, like a reluctant bull, and sent him sprawling down the front steps. Josh whirled and sidestepped the next biker, throwing a knee into his gut. The biker grunted and bent over. Josh kicked him in the ass as the third biker picked up one of the wooden kitchen chairs on the porch and swung it at Josh's head. Josh went under the chair, tackled the biker and took him to the ground, landing with a knee on his sternum, and transitioned into an arm bar as he'd been taught by Nelson Ferreira of the Zhong Yi Kung Fu Academy in Madison.

Technically, it wasn't Zhong Yi, it was Brazilian jiu-jitsu. Nelson taught a little bit of everything.

As the biker grunted, Clarence stepped out of his bar cradling a shotgun. Several other patrons came out with him.

Josh said, "If I break your arm, you won't be able to ride."

"Uncle," the biker said. Josh let him up.

Buddha got to his feet and plucked a shard of broken glass from his arm, fixing Josh with a basilisk stare. "You're dead, motherfucker. You ever hear of the Jesuit? Huh? No? Well he's our brother."

Clarence ratcheted a shell into the chamber. "The cops will be here any second."

They heard the wail of a siren getting closer. The Assholes got on their chops, started their engines with a cacophonous roar and left the parking lot amid a haze of exhaust. They turned left on the highway and motored down the road. Minutes later a Dane County sheriff's car pulled into the lot, light bar flashing. Clarence and Josh walked over as the big deputy got out, wearing a Smokey hat.

"What happened?" he said.

Clarence told him. The deputy spoke into his shoulder mike. "Dotty, this is Phil. We have three Insane Assholes headed east on BB, possibly armed and dangerous and carrying controlled substances."

He got back in his whip. "You boys be good now." He pulled out as a girl on a red Honda Hawk GT pulled into the lot. Despite a full-face helmet, Josh could tell it was a girl from her svelte frame, the ponytail peeking out behind and her pink Hello Kitty backpack.

Clarence went back in as the girl backed her bike up to the rail, got off and put it on the center stand. She took off her helmet and shook out her blond hair. She was in her mid-twenties and beautiful, wearing a short red leather jacket and girl's khakis that cupped her ass like aggies in a velvet bag. She came up the steps.

"I'm looking for Josh Pratt," she said.

CHAPTER 3

FIG NEWTON

"I'M PRATT," JOSH SAID.

"I'm Charlotte Newton. Are you a private investigator?"

"When I can get work."

"Can I talk to you for a minute?"

Josh looked around. All the patrons had returned to the bar. Bob Seger boomed from inside. "Sure."

"Two weeks ago my brother, Stan died on the way home from a State Street bar. The cops say it was accidental but I think he was murdered."

Josh gestured to a slat bench and sat. "Tell me about it."

Charlotte shrugged off her backpack and sat. "He drowned. Stan was an excellent swimmer. He wasn't stupid and he didn't skinny dip."

"Was he naked when they found him?"

"Yes. They found his clothes piled on a pier nearby but

his wallet was empty. And his class ring was gone. He never took it off. The cops say some passing shitbird probably cleaned him out." She passed him a much folded, frayed magazine scrap. It was an ad for the UW class ring for 2015 with a brilliant red stone.

"How did you hear about me?"

"Detective Calloway. He's in charge of the case, and he told me if I wasn't satisfied with the investigation I should talk to you. He also told me to save my money."

"Why do you think he was murdered?"

Charlotte fixed her intense green eyes on him. "In the last ten years, fifteen college athletes have been found drowned. All of them were on their way home after a night of drinking. All the campuses are near water. In almost every case cops found a smiley face drawn on a nearby wall."

"The Smiley Face Killings?" Josh said. "That's been investigated. They said it was a hoax."

Charlotte gripped Josh's wrist. "Calloway said that if anybody could get to the bottom of this, you could. I will pay you."

"I get two hundred a day plus expenses."

Charlotte reached into her backpack and withdrew a man's wallet, peeling out six hundred-dollar notes. "Here's an advance."

Josh tucked it into his Harley wallet. "Would you like a receipt?"

"No thanks. I trust you."

"Why?" Josh said.

"Calloway told me a little about you. You're born again, right?"

Josh nodded.

"That's good enough for me."

"Are you Christian?" Josh said.

"I'm a lapsed Catholic. But I'm not stupid enough to ignore what religion can do for a man. Especially those who find God in prison."

"Calloway told you I was a con?"

"No. I googled you. I read about that business last year with the Munz family. Such a tragedy. It was an article in the *Wisconsin State Journal*, I think, that mentioned you'd done time."

"I was very fortunate that Frank Dorgan was the chaplain."

Josh hadn't spoken with Dorgan in over a year. He vowed to talk to the man who had brought him into the light and introduced him to the blues.

"Well I've met a few born-agains that came out of prison, and they were all solid citizens. My father's a developer too. Ludlow Newton. He built Zebrawood and right now he's got a fifty-four-acre site under development in Mazo. My dad's no Bible-thumper but he believes in giving people second chances. He's employed dozens of ex-cons over the years, and no one who was born again has ever burned him."

"Any of 'em come from Waupun?" Josh wondered if Chaplain Frank had worked his magic with them too.

"Probably."

"Does he employ ex-cons now?"

"Sure. Why?"

"No reason."

They stopped as two Harleys rumbled into the lot. The bikes were new and shiny and cost over twenty-five grand apiece. The pot-bellied, tatted, bearded dudes who got off were two lawyers Josh recognized from a bar association meeting he'd attended at the request of Steve Fleiss, his go-to lawyer. Fleiss funneled process work to Josh, and had even talked about getting the Discovery Channel to do a reality show.

An ex-con, born-again, motorcycle hoodlum process server. It was a natural.

One of the lawyers recognized Josh and waved. Josh waved back.

Charlotte reached into the backpack and withdrew a manila envelope.

Josh shook it out. It contained black-and-white glossies of Stan, with a football, with a basketball, with a bicycle, a list of his friends and contact information, a copy of the police report and Charlotte's card, which read, CHARLOTTE M. NEWTON, ALGORITHMS, INC.

He tucked it away and handed her one of his. "I report every couple of days. If there are important developments I'll contact you as soon as I can. How do you like that Hawk?"

"I love it! It's like a ten-speed. I can park it anywhere. Which one is yours?"

Josh pointed to his modified Road King.

Charlotte stood. "Sweet. Call me Fig. Everybody does."

THE SMILEY FACE KILLINGS

Wary of possible retaliation, Josh took a circuitous route home to his modest ranch house on Ptarmigan Road, on Madison's far southwest side. When he'd moved there it was the only residence for a half mile in either direction, surrounded by farmland. Since then developers had transformed the landscape with million-dollar McMansions, whose owners now regarded him as a threat to property values.

It was just past one as he eased his heavily modified Road King into his two-car garage, which housed three motorcycles and parts for several more. His gray, ten-year-old Honda Accord sat in the driveway. It was so old it had crank windows. He entered his home from the garage and thought about getting a dog who would greet him with leaps and licks. A year ago he'd agreed to locate his neighbors' two missing schnauzers, which led him to an encounter with a hoodlum named Moon and a certain degree of notoriety.

They were Dave Lowry's dogs, and Dave was the only guy on the street who hadn't signed a petition to the Madison City Council demanding that Josh remove the '68 Camaro on cinderblocks from his front yard, control the weeds and mow the damned lawn. In fact, Dave had threatened petition signers he knew with exposure. Dave raised funds for UW. He had a lot of dirt on the town. It was a regular Peyton Place—the bank president who snorted coke, the insurance exec who was screwing his son's girlfriend.

Josh had been lucky to have avoided domestic surveillance jobs throughout most of his short career. Even so, he had learned and seen things that would gag a dog off a gut wagon. He had to live with what he'd seen. It wasn't always easy, and sometimes at night he took Benadryl and Trazodone to help him sleep. When nothing else worked he bowed his head and said, "It's in your hands, Lord."

He lay in bed a long time, thinking about the Assholes, the case and Fig. He thought too much about Fig. There was something about a girl on a bike.

He slept until nine, made a pot of coffee, put on his sweats, ran five miles, showered and made himself breakfast of toast and peanut butter. By then it was ten. He phoned Madison Detective Heinz Calloway, his go-to guy on the force. It went to voicemail. Josh went online and researched the Smiley Face Killings.

Two NYC police detectives, Kevin Gannon and Anthony Duarte, believed that over a dozen university students who had drowned near their campuses had been murdered by either a serial killer or a gang. In each case, smiley face graffiti had been found near the bodies. The LaCrosse, Wisconsin, police, in charge of eight of these investigations, insisted that the men had all drowned accidentally because they were drunk.

The FBI had issued the following statement:

The FBI has reviewed the information about the victims provided by two retired police detectives, who have dubbed these incidents the "Smiley Face Murders," and interviewed an individual who provided information to the detectives. To date, we have not developed any evidence to support links between these tragic deaths or any evidence substantiating the theory that these deaths are the work of a serial killer or killers. The vast majority of these instances appear to be alcohol-related drownings. The FBI will continue to work with the local police in the affected areas to provide support as requested.

He googled "Jesuit" and got the usual information on the Society of Jesus and the Franciscan Order. When he combined it with motorcycle gangs, he uncovered two Jesuit MCs, both composed of Catholic bikers.

Calloway phoned back at eleven and they agreed to meet for lunch on the Student Union terrace. Slipping into a backpack, Josh headed downtown at one, parked in one of the cycle slots across the street and crossed Langdon to the Student Union, passing informational tables for Queers for Palestine, the Young Communist Alliance and the Ban Fracking movement. A girl with a big cardboard box filled with kittens held one out as Josh passed.

"Do you need a kitten?"

"No thanks," he said.

Josh made his way through the crowded Union, passing a long line at the Babcock Ice Cream counter, through the gloomy Rathskellar, out the double doors onto the terrace, chockablock with students, teachers, lawyers, government officials and aged hippies who still hadn't weaned themselves off the university thirty years after they'd dropped out.

Calloway motioned to him from a table down by the waterfront and stood as Josh approached. Calloway, the MPD gangs expert, was a six-foot-four black man with graying hair, a summer-weight gray suit and a wandering eye that put Marty Feldman to shame. A fresh brat and a beer in a plastic cup waited. Josh took off the backpack, set it on a chair and sat.

"Thank you sir," he said, picking up the brat.

Calloway dug into his second brat. After a while he said, "What?"

"Charlotte Newton asked me to look into her brother's death. I know you wouldn't have sent her to me if you didn't have unanswered questions, so the question I have is, have you guys given up on the investigation?"

One eye looked at Josh, the other stared into the sky. "Coroner says accidental death. Case closed."

"But you don't believe it."

"We were never called in to investigate. Now I don't buy into this smiley face crap, but I do find it peculiar that a gifted athlete could drown in four feet of water, even if he was shitfaced.

His fraternity brothers say no way. Said Newton could hold his beer. Said many's the night they'd seen him stumble home without a problem. Hey, the little lady's got money and you need the work. Or do you like bouncing?"

"May I see the coroner's report?"

Calloway boosted his old-fashioned leather barrister's case onto the table and took out a manila envelope. Josh slipped it into his backpack.

"Did you find a smiley face?"

"We didn't look for one."

"And where was this?"

Calloway nodded toward the capitol. "Right up the street. You can walk over after lunch."

SHRED HUSL

JOSH TOLD CALLOWAY ABOUT HIS ENCOUNTER
the previous night.

"They got those three Assholes in County right now,"
Calloway said. "Picked 'em up in Waunakee on a traffic
violation. Two of 'em are brothers. The Culligan brothers.
A two-man crime wave. Don't worry. They won't be going
anywhere soon."

"What are they doing up here?" Josh said.

"We found a half key of meth in a saddlebag. Probably
on their way to the Dells to do a little business, steppin' on
T-Bird toes. We're getting reports of other Assholes in the
Upper Midwest and rumors that the T-Birds aren't about
to sit back and watch these carpetbaggers steal their turf."

"Is there going to be trouble?"

Calloway shrugged. "Ho-Chunk doubled their security.
More bikers than usual." He looked at his watch.

"Gotta go. You find anything you let me know, right?"

"I will. Thanks for the referral."

Disposing of their trash, they parted ways at the parking lot. Josh headed up the lakeshore path to the drowning site, readily visible from behind the Union. He walked behind Lowell Hall to where the pier jutted fifty feet into Lake Mendota, walked to the end of the pier, squatted and looked down. There was too much algae to see the bottom, but Josh knew from experience it was only about four feet deep. From his crouch he looked back at the shoreline, with its piers sticking into the green water in a gentle curve ending at the Edgewater Hotel a quarter mile up.

Most of the buildings belonged to the university. The rest were fraternities and sororities. It was university policy to remove graffiti immediately, the others not so much. It had been two weeks since Stan's death. Josh walked back to shore and worked his way methodically toward the Edgewater, examining the graffiti, which ranged in scale from simple gang signs on transfer boxes to more elaborate murals sprayed in the dead of night on the backs of the fraternity houses. Two kids in cutoffs stood on scaffolding painting over graffiti on the back wall of the Delta Tau house. They'd started from the top down and hadn't got very far, leaving most of it visible.

"Hey you guys," Josh said. The painters, who stood about ten feet off the ground, turned to look. Typical jock college students, no shirts, sockless tennis shoes, a hank of blond bangs on one, buzz cut on the other.

"Whassup, man?" Buzz Cut said.

"How long has this graffiti been here?"

"Couple weeks. Why?"

"Mind if I take a look?"

"Knock yourself out," Buzz Cut said.

"A portion of tarp hung over some of the defacement. Long, looping letters spelled SHRED HUSL in red and gold, like incomprehensible hieroglyphs on a modern tomb. Josh stepped under the scaffolding and lifted the edge of the canvas tarp. More incomprehensible lettering, and tucked up beneath a window frame, no larger than a saucer, a smiley face with Xs for eyes.

He stepped back, pulled out his cell phone and took a picture.

"What are you doing?" the guy with bangs said.

"Doing a study on gang graffiti," Josh said.

Bangs wrinkled his nose. "Gangs? Only gangs around here are frats."

"Maybe. Who wrote 'Shred Husl?' You guys know a Shred Husl?"

They looked at each other. "Nope," Buzz Cut said. "Could be anyone. Lotta skaters come down here from the burbs to look at girls and smoke dope on the terrace."

Josh thanked them and booked. He walked between buildings up to Langdon and emerged opposite the Hillel Building, where two dark-haired students were scrubbing away at a swastika.

Outside the Student Union, Josh paused at a kiosk for flyers and posters. As he watched, a trim young man in slacks and a knit shirt with neatly combed hair stapled a poster to the kiosk. UW YOUNG REPUBLICANS it said, with a date, time and address. As soon as the stapler moved off, a kid who'd been sitting on a bench rolling his skateboard back and forth sprang up, tore down the poster and tossed it in a trash can.

At home Josh went online and googled the X-eyed happy face. There were numerous versions but none quite like the one he'd photographed. He went to the FBI website and examined gang symbols. He sent a copy of his photo to the LaCrosse police, asking them if they'd seen anything similar.

Josh e-mailed Calloway asking if he'd ever heard of Shred Husl. A google search produced a Wikipedia entry: Shred Husl is the fictional hero of a series of hard-boiled crime novels written by the pseudonymous "Curtis Mack," from 1974 to 1978. All are set in the world of black pimps, players, and private eyes, and were published by the Onyx Press. Titles include Tear the Roof Off the Sucker, Take It to the Max, and Stop Killing Me. Modern scholars compare Mack to Donald Goines, Icepick Slim, and Malcolm X.

Josh requested the police reports on three accidental drownings from the LaCrosse PD.

He was back at Crazy Jack's by seven; still light out, with plenty of time for dinner.

CRAZY JACK'S

JOSH EASED HIS WAY THROUGH A SCRUM OF yuppies at the door, youngsters in cargo shorts, Crocs, Birkenstocks and knit shirts.

"Excuse me," he said, parting the crowd with his palms pressed together in front of him. Crazy Jack's offered 150 brands of microbrews, with two dozen on tap, and had been featured in *Madison* magazine as a "place to be seen." It was early Sunday evening and at least two dozen patrons filled the bar, playing darts and pool and drinking beer. Brewers vs. Rockies played silently on four flat-screens suspended from the ceiling. Josh made his way to the bar and caught Cassandra's eye.

"What'll it be, Josh?" she said.

"Can I get a cheeseburger and a root beer?"

"What kind of root beer? We've got A&W, American National, Badger, Barq's, Bayer's, Bells, Big Daddy, Big Frosty, Big K, Big Y, Billy Goat, Bingo, Blue Sky, Bob-by's..."

Josh held a hand up. "Badger."

"How do you want that burger?"

"Medium."

Cassandra turned her order in and Josh turned around, elbows on the bar, and surveyed the crowd. Clarence came over and set a foaming mug in front of Josh and said, "Mellow crowd tonight."

"I'll take it."

"Don't get me wrong," Clarence said. "I don't mind bikers. Hell. This bar was built by bikers and they can be sweet as pie."

"Soon you'll be hanging ferns and showing soccer games," Josh said.

Clarence laughed. "Not as long as I'm here. You couldn't pay me to watch soccer." Clarence had a devilish gleam in his eye.

"What?" Josh said.

"Nothing. Here comes your burger."

Cassandra set the white plate down on the bar. It held a fat burger with lettuce and pickles peeking out, a side of cole slaw and a bag of chips. Josh reached for his wallet.

What the fuck?! His wallet was gone!

Clarence and Cassandra laughed. Clarence held out his hand. "I told you!"

Cassandra reached into her apron, removed a five and slapped it to Clarence.

"Where's my wallet?" Josh said.

Clarence motioned and one of the yuppies from the entrance came over. He was in his early twenties, long brown hair gathered in a ponytail, grin displaying big horsey teeth. He reached behind him and slapped Josh's oversized Harley wallet, chain dangling, on the counter.

"Josh," Clarence said, "meet Elliott Homolka. Elliott's a prestidigitator."

"A what?" Josh said.

"A master of sleight of hand," Elliott said. "One who practices legerdemain. How do you do?"

They shook hands.

"Elliott also does card tricks and magic," Cassandra said.

"I'll be at the Cardinal Friday and Saturday night," Elliott said. "Bring your friends!" He held his hand up and snapped his fingers, and a business card magically appeared. He handed it to Josh.

ELLIOTT HOMOLKA

PRESTIDIGITATION, SLEIGHT OF HAND, LEG-
ERDEMAIN, CARD TRICKS, MAGIC

Josh slipped it in his wallet and gave the magician one of his.

"I could disappear things and hand your card out to people," Elliott said. "Fifteen percent, that's all I ask."

"Let me think on it," Josh said.

A cheer rose as the Brewers scored a run. Josh periodically checked his phone but it was Sunday evening and nobody had gotten back to him. When Clarence came over Josh said, "Clarence, I won't be here tomorrow. I'm working a case."

Clarence nodded. "Okay. I'll call Joe."

Two hours later several dozen people surrounded Elliott as he did card tricks, pulled things from peoples' ears and slid shot glasses around on the tabletop, daring people to pick the one over the silver dollar. Even when they thought they saw the silver dollar under the shot glass, they were wrong.

Josh stayed until twelve thirty, closing time, then split. Once again he took a roundabout route just in case.

STRANGE

AFTER HIS MORNING RUN JOSH SHOWERED and went online. A LaCrosse homicide detective named Bart Strange had responded to his inquiry.

Dear Mr. Pratt: I was chief investigator in the drowning death of Theodore Grant, a senior at the University of Wisconsin, LaCrosse, who was found drowned on July 16, 2011. Although my partner and I suspected homicide, we were overruled by the district attorney at the time. We found graffiti identical to what you sent us on a wall not far from where Grant was drowned. LaCrosse has seen increasing gang activity over the years, most of it due to an influx of gang members from Chicago. Most notably, there is a strong Black Disciple presence in the city as well as members of a Latino gang called Los Machados.I would be happy to compare notes with you if you are interested.

Josh phoned Strange and arranged to meet him in La-Crosse at one. LaCrosse was two hours away via interstate, three hours the way Josh rode, through the Kettle Moraine country that was southwestern Wisconsin. The glaciers had stopped about halfway down the state, and their runoff had created a wonderland of wooded hills, streams and valleys. Josh never tired of it.

He checked his tires, gassed up, assed up and headed west on 14: Cross Plains, Black Earth, Mazomanie, Spring Green, Gotham. There was no statue of Batman in Gotham, population 200. He reached LaCrosse at twelve thirty and rode down to the waterfront to take a look at where they'd found Grant, off East Avenue across from Green Island. The city maintained a park on the Mississippi across from the bluffs of Minnesota.

The UW campus was inland, not far from the river. You could jog from campus to the river in five minutes. Nothing was far in LaCrosse. In addition to the UW, LaCrosse was also home to Western International University and Viterbo, a Catholic Franciscan college.

Josh kicked out in a narrow parking lot fronting the water and walked to the levee. A bronze plaque noted that it was the site of one of the earliest French trading forts, dating back to 1789. According to the police report an early morning jogger had noticed a body in the water. It was the fifth drowning of a college student in the past five years in LaCrosse. Of the five, four had been students either at UW or Western Reserve. All were ruled accidental, or "death by misadventure."

Four of the victims had high levels of alcohol in their blood. The fifth had been in the water too long to tell.

Josh turned his attention to those surfaces that invited graffiti. The LaCrosse Parks Department maintained the place in sparkling condition. Graffiti disappeared overnight. Still, Josh managed to find some, most of it on the sides of the concrete level where someone had to go out on rocks, constantly swept with river water, to reach those surfaces. Or they might have done it upside down lying on their belly.

The graffiti looked like alien lettering to Josh but he took photos anyway.

Josh arrived at Culvert's Restaurant at one thirty. There was a city charger with a light bar in the lot. Strange was a big, pink blond Swede who stood as Josh entered. Strange wore a gray seersucker sport jacket over a white shirt, had a hand like a boxing glove.

"Thanks for seeing me," Josh said, sliding in opposite.

"If you want something, you got to go to the counter," Strange said.

Josh got a coffee. As he sat, Strange slid a manila envelope across the Formica tabletop. "There are the autopsy and police reports on five drownings that occurred here in LaCrosse during the past five years, all involving college-age white males. No signs of violence on any of the bodies."

"But you don't think they were accidental."

Strange shrugged. "I wanted to pursue it but my chief said no. He said the FBI already gave it a shot and came a cropper. It bothers me, I don't mind telling you.

I've got a kid in college in Minneapolis. Football scholarship. I told him to watch his drinking and don't stay out at night, but he's nineteen, y'know? Thinks he's immortal."

"What about the smiley face?" Josh said.

Strange leaned in, his pale blue eyes intense. "I saw it. Montgomery Hastings, three years ago. We found him in the river off Bainbridge Street on French Island. He'd been out late drinking. I walked the scene and I saw the face you sent on a concrete abutment on I-90 where it crosses French Island."

"Who's your gang guy?"

"That would be Emmett Rawlins. Good guy. Let me give you his phone number."

Josh took out his pad and pen. "You know about the deaths nationally."

Strange nodded. "I looked into it. I contacted the FBI. They said it was not a priority."

"Okay," Josh said. "I've thought about this and for all these murders to occur in all these places, somebody had to get the word out. And all I could think of was the internet. So suppose you were a criminal mastermind and you had a hard-on for white college-age males. How would you do it?"

Strange nodded. "I came to the same conclusion. I contacted the FBI's cyber unit, and while they didn't know squat about the Smiley Face Killings, they had a lot to say about disseminating information."

Strange's cell phone chimed. He looked at it. "The FBI said someone would most likely use an invite-only authenticated web forum. Whoever controls the forum can give out passwords so only the people he wants can read what he posts. He would send his message as an encrypted data file via a torrent program. Each recipient can download and view his message with little effort. You would never be able to find this forum without knowing where to look. There's a lot more and it's highly technical, but that's the gist of it."

Josh handed Strange his card. Strange took it and gave Josh one of his.

"Could you send me the report discussing those forums?" Josh said.

"Sure. Will you keep me up to date on your investigation?"

"No problem."

Strange stood. "Nice meeting you. I have to get going."

FRAT HOUSE

JOSH WAS BACK IN MADISON BY THREE THIRTY. He rode downtown, rolled his bike up onto the Delta Tau sidewalk and kicked out. Several members came out to admire the bike. Josh took out his card.

"Dudes, Stan Newton's sister, Charlotte, hired me to look into his death."

"Right on," said a tall, gangly kid with knobby knees, wearing a gray sweatshirt with the sleeves cut off. "None of us believes he drowned accidentally."

"Even when he was drunk, Stan could slam dunk," said another.

"Any of you guys know if Stan had any enemies?"

"Come in the house, why don'tcha," said the gangly kid. "You want a beer?"

They led Josh to a man cave living room with an enormous flat-screen, various game yokes and consoles, a shelf filled with athletic trophies and a collection of mismatched furniture. Josh planted himself on a busted sofa among four frat bros and took out his notepad.

"Who wanted Stan dead?" he said.

"That bitch Wanda, but I doubt she'd have the strength to drown him," said a kid with a shock of red hair.

"That guy Randy something who he beat out for running back," said another. They wanted to help, but there were no serious threats to Stan among anyone they knew. It was all conjectural.

"Are you guys aware of the so-called Smiley Face Killings?" Josh said.

They looked at one another and shrugged.

"Were any of you with him the night he died?"

The gangly kid raised his hand. "Morris was too."

"Mind if I take a look at his room?"

The redhead stood. "Sure. But the cops came by and then his girlfriend came by and then his sister came by and pretty much cleaned it out."

"Stan's sister is hot!" the gangly kid said.

"I'd fuck her," said another.

Josh followed them up the stairs to the second floor, where they showed him a dorm-sized room in the back with a view of Lake Mendota. Wall posters included UW football, Ronda Rousey and Megyn Kelly. The room contained a monastic bed, a wooden desk and a shag rug. A copy of *The Last Days of Krypton* lay on the bed table. Gangly stood in the doorway, hands on hips, while Josh searched. He lifted up the mattress, got down on his knees and looked under the bed. Nothing but dust bunnies. He checked the closet.

"Ellie took everything," the kid said. "And what she didn't take, the sister did."

Josh sat down at the desk. There was a gooseneck lamp and a small stack of magazines, including *American Lawyer*, *Sports Illustrated*, *Maxim* and *The American Spectator*. He pulled out the center drawer: paperclips, rubber bands, pens, a flash drive and a cardboard folder containing the previous semester's class schedule. Josh held up the folder.

"May I take these?"

"Sure," Gangly said. "Does Charlotte, like, think Stan was murdered?"

Josh shrugged. "That's what we're trying to determine."

"I'm Luke," the kid said.

They shook hands. "Nice to meet you, Luke. What about that night? Did you notice anything unusual in the pub? Anybody giving Stan the stink eye? Did he get in a tiff with anyone?"

"No. Nothing like that. We were so blitzed I wouldn't have noticed if they'd served me a glass of peanut butter. I got home about an hour later and went straight to bed. So did Morris. He was the other guy with us. He's not here right now."

"What was Stan studying?"

"Business. I think he wanted to join his old man's firm. He wasn't a slacker or anything. Stan was a smart guy—he knew there was life after football, and he didn't kid himself he could make it in the pros."

Josh wrote it down, thanked Luke and left. He stopped at a Rocky Rococo and bought a "personal" pizza, stuck it in his tank bag and went home, where he sat out on his back deck, ate the pizza and looked at the course schedule.

INTRO TO ACCOUNTING 601
STATS: MEASUREMENT IN ECONOMICS 641
CONTRACTS 711
APPLIED STATISTICS FOR ENGINEERS 491
POLITICS IN MULTI-CULTURAL SOCIETIES 201
INTRO TO FILM NOIR 102

Well, a kid had to have some fun. Total credits: 16. An ambitious program for a young man who also played varsity football. The schedule listed Stan's student advisor, Avery Waldrop, the Hewlitt Bascom Professor of Law.

Josh saw nothing that shined light on the situation. He went online and compiled a list of young men who'd drowned on campuses, searching for a link. They were all remarkably similar: white, athletic college students on campuses close to water. All the killings save one occurred on the weekend. Didn't college athletes drink during the week?

Josh read the report by FBI agents Gannon and Duarte. There were over fifteen victims in eleven states. As a group they were cleaner than a decontamination chamber. None of them had police records, and most had also been high school standouts.

Josh knocked off at eight, went out on his back deck and kicked back with a beer. Fireflies began to appear. He'd never chased fireflies as a kid. He hadn't played much. He was too busy dodging his old man.

Josh finished the beer and went to bed.

CURTIS MACK

ON TUESDAY JOSH RAN FIVE MILES, SHOWERED and phoned Stephen Fleiss, the lawyer for whom he often worked. It was just past nine and Fleiss was in his office on King Street just off the Capitol Square.

"What?" the lawyer barked.

"Steve, you went to UW Law, right?"

"Yeah."

Josh looked at Newton's course schedule. "Do you know a Professor Czyrney, a Professor Austin, a Professor Franklin or a Professor Waldrop?"

"I took Czyrney's contracts class. Every law student has to take that. I don't know Waldrop. Why?"

"I'm working a case here and I need to get some background on these people. Can we get together?"

"I'm in court until one and then I have clients all afternoon. You want to hook up around five at the Cardinal?"

"Sure."

"I might have some work for you."

Josh thanked him, went online and looked up the Newton Corporation: "Elegant homes from a half million up." Zebrawood was their most notable accomplishment, sixty-five acres west of Madison—home to the UW athletic director, two retired Packers, the president of Wisconsin Physicians Service and other movers and shakers. Josh looked at the homes. They beggared the modest McMansions on his own street.

Taliesin Associated had designed Newton's home, which resembled a Frank Lloyd Wright design on steroids, with soaring wings and a shake roof reaching for the ground, a tree growing up through the living room. Of course there was no zebrawood in Zebrawood unless it had been imported from Africa.

Josh worked from an office he had created from a spare bedroom in his house. It consisted mainly of a table set beneath a window looking out on the backyard and a line of trees, through which he could see his neighbor's 5,000-square-foot mini-manse and swimming pool.

Not far away, the UW campus called. The coeds weren't hard to look at, the beer was cheap and the terrace was cool. But there was something else as well that Josh always noticed there, an invisible struggle for the souls of students being fought by an entrenched university establishment against "traditional values." Josh grew up in the eighties as an outsider, never staying in one place long enough to make friends.

His old man was a rake and a ne'er-do-well who had abandoned him at a Bosselman's Truck Stop when Josh was fifteen. He'd bounced from foster home to foster home, never really connecting. Some of the families were all right and he was grateful they'd taken him in, but he had no friends to show for it, and kids his age were more concerned with getting laid, getting high and getting style than they were with the meaning of life or doing the right thing.

Josh left the house and rode downtown, parked opposite the Union and went to the kiosk. There were posters soliciting roommates, seeking lost pets, describing the Society for Creative Anachronism and other frivolities. There were posters urging students to demonstrate in support of a black kid shot in Kentucky, to End the Wars and to impeach the governor. Josh sat on the slot bench near the main steps, as out of place as a brick on a table setting. He wore Ray-Bans and spread his tatted sleeves across the back of the bench. Goth coeds smiled at him. Guys ignored him.

Across the street on Library Mall, panhandlers mingled with board punks from the burbs. A refugee from the sixties in serape and ponytail strummed protest songs, hat out for donations. Across the mall a food truck was selling falafel.

Josh used his phone to look for Curtis Mack on Amazon. There was one copy of *Stop Killing Me* in fair condition for $245. Josh had only read one novel in his life, *Huckleberry Finn*, and only because it was required in the prison course he took. Josh liked hard rock, heavy metal and gangster movies. His three favorite movies were

The Godfather, Scarface and *Carlito's Way*, all starring Al Pacino, whom Josh considered America's greatest living actor.

Josh assed up and headed out East Johnson. He'd passed The Little Read Book store countless times since moving to Madison but this was the first time would be going in there. Situated on a commercial block across from a three-story redbrick apartment building, sandwiched between The Rock Shop and Amy's Cafe, The Little Read Book store still sold Chairman Mao's *Little Red Book* as well as the complete works of Howard Zinn, Noam Chomsky and Larry Gonick. A shaggy cat was sleeping in a cat bed in the window next to a cactus and a display of books that hadn't changed in ten years: *Steal This Book. The Wretched of the Earth. The Autobiography of Malcolm X.*

The old door creaked and a bell jingled as Josh entered the small, close space, which smelled of dust and books, oddly pleasing. The store had no air conditioning but remained relatively cool due to its location. Pots of dusty ferns hung from the ceiling. Floor-to-ceiling shelves lined three walls, with one long rack going down the center. Ancient, bent, dusty hand-lettered signs indicated Fiction, Atheism, World History, American History, Homeopathy, Queer Theory, Race Theory and White Privilege.

A long cardboard box held comic books in plastic slips. Josh flipped through Avengers, Savage Dragon, The Badger, Teenage Mutant Ninja Turtles. The only comics he'd ever read were borderline obscene, circulated in prison.

Josh picked up a newly minted pamphlet: *Queer Migration Politics* by Gaia Ruiz, an assistant professor of rhetoric, politics and culture at UW-Madison. Filthy curtains dividing the store from the back parted as a man emerged, five ten with long brown hair like Lennon in his peace phase, smelling of marijuana. The man wore wire-rimmed round glasses and had a beard.

"Help you?"

"Got anything by Curtis Mack?"

The man grinned like Tom Cruise. "Curtis Mack! One of my favorites. His books are very hard to get, you know. I wish someone would republish them, but I think I may have one. Let me check."

The old hippie parted the curtains. Josh heard rummaging, the susurrus of cardboard, and the man re-emerged clutching a book. Put a wizard's hat on him, he could have appeared in *Lord of the Rings*. He laid a weathered paperback on the counter. The cover showed a mack daddy in a full-length leather duster, 'fro peeking out from under his wide-brimmed hat, Fu Manchu, high cheekbones, cool slitted eyes, holding a .45, with a beautiful girl crouched by his feet clutching one of his legs and wearing white go-go boots, hot pants and a halter top, 'fro out to here.

Tear the Roof Off the Sucker by Curtis Mack, published by Onyx Press.

"That's his first book," the man said reverently. "He only wrote four, and the last one, nobody's seen a copy in years."

"How much?" Josh said.

"You gotta understand—this is a collector's item virtually unavailable anywhere."

"How much?"

"Twenty bucks."

Josh peeled off a twenty and gave it to the man. "Got anything else by Curtis Mack?"

"Maybe in the archives. I'd have to go digging."

Josh gave him one of his cards. "If you do, please give me a call."

The man stared at the card. "You're a private investigator?"

"Yes sir."

"Could you find a lost cat?"

Josh laughed. "No. But I know where you can get a new one."

PROCESS

THE CARDINAL BAR HAD BEEN A MADISON institution for decades, a favorite gathering spot for politicians, journalists, gays, musicians and jazz aficionados. Josh parked his bike around back in a place reserved for cycles and went in through the back door on Butler Street. Ben Sidran was playing piano with bass and drums. Ben Sidran had been in the Steve Miller Band and written "Space Cowboy" and "Seasons." Fleiss was at the bar with Dan Dunn and Dave Mandel, two criminal attorneys.

"There he is," Fleiss said as Josh approached. The other two attorneys greeted him. Fleiss bought Josh a beer and they turned toward each other. Fleiss reached inside his jacket pocket and withdrew a legal envelope.

"Give this to Emory Bostwick. His addresses are inside."

Josh took the envelope. "Guy who runs North Country Choppers?"

"Yeah. Right up your alley. His partner's suing him."

"Great," Josh said, stuffing it in his cargo pants. Emory Bostwick was a well-known bike customizer, drunk, meth addict and bully who beat his girlfriends.

"Hey," Fleiss said. "That's why we pay you the big bucks."

Josh put his elbows on the bar and listened to Sidran play Monk, then finished his beer, assed up and booked. On a warm summer Tuesday evening, North Country Choppers, located in an industrial mall in Monona, would still be open.

North Country Choppers occupied an industrial space behind a storage facility between a game company start-up and a cut-rate recording studio. Josh kicked out in front, next to a chopper with an eighty-inch wheelbase, tank painted with skulls, bats, the grim reaper. He entered the showroom, where three hardtails gleamed beneath fluorescent lighting. Bostwick, a hulking man with a gut spilling over his plate-sized buckle, was working a wrench on a bike toward the back. His white hair was a ponytail in back and a beard in front, arms tatted up. He didn't look up.

"Help you?"

Josh walked over. "Are you Emory Bostwick?"

Bostwick looked up with mean little meth-addict eyes. "Who wants to know?"

Josh handed him the envelope, which he automatically took. "This is for you." He turned and walked toward the front.

Bostwick stood. He was six two and weighed about three hundred. "Hey. Hey, motherfucker! I'm talking to you!"

Josh walked through the front door into the evening heat. Bostwick followed.

"You come into my shop and serve me fucking papers?"

Josh got on his bike and started the engine. Bostwick came over and flipped the kill switch.

"What about it, motherfucker? Give me one good reason I shouldn't spread your brains all over the parking lot."

A four-man punk band from the recording studio stood outside taking a smoke break, watching.

Sighing, Josh got off the bike, stepped sideways and around so he couldn't be pushed over his own bike, and stood in Bostwick's face. "Let's go."

Bostwick blinked and stepped back. "Get the fuck outta here."

It was six thirty by the time Josh got home. A student was mowing Dave Lowry's lawn across the street. Josh left his bike in the driveway, went inside and nuked a pizza, which he ate on the back deck with a glass of water, watching a deer pick its way through the narrow stand of trees. He went inside, went online and checked his e-mail.

hello. I AM Larisa IN SEARCH OF A MAN WHO UNDER-STANDS THE MEANING OF LOVE AS TRUST AND FAITH INEACH OTHER RATHER THAN ONE WHO SEES LOVE OF WHAT THE WORLD IS ALL ABOUT AND

AFTER READING YOUR PROFILE I TOOK INTEREST IN YOU SO REPLY TO ME WITH THE SEND TO ME WITH e-mail AND I SEND YOU MY PIC ON ME OK MY EAMIL ADDRESS AT

Hello my dear

my name is ROSE How are you and how is your work hope all is moving fine. i

seek for honest partner and i saw your profile while am browse in [facebook] so i diced

to write to you, in your e-mail address. i will be very glad to read your mail with

all pleasure. it will be nice to meet you and also read from you.

please do honor my invitation so that we can exchange our pictures and

maybe become partner because i have something to tell you. Remember the

distance does not matter what matters is the love we share with each

other. i wait to hear from you soon.

kiss Regards Miss ROSE

There were more. He blocked them all, wondering how they'd got his e-mail address. There were also letters from the wives of recently deceased Nigerian generals trying to give him $6 million if only he would provide certain personal information.

Amid this clutter Bart Strange had sent him the La-Crosse Gang Task Force list of gang activity. Most were black gangs from Chicago but MS-13 had recently appeared and begun marking their territory. Strange had included an attachment identifying certain gang symbols. Josh printed it out to compare with those found in Madison.

He went on Facebook and responded to a friend request from Charlotte Newton. As soon as he did, she instant messaged him. "How's it going?"

"Met with LaCrosse detective investigating college athlete drownings. Part of a pattern."

"I'm aware of the FBI study. What are your feelings?"

"Although I have no hard evidence yet, my gut feeling is it was murder. Do not worry. I have only just begun this investigation."

"Thank you."

Josh knocked off around nine and took *Tear the Roof Off the Sucker* into his bedroom

CHAPTER 11

TEAR THE ROOF OFF THE SUCKER

I SHOULD HAVE KNOWN NOT TO GO THROUGH Baxter, South Carolina. I should have stuck to the interstate, never mind the motherfuckin' pigs cruising up and down the eastern corridor looking for drug runners. I had five keys of Bolivian marching powder in the door panels of my Eldo. It wasn't even tricked out. Just a plain brown Eldo like any square John might drive. I shoulda known a black man don't get no slack. Maybe he'd have let me go if I'd been drivin' some piece of shit Pinto, but he weren't 'bout to let through no nigger in a Cadillac, a car reserved for white folks. Them crackers go into a frenzy, they see a black man in a Cadillac.

So there I was cruising motherfuckin' Main Street in motherfuckin' Baxter and sure as shit a motherfuckin' pig pulls up behind me, hits the lights and the siren. One big yawp. Well I been down this street before. What black man hasn't?

I pulled over, lowered my window, got my license and registration ready to go. And I see this ofay motherfucker get out his Crown Vic. And I think fuck me runnin'. 'Cause this cracker is Baby Huey sized, got a face like a cut ham, a mustache looks like a dust mop and mean little blue eyes. Born in a Cracker Barrel. So I just sit there while he comes up and stands next to me breathing through his mouth.

"License and registration."

I fork 'em over. See his name is Billings. See he's the chief.

"You know why I stopped you, boy?" he says.

"No sir," I says. I sure as shit wasn't breaking any traffic laws.

"You got a faulty taillight."

This is news to me. "You sure, officer?"

"You want to step out the car I'll show you."

So I get out the car real careful like keeping my hands in plain view. Officer Billings got his mitt on the butt of his service revolver. He steps back, nods toward the rear of the car. I walk back there. Pig unlimbers his fucking baton and smashes one of my taillights.

"Like I tell you. That's a fifty-dollar fine right there."

I see where this is going. Crackers gotta eat. So I reach in the pocket of my purple velvet jeans and take out my ostrich skin wallet and I peel off a C-note. "Officer, I sincerely apologize and I hope this will cover the fine." And buy some motherfuckin' donuts.

Pig smiles a little bit and vanishes that C-note like a ho snortin' a line. "Best you get that taillight fixed, boy."

And he's giving me the death eye, looking at my hair out to here, and my silk shirt with the arrow lapels, and my snakeskin boots and the gold chains around my neck and you just know he would love nothing better than to beat me to death with his motherfuckin' taillight breaker.

I get back in my short and ship, thinkin' I will never drive through that fucking cracker-ass burg again.

How wrong I was.

WEDNESDAY

WHEN JOSH RETURNED FROM HIS RUN, HE found a message from Fleiss. Another summons. Josh showered, shaved, ate some stuff and rode downtown, parking in the lawyer's tiny lot off King Street. The two-story stucco building was all legal, with two ambulance chasers on the ground floor and Fleiss, who owned the building, on top. Josh went up the turning staircase beneath a VW-sized skylight and entered Fleiss Law Offices through a glass door with gilt script.

Marcia Haynes was behind the reception desk. She was a svelte fortysomething with short blond hair and ruby-colored glasses. "Go right in, Josh. He's expecting you."

Josh went in. Fleiss leaned back in his high-zoot black mesh chair and stretched. "You know, just the sight of you is enough to make people pay. Got a friend needs collection work."

"Not interested. What else you got?"

Fleiss slid a white envelope across the desk. "This might take a little work. Keep track of your expenses. Aaron Kofsky, CEO of Dovetail, a defense contractor. Lives in Zebrawood but no one's seen him in a week. He has a condo in Cabo."

"I'm involved in a case right now, Steve. Don't know if I can leave town for any length of time."

"What length? Listen. These guys are willing to pay you ten thousand dollars if you can find him and bring him back."

Dollar signs lit up in Josh's skull. "Steve, you know I have no authority to do that."

"Use your powers of persuasion. You can be very persuasive. The ten grand is in addition to your per diem."

Two hundred a day plus expenses added up after a long dry spell. There was no reason he couldn't pursue both Newton and Kofsky. "What's the skinny?"

"All right, this is classified but here's what I know. They got a contract to develop software that can detect darknet and private forums that jihadists might use. They have a hard deadline in two weeks. Kofsky, who was supposed to be leading the charge, went off-radar. His partners say he's one of those creative genius types. He's a little erratic. They figure the pressure got to him and he just bailed, like some kid running away from home. He was seeing a Realtor named Sandy Meyer but she don't know nothin' from nothin'."

"What's darknet?"

Fleiss poked at his computer and read, "'A darknet is a private network where connections are made only between trusted peers—sometimes called 'friends'—using non-standard protocols and ports. Darknets are distinct from other distributed peer-to-peer networks, as sharing is anonymous and therefore users can communicate with little fear of governmental or corporate interference. For this reason, darknets are often associated with dissident political communications and illegal activities. More generally, the term 'darknet' can be used to describe all non-commercial sites on the Internet, or to refer to all 'underground' web communications and technologies, most commonly those associated with illegal activity or dissent.' Thus sprach Wikipedia."

"I go to Cabo, it could add up."

Fleiss waved a hand. "These guys got deep pockets. They say Kofsky likes to gamble. He embezzled $750,000 and they want it back"

"Do you want me to bring him back?"

"That would be ideal," Fleiss said.

"I have no legal authority," Josh said.

"Use your imagination."

"Can't they track him with his cell phone?" Josh said.

"You've been watching too much television. He has a black phone, impossible to track."

Josh opened the envelope and removed several pictures showing a prematurely balding, somewhat plump young man with a halo of frizzy hair and glasses.

"I served Bostwick," Josh said.

"He give you any trouble?"

"No."

"Okay. Thanks, Josh. Mar and I will have you over for a barbecue real soon."

Mar was Fleiss's girlfriend, a public defender. They'd been together fifteen years.

"Cool."

In the parking lot Josh checked his phone. Calloway had called. "Just a heads-up—Insane Assholes bonded out of County yesterday. Shiny side up."

Josh rode down to campus and parked across from the Union again. He couldn't explain his compulsion. He was looking for something but he didn't know what. He got a kick out of the reaction he elicited from coeds and other students. He was obviously older than the average student, and didn't look like one.

There were five other bikes in the narrow slots: two Suzuki X-somethings, a Honda 600 RR, an R1 and an ancient CB 650. Jocks rode those bikes in flip-flops, Gargoyles, tank tops, shorts and ball caps. Until they went down. The old 650 was the only bike Josh could identify with. All the modern sport bikes looked alike, all the mechanics buried under yards of fiberglass. You couldn't tell them apart except for the color. A motorcycle should show motor.

Josh walked across the street.

A board punk with tatted sleeves and a painting of Heisenberg on his board rolled at him and did a flip dismount, catching the board in his hand. "Dig your ink, man."

"Yours, too."

The kid went into the Union. A slim coed in shorts and halter top, draped in long brown hair, approached him with a smile and a clipboard. "Hi! Are you registered to vote?"

"Yes I am, thank you, ma'am."

"You know we have a city council election coming up. It's very important to elect progressive-minded candidates so we don't lose all the gains we made during the last administration, don't you agree?"

"Couldn't agree more."

She handed him a pamphlet extolling the virtues of Amy Salicrup-Goldstein. "My name's Beth, by the way. What's yours?"

"Josh Pratt."

"Are you a student?"

"No. I hope you're not going to report me."

Josh wished she'd go away.

"Do you go to school here?"

Josh became aware of a disruptive force as a woman cruised by on a bright red Hawk GT, pulled into the slots next to the Historical Building, removed her helmet and shook out her long blond hair. Josh's gaze was elsewhere and the canvasser got the message.

"Well, nice meeting you!"

Josh watched as Fig crossed the street in front of the Union, saw him and switched direction. "What are you doing here?"

"I'm observing, I'm taking notes. What are you doing here?"

Fig made a guffaw face with a delightful overbite. "I'm studying business. I have a class at two. I just stopped by to grab some lunch."

Josh stood. "I'll join you."

ON THE TERRACE

THEY GOT THEIR BRATS AND SODAS AND found a seat beneath the ancient oak that served as the terrace centerpiece.

"How were Stan's grades?"

"Three point seven," Fig said with her mouth full. "He made the Dean's List last year."

"Could someone have been so jealous of him they wanted him dead?"

Fig looked up. She'd put on a Brewer's cap and her eyes were in shade. "I guess so, but that's pretty flimsy. If that were the case...I don't know anyone. Have you asked Ellie?"

"Not yet. I hope to speak to her today. Were you close?"

"We were extremely close. Stan idolized me and I couldn't be prouder of him. We were both jocks. The only place we differed was politics. We didn't talk politics."

"How did you differ?" Josh said.

"I'm a screaming lib. Stan was conservative. He and Dad always used to wonder how I came out of our family."

"So how come they're conservative and you're a lib?"

Fig smiled. "I chalk it up to my college experience. I went to Michigan State but I'm getting my master's here. I had liberal professors. They taught me the value of seeing every point of view and not adhering to a rigid structure."

"So why are you majoring in business?"

Fig's laugh sounded like silver coins falling into Josh's palm. "I'm not stupid! I want money and I don't just want Daddy to groom me for a position in his company, although he would like to. I'm starting my own business."

"What kind of business?"

"I could tell you but then I would have to kill you."

Josh smiled. "Product or service?"

"Product," she said.

"But you believe in God," Josh said.

Fig rolled her eyes. "God! Now you sound like my faculty advisor."

"Did you know Stan's student advisor, Avery Waldrop?"

"He's my advisor."

"How does that work?" Josh said. "Stan was in law and you're in business. How can you both have the same advisor?"

"Avery teaches Western philosophy, which touches on both disciplines."

"Did the cops talk to him?"

Fig shrugged. "I wouldn't know. I could ask. Why?"

"I'm just gathering data now. I don't know what it means. Don't worry. I'm not going to pad your bill but I'd like to meet this professor."

Fig pulled out her phone. "I wasn't worried." She dialed. A moment later she handed the phone to Josh.

"This is Avery Waldrop," said a voice.

"Mr. Waldrop, this is Josh Pratt. Miss Newton has hired me to look into her brother's death. I wonder if I could speak to you."

"We were all devastated by Stan's death. By all means. Let me look at my schedule. Hmmm. Tell you what, there's a faculty party tonight in Shorewood. Could you possibly come by then?"

"Sure. Where and when?"

"Fig knows. Let me talk to her."

Josh handed back the phone. A minute later Fig put it away.

"Okay. I'll meet you there. It's on Lake Mendota Drive in Shorewood. You know how to get there?"

Josh nodded.

"Those people are going to shit," Fig said.

"What do you mean?"

"When you show up. Will you ride your Harley?"

"Of course."

"Radical chic. It's what they used to call it when university eggheads rubbed shoulders with the Black Panthers. Now we got bikers. They're gonna love it."

ELLIE

FIG LEFT AND JOSH PHONED ELLIE SWANSON, Stan's girlfriend. She was distraught but agreed to meet with him between classes at the Lincoln statue outside Bascom Hall in fifteen minutes. Josh vacated his table, which was immediately seized by loafers in waiting, then deposited his trash in the barrel, grabbed a *Daily Cardinal* and walked up Bascom Hill. It was a beautiful summer day, with students studying beneath the shade of the ancient oaks and elms, others tossing Frisbees, and high school kids racing down the inclined walk on their boards.

Lincoln faced east in front of a semi-circular marble bench with an unusual property. Persons sitting opposite each other separated by the statue and twenty feet could whisper to one another by speaking close to the curving marble, which carried sound better than most phone companies.

Josh sat on the bench and read the *Cardinal*. The Badger football team was expected to do well in the coming season. Ethnic food was popular at the mall. He became aware of a woman walking toward him. She was young, a redhead with pale skin and freckles. Josh stood.

"Ellie? I'm Josh Pratt."

They shook hands and sat on the bench.

"Do you think Stan was murdered?" she said.

"I'm looking into the possibility. Did Stan have any enemies? Anyone who might have wished him dead?"

"No! Everybody loved Stan!"

"Everyone?"

"As far as I know. Sure he had his detractors. People who were jealous and resentful, but nobody serious."

"When was the last time you spoke to him?"

"We talked the night he died. He phoned me to see if I wanted to go hear a band the next day." She stopped, her face crinkled and the tears flowed.

Josh watched helplessly as she rummaged in her backpack for a tissue, which she used to dab her eyes.

"I'm so sorry," he said.

"I know, right?" she said through a mirthless smile. "You're cruising along on top of the world, everything seems to be going great and then all of a sudden this thing comes in from left field...I just can't get over the fact that he's dead!"

The floodgates opened and Josh held her. "He was such a good man!" she sniffled. "It wasn't just about being a football star—he was thinking ahead!

That's why he studied construction and business. He wanted to join his father's firm and not just to make money, either. Stan wanted to help people. He had all these plans for cheap but good modern houses, based on Frank Lloyd Wright's Usonian ideas. Stan loved Wright. He took me to every Wright building in Wisconsin! And he wanted to be able to invest in his sister's business."

"What business is that?" Josh said.

"I don't know."

"Have you received any suspicious communications? Does the phone ring and when you pick it up no one's there?"

"No," she said, honking. "Nothing like that. My friends and family have been nothing but supportive. We were going to get married. We were going to have kids."

She bawled. Josh put an arm around her shoulder and she turned into him, soaking his shirt. He let her sob. After a while she pulled back, dabbing at her face with a fresh tissue.

"I'm sorry. I'm not usually this way."

"Nothing to apologize for." He took out his billfold. "Here's my card. If you can think of anything that might help or if you get any new information, please call me."

Ellie tucked the card in a backpack pocket. "Thank you, I will. I've got to pull myself together. My next class is trigonometry."

Josh watched her go, tall and elegant, and then he rose and walked down the hill to his bike.

FACULTY PARTY

THE HOUSE WAS EASY TO SPOT. MERCEDES, lexuses, BMWs and Audis flanked it on both sides of Lake Mendota Drive. Josh backed his chop between two sedans and walked over a plank bridge to reach the front door of the lakeside, Prairie-style dowager directly across from the Bishop's Bay Golf Course. Lights, laughter and the tinkle of glass emanated from the multi-decked house as Buffalo Springfield segued into Kylie Minogue. Josh wore a long-sleeved cotton pullover from Western Slope that covered his tats. The only visible ink was the tip of the dragon's tail crawling up his neck. He wore creased khaki Dockers and deck shoes. Only his overt muscularity and shaved head indicated he was not faculty.

Stepping down to the main entrance, he entered a broad room encompassing a kitchen and dining area. University types stood in clusters in animated discussions, clutching drinks.

A grad student in black slacks and white shirt dispensed drinks from a built-in bar. Josh went over, got a beer and slipped a buck into the tip glass. Back to the bar, he surveyed the crowd, a Whitman's Sampler of diversity. About two dozen people milled and yakked, with more on the lower deck overlooking the lake. Josh didn't see Fig so he took his drink, went down four steps to the living room and through the sliding glass patio doors onto the deck. At seven the sky was still bright blue over the water, with tiny white sails heading for the Hoofer's dock to his right. He went to the rail and looked out. Seconds later he felt a hand on his arm and turned.

Fig wore a strapless white cocktail dress, her hair fixed in a bob. She looked like a cover girl and smelled of honeysuckle. "Hi!" she said. "Avery's here and he's dying to meet you."

Josh looked her up and down. "You didn't ride your motorcycle."

"No, I got a ride. Come on." She took his hand and led him across the deck.

They came to a group of four, two men and two women, in a heated discussion. One man was tall, with a pronounced Adam's apple, white goatee and glasses, wearing a tweed jacket with leather elbow patches. The other was younger, with brown curly hair, bit of a pudge. The two women were a study in contrasts, one black and built like a linebacker, the other Asian and thin as a drinking straw.

Josh and Fig hovered at the rim.

"That's nonsense, Yvonne, and you know it," the tall man said to the stout woman. "If my wife consents to have sex with me, how is that rape?"

Yvonne crouched like a border collie. "You fail to understand the full implications of patriarchy. Of course you don't get it! You're a man! How can you possibly understand what it means to be imprisoned by your sex?"

The younger guy turned. "Oh there you are! Folks, Fig is one of the good ones. She's studying business administration."

Yvonne wrinkled her nose. "Business administration? What for?"

Avery Waldrop continued. "Fig, this is Yvonne Hargreaves, Associate Professor of Gender and Women's Studies. She teaches Introduction to Gay, Lesbian, Bisexual and Transgender Thought. And this is the charming and erudite Jessica Wong, our distinguished Arkham Professor of Anthropology, and this tall drink of water is Archie Simmons, Professor of Atmospheric and Oceanic Sciences. And this is Fig Newton, who is pursuing her master's in business. And you must be..."

"Josh Pratt, sir," Josh said, sticking out his hand.

"Josh is a biker," Fig said. "Show them your arms."

Josh rolled up his sleeves and the group oohed and awed.

"That is so tribal," Yvonne said. "What do they mean?"

"Well these are just design work but this one here"—he indicated a furious cartoon character—"is the Badger, Wisconsin's own superhero." He turned to show them the other arm.

"And this, of course, is Christ's heart."

Yvonne wrinkled her nose. Jessica rolled her eyes.

"Fig tells me you're a detective," a smiling Waldrop said.

"Sorta."

"You mean like a private *dick*?" Yvonne said.

"I prefer shamus, gumshoe or peeper," Josh said.

"Do you do divorce work?" Jessica said.

"Mostly I just deliver summonses," Josh said.

"Hmmm," Simmons said. "I can see where you might be good at that."

Fig put her hands through Josh's and Waldrop's arms.

Waldrop said, "Excuse me" and allowed himself to be pulled across the deck to an empty spot at the rail looking toward the lights of Middleton. They leaned on the rail.

"Fig tells me you want to talk about Stan."

"Yes sir."

Waldrop let out a deep sigh. "I'm still trying to deal with that. I've seldom had a student with as much potential as Stan. He was seriously a good person. I would very much like to know if he was murdered. How can I help?"

INDIAN

"DID THE COPS EVER TALK TO YOU?" JOSH SAID.

"No," Waldrop said. "I never called them. I didn't think I had anything to add. But I'll do whatever I can to assist you in your investigation."

"Okay. Let's start with the obvious. Did he have any enemies, anyone who might wish him harm?"

"Stan was the sweetest guy in the world. On weekends he coached Pop Warner. Never talked about it, just did it. I've racked my brain trying to come up with a reason. I know he didn't drown."

"Why do you say that?"

"'Cause even drunk, Stan could handle himself. Believe me I know. And why would he suddenly go skinny dipping in the middle of the night? And why not off his own pier? Why down the street?"

"Are you aware of the Smiley Face Killings?"

Waldrop nodded. "I looked them up. But there was no mention of a smiley face concerning Stan."

Josh took out his phone and brought up the picture. "I took this outside the Delta Tau frat house, in the back. Lakeside. Two guys were cleaning it off. I took it this weekend."

Waldrop scrolled through the photos. "Who's Shred Husl?" he said.

"Shred Husl was the hero of several blaxploitation novels from the seventies by Curtis Mack."

Waldrop turned toward him and raised his shaggy brows. "Seriously?"

Josh nodded. "It may not have anything to do with Stan. One thing bothers me. All these victims, all white, upper middle class, gifted athletes. They represent a symbol, don't you think?"

"Yeah," Waldrop said. "I did think that. Like maybe it's a terrorist plot. All these drownings all over, someone would have to direct them. And that place could be anywhere. It could be in the Middle East or in his mother's basement in Belarus."

"But who are they talking to?" Josh said.

"Well if I were a jihadist," Fig said, "I'd think this would be a great way to demoralize the Great Satan. Order the faithful to kill off their sons."

"The FBI considered that angle," Josh said. "There was just no evidence. But they never did figure out how whoever is doing this gets the message out."

"It has to be the internet," Waldrop said.

"Yeah I figured. But how do you search for something like that? I can barely operate this smartphone. This smartphone is smarter than me."

"I don't know," Waldrop said, shaking his head.

"Seems to me," Fig said, "jihadists like to take credit for their work. They take credit every time there's a disaster. Wouldn't they take credit for this?"

"I don't know," Josh said. "Maybe it's a new phase. Stealth jihad. Maybe it's been going on for a while. There may be some commonality we're missing."

"What did all these boys have in common?" Waldrop said. "They're all white, young, good athletes, liked to party."

"What were they all studying?" Fig said.

Josh and Waldrop looked at her. "I'll take another look," Josh said. "But anybody who would incite random murder probably doesn't go that deep."

"How would they do it?" Waldrop said. "Exactly what do you say that makes a perfect stranger go out and kill someone?"

"More appropriately," Josh said, "who do you say it to?"

A guy who looked like Volstagg from the Thor comics headed their way holding a drink in each hand. "Is that your Road King out front?" the man boomed in a stentorian voice.

"Hello Walt," Waldrop said. "Josh Pratt, Fig Newton, Walter Pandome. Walter's head of Theater and Drama."

"I just got a new Indian. Like your bike! What modifications have you made?"

"Engine: 88 with oil cooler. Changed the cams to S&S gear drives with .510 lift. Took out the fuel injection and replaced it with an S&S Super E, Yost Power Tube, S&S manifold and Pingle high-flow petcock. S&S teardrop air cleaner cover with a K&N filter. Screamin' Eagle Hi-Performance ignition unit with a 6200-rpm rev limiter. Accell Super Coil, FireWire plug wires and spiral wound metal core wires. Accell platinum-tip plugs. Five-speed tranny with Barnett Kevlar clutch, self-adjusting hydraulic chain tensioner. Screamin' Eagle dualies. Progressive springs in front with higher viscosity, Progressives in back. Changed the rear swing-arm bushings to STA-BO nylon high density. SBS semi-metallic disc brake pads, and the brake lines are stainless steel braids. Went to tubeless wheels."

Walt looked like a child on Christmas morning. "Nice!" he declared. "We've got a little group, The Drama Queens, toy drives, weekend jaunts, that sort of thing."

Josh was going to ask about the Indian, but he caught Yvonne headed their way with two other unhappy-looking faculty whom he'd never met. She came right up to Walt.

"Walt, what are you doing talking to this guy? He's a Christer."

Walt turned toward her. "I beg your pardon?"

"Oh yeah. He's born again, isn't that right, Pratt?"

Pratt nodded.

"Show him your Christ heart," Yvonne said.

"Maybe some other time," Josh said.

Yvonne turned on Fig. "Why'd you bring him?"

Fig snaked her hand through Josh's arm. "Come on. Let's go."

She led him up the steps across the bridge to the street. A man zipped up in a silver Boxster with the top down, blipped to a halt and expertly parallel parked near the house. He got out and came their way, a trim middle-aged man in a navy blue blazer with gold buttons, a white silk turtleneck shirt, blue jeans, long silver hair gathered in a ponytail and wraparound shades. He looked like the Silva Thins Man. He passed them without acknowledging them.

Fig turned to Josh. "Can you give me a ride home?"

"I'm on a bike," Josh said.

Fig leaned down, gripped the hem of her little white cocktail dress firmly in both hands and ripped it upward to mid-thigh. "There," she said with a dazzling smile.

CHAPTER 17

MR. P'S PLACE

WITH FIG NEWTON PRESSED AGAINST HIS BACK, her arms around his waist and her honeysuckle floating in the air, Josh wished the ride would never end. She lived in a little redbrick house halfway up a hill on Clifton Drive near Hilldale. Josh stopped at the base of the steps as Fig semaphored one long leg over his head and got off.

"You rent?" he said.

"I own it," she said. "Bought it last year."

Josh wondered where the money came from but she was a business major.

She smiled at him as if reading his mind. "My product."

"Maybe one of these days you'll tell me what that is."

"Maybe, but not tonight. Got too much to do tomorrow." She leaned over and kissed him on the cheek, turned and sashayed up the stairs. Josh watched until she was inside her house before leaving.

He was far too riled to sleep, so when he got home he stripped to his skivvies, got a glass of iced tea and holed up in bed with *Tear the Roof Off the Sucker*.

When I got close to my crib I heard Marvin Gaye and Tammi Terrell crooning "Your Precious Love" through the door and I knew what to expect. I unlocked the two deadbolts and let myself in. My pad was cool, creamy and dark with dozens of candles lighting the living room, my black velvet painting of James Brown poppin' on the mantel. Just as the song ended, the beaded curtains to my bedroom parted and Yolanda stepped through wearing a silk gray peignoir that clung to her like a mountain road. Her luscious red lips barely parted as she pinned me with her violet eyes.

"Hello, sugah."

I cascaded into her like the mighty Mississippi, clutching the back of her beautiful black bouffant, thirteen inches in diameter, smelling of Shalimar. She gripped my twelve-inch johnson through my purple velvet pants and led me like a horse into the bedroom. The black lights made my black velvet paintings of Aphrodite, Lady Cocoa, and Tamara Dobson really pop. I undressed her slowly, letting each fold linger on her skin as I pulled it off.

Josh skipped ahead.

As we lay on my silk sheets in my round bed looking up at our reflections in the mirror, Yolanda lit a cigarette and placed it between my lips.

"Sugah," she said. "Is it okay if my cousin Tyrone stay with us 'bout a week?"

"Tell me about Tyrone," I said.

"He studying karate or some such. He gone 'bout as far as he can down in Mecklinburg, now he want to come up here study with some El Rukns Grand Master here in the Bronx. Some kind of kung fu he says."

"What kind of man is he?"

"Tyrone? He always been so serious, always wanted to be a kung fu expert, been studying since he was in the sixth grade. He eighteen now, thinking about joining the Marines and seeing the world. But before he go he want to get that black belt or whatever in this weird form of kung fu. Tyrone always been serious, always got good grades, never did like to hang out, drink or carouse. That don't mean he some kind of saint. He got a beautiful girlfriend, know how to work. He always had a job. You got that spare room in back, he won't be a hindrance."

"All right," I said. "When's he thinkin' of coming up?"

"Well sugah, he never been to New York before and I gotta go back for my grandma's birthday on Sunday. I was thinkin' of just bringing him back with me."

"I guess. Maybe he can teach me a trick or two."

Yolanda threw her arms around my neck and started kissing me, her perfect breasts hanging down brushing my chest. Just then the phone ring. I pick it up.

"Yeah?"

"Shred, where you at, man? I been waitin' on you forever."

It was P. His real name is Percy Carter but everybody call him P. I told him I'd bring him some choice pearl, and I always keep my word. "Hang on, P," I said, swinging my legs out of bed. "I'll be there shortly."

Mr. P's was poppin' when I got there. I eased my whip into my usual space and got waved in by Tiny, Mr. P's six-foot-seven 350-pound bouncer, L.K. "Tiny" Scroggins, All Pro linebacker for the Pittsburgh Steelers.

"How you doin', Mr. H," Tiny said with a dap to the fist.

"Low and slow, Tiny. P in?"

"Yeah, P's up in his catbird seat. I'll call 'im and tell 'im you're comin'."

I entered the club beneath the striped awning, tossed my Dobbs to Sweet Jessica at the coat check. She blew me a kiss.

"You bring yore sweet self over here, Shred!"

"Can't, Jessica honey, gots to see the man. I'll be back."

I boogied through the club to a disco beat, the O'Jays on the speakers, throbbing neon outlining the art deco booths and bar, strobe lights skippin' on dancers doin' the Frug, doin' the Mashed Potato, doin' The Peppermint Twist, slippin' skin, slappin' backs and trading kisses. Took me five minutes to walk fifty feet back to the stairs leading to P's sanctum sanctorum, a velvet-lined nest overlooking the main floor.

Everybody wanted a taste but I wasn't there to do retail. Never do retail. Any Jew can tell you that. Men pressed money into my hand. Women rubbed their pussies up and down my leg.

Everybody wanted a piece of me. I eased my way among them and glided up the winding stairs. P chilled on a custom Italian black leather sofa, one arm around a sensual redhead in a black shift, the other around a jiggy Eartha Kitt-looking momma. P's face lit up like Times Square when he saw me.

"My man, my man!" P said, putting hands on the girls' knees and getting up to crush me in a bear hug. "You just in time for the party!"

"You bring them party favors?" he whispered in my ear.

"They in your pocket," I said.

"Shyneeka," P said. "Get my man Shred Husl a rum and coke."

Eartha Kitt unfolded from the sofa like smoke rising and went to the wet bar. P took the bindle I'd slipped into his pocket, sat down on the sofa and shook a mound of white powder out on the black marble surface. The redhead squealed and clapped her hands.

P pulled out a butterfly knife, spun it around and commenced to chopping up lines. He reached into his violet Van Heusen and pulled out a tiny gold coke spoon on a gold chain, scooped some up and hoovered up his nose. He sat back and pointed ten fingers to the sky.

"Sweet Mother of Jesus, that's the real deal!"

"Ooh! Let me!" the redhead squeaked.

"This here Angela Levine," P says and winks at me. We all know 'bout them Jewish girls.

P took the chain from around his neck and handed it to her. Shyneeka handed me a rum and coke in a cut-glass snifter.

I waited for the babes to get their freak on before leaning over that black marble table. I ain't lyin', I was flyin'. I get my shit from a Cuban cat down in Miami who gets it straight from Bolivia.

"Disco Inferno" pumped from the concealed KLH speakers. I looked over the rim of P's velvet-padded nest and see my man Scarecrow workin' that deejay thang. Angela and Shyneeka get up and dance and me and P jes' sit back and watch. They knew what they was doin'. After a while Shyneeka pirouettes and lands in P's lap and Angela throws her bad body right down next to mine and grabs my arm.

"I heard a lot about you, Shred."

"Oh yeah? Whatchoo hear?"

"I hear you're a real stud. Is it true what they say about you? That you can keep a woman happy all night long?"

"Show, don't tell," I said. "That's my motto." And I get up, take her by the hand, and lead her into one of Mr. P's back rooms.

Josh quit reading and turned out the light.

THURSDAY

ALTHOUGH TECHNICALLY GUILTY OF SECURITIES fraud, Aaron Kofsky had not yet been charged and there was no warrant out on him. The partners wished to deal with him with as little publicity as possible. Therefore the FBI and the Justice Department had no interest in him. Finding him was up to Josh.

Aside from a brief bio on Dovetail and Wikipedia, Kofsky had virtually no web presence. He wasn't on Facebook or Twitter. The only e-mail address was for general inquiries to Dovetail. Fleiss had told him there was no point contacting board members. They had no idea where he was, no way to get in touch with him.

After his run and shower, Josh went through his Kofsky file.

Kofsky lived alone except for sometime-girlfriend Sandy Meyer, a hard-looking blond Realtor who hung up when Josh called.

Josh scoured her Facebook page for clues but there hadn't been any word about Kofsky for at least a month. If he'd dumped her she might have a motive to find him, if for no other reason than having the satisfaction of seeing him dragged through the courts. Meyer wasn't hard to find. She maintained offices in Group Realty on Excelsior in Middleton and worked out at the Madison Club on the West Beltline. Josh waited until she posted from the Madison Club and headed over.

The Madison Club was a new, three-story redbrick structure with tinted glass walls so the good burghers of Madison could look out on the city as they worked their abs, lats, deltoids and thighs. Josh kicked out in the lot, went into the frigid building and smiled at the buff brunette behind the counter.

"How can I help you?" she said with a dazzling smile.

"I'm thinking of joining. Mind if I look around?"

"Certainly, sir. Let me give you a guest pass and please sign our visitor's book."

Josh took the stairs to the second floor, where the workout machines were arranged in an outward-facing perimeter, the center of the room reserved for dead weights, kettlebells and personal trainers. Flat-screens hung from the ceiling every ten feet over the windows, some tuned to CNN, some tuned to ESPN. Sandy wasn't hard to spot, her platinum helmet of hair gleaming in the fluorescent lights. She wore a light blue jumpsuit with red piping. Josh could see her determined expression reflected in the east-facing glass as she worked the treadmill.

Josh sat on a bench behind her and smiled at her in the window. She smiled back. When she finished she stepped off the treadmill, flipped a white towel around her neck and turned around.

"Hello, cutie," she said.

Josh stood. "Miss Meyers."

She came up to him, taut as a panther. "Do I know you?"

"Josh Pratt. I'm a private investigator. I've been hired to find Aaron Kofsky."

Sandy rolled her eyes and flipped the towel. "That prick! Well I'm sorry, I have no idea where he is. I'd like to know. He owes me money, too."

"Would you let me buy you a smoothie?"

The hard eyes softened. "Sure."

The smoothie bar was on the top floor, with an expansive view of the West Side, the capitol dome a tiny silhouette on the horizon. Sandy ordered some blueberry, banana, almond/soy disaster and Josh had pasteurized orange juice. They sat at a table at the window looking out on eight lanes of traffic.

"Did you invest in Dovetail?" Josh said.

Sandy sighed and rubbed her forehead. "Yes and I should have known better. Aaron always seemed just a little too good to be true, if you know what I mean. I'm not a stupid woman but he sure snowed me. The cars, the clubs, the homes."

"If after a certain amount of time he fails to respond to a court summons, the court can put his assets up for sale and disperse them to the plaintiffs, if it finds for them."

"Have they charged him?" Sandy said intently.

"Not yet. They prefer to avoid the limelight. They prefer to keep this a civil matter. Where do you think he might be?"

Sandy shrugged. "I have no idea. He could be anywhere. But if he's fled the country, chances are he's not coming back."

"What about his homes here? Would he just abandon them?"

"I don't know."

"I sure would like to take a look at them," Josh said.

"I have keys to both his places," Sandy said. "If you wait while I change, I'll go with you."

A yard crew was mowing Kofsky's emerald greensward in Zebrawood when they arrived fifteen minutes later. Zebrawood was the jewel in the Newton crown, their first and most successful development. The house itself was an attractive but undistinguished hodgepodge of SW stucco, tile roof, bay windows and four-car garage.

Josh had left his bike at the club and ridden with Sandy in her Grand Cherokee.

"I guess the yard service didn't get the word," Sandy said. "Should I tell them?"

"I would," Josh said getting out.

They walked up the flagstone path to the arched main entrance. Sandy removed a thick key ring from her feed bag and opened the right half of the double front door.

They entered a foyer finished with Italian marble with a fountain directly beneath a free-form wrought iron chandelier that reminded Josh of car ribs after a fire. The house was cool, air conditioning on, but a fine layer of dust covered most surfaces. It felt empty.

Sandy walked to the arched entrance to a book-lined room with a bay window looking out on a garden. "This is his office. There's a wall safe behind that painting but it's empty."

The painting was of a black blues guitarist wearing a blue suit in blue club light as he bent backwards in an ecstasy of riffing.

"What's this?" Josh said.

"Some blues guy. Aaron loves the blues."

Josh swung the painting out on hinges revealing an inset, round steel wall safe. It was unlocked and empty. He shut it and swung the picture back. There were also framed posters of Otis Rush, Muddy Waters and Son Seals.

Chaplain Dorgan had taught Josh you could learn a lot about a person by the books he reads and the music he likes. Josh looked at the bookcase on the other wall: novels by Marc Olden, William H. Hallahan, Geoffrey Household. The only one Josh was familiar with was Rex Miller, who had written a series of novels based on a lurid serial killer named Chaingang, and only because certain books had been popular among inmates.

There were also volumes by Mark Twain, Leon Uris, Stephen Hunter and Ayn Rand.

"Were you ever at his place in Cabo?"

"Once. It's nice. Azure Oasis it's called. It's on the gulf."

"Think he's there?"

"If he is, he's not coming back."

Josh methodically went through the desk drawers and files. The bottom left-hand drawer was for hanging files. Josh rifled through the titles: house insurance, car insurance, health insurance, DD contracts, warranties. Hanging files filled the space front to back like a compressed accordion. He rolled the whole file out and lifted it out of its grooves, exposing the hardwood floor beneath and a small cardboard jewelry box. He opened it. Inside was a flash drive, which he slipped into his pocket.

"What was he like?"

"He was a lot of fun when he wasn't coked to the gills. He took me to blues clubs. Funny. Erudite. That's why we broke up. I couldn't take his binges. He'd go through an eight ball and a bottle of vodka a night. I couldn't keep up. I mean I used to like coke. Sure, who doesn't, right? But after a while it just gets to be a drag. It wasn't fun, it was something you did so you could do more. Lying awake all night listening to my heart beat, who needs it?"

"I hear ya," Josh said. He felt the same way. "You think the money went up his nose?"

"How much can one man snort?" Sandy said.

Josh looked around. "Where's the hard drive?"

ASSHOLES RECRUDESCENT

THERE WAS NOTHING IN THE HOUSE INDICATING where Kofsky might have gone. Sandy had a showing, drove Josh back to the Madison Club and dropped him there. He rode home and made himself some lunch. Suddenly Salad represented the apogee of his culinary skills, infused with microwaved bacon. Anything infused tasted better. There was a knock at the front door, which he'd left open, leaving only the screen. Josh got up and looked. It was his neighbor from across the street, Dave Lowry, whose two schnauzers he'd saved from a dogfighting ring.

Josh opened the door. "What's up, Dave?"

Dave came in wearing Bermuda shorts, a knit Lacoste golf shirt and white Nikes. "Do you know the Insane Assholes?"

Josh's heart tumbled out of its slot. "What happened?"

"Nothing happened, it's just that a while ago I was mowing my lawn and this greasy-looking outlaw pulls up in front of the house and waves me over. You can imagine how well that went over so I waved him up. Got off his bike and came up the lawn, George and Gracie are going crazy, I'm sure if Louise saw she'd have dialed 911. 'Big Lennie' it said on his vest. Points across the street. 'Is that Pratt's place?' I told him I didn't know. He stared at me and for a second there I thought I'd have to fight him off with the lawn mower but he went away. I think he was high on something."

"Did you tell the cops?"

"No. Should I?"

"Don't worry about it, Dave. I'll take care of it."

"What's going on?" Dave said. He was an aging athlete gone to seed and the only neighbor Josh trusted.

"I had to kick them out of a bar last week, and now they've got their panties in a wad. Don't worry about it. There will be no trouble, I promise you. How can they be so fucking stupid to think they can come into a neighborhood like this? That's what drugs do to you, Dave. Stay away from them!"

Dave laughed. "Hey, want to join us Sunday? We're just grilling some hamburgers."

"Sure. I'll be over around five."

Josh went into his office, pulled the flash drive from Kofsky's desk from his pocket and plugged it into his hard drive.

Naked kids. The most appalling shit. He forced himself to watch all of it. Was this why Kofsky had gone to Mexico? How could he have left this flash drive unsecured? He forced himself to watch the whole thing, hoping there was nothing incriminating Kofsky because it would make dealing with the man an ethical dilemma. Fortunately, Kofsky never entered the picture, which didn't mean he wasn't a sexual predator. It only meant there was a chance he wasn't a sexual predator.

Josh went to the basement and locked the hard drive in his gun safe.

He mowed his lawn. It was a wonder what a little lawn food could do. He showered and spent an hour online learning as much as he could about Dovetail, a web security company that had only been in existence a year.

Josh phoned the MPD on McKenna and told them about the biker. They told him they'd increase patrols. Numerous captains of industry, government officials and university bigwigs lived on Ptarmigan Road and they would suffer no dregs of humanity.

Josh had been around bikers half his life and knew there were members of that tribe barely smarter than a paramecium, violent elemental creatures who would throw their lives away on a dare or a grudge. They were an extreme minority but their shadow hung heavy over every motorcyclist.

Josh phoned Clarence Peet.

"Have the Insane Assholes been bothering you?" Josh asked.

"They came back once, last night, but I had an off-duty WHP guy on duty and they went away. They were looking for you."

"Thanks, Clarence. Sorry about the inconvenience."

"Not your fault. You were only doing your job."

"I just can't believe how stupid they are."

Josh went online and checked Facebook, uploading a picture of him slouching on his motorcycle, taken by Cass Rubio, who'd been his girlfriend for a month before Moon killed her. A heart valve missed a beat. It had been one of the longest and most satisfying relationships he'd ever had. He'd long ago concluded he'd had terrible taste in women. Hanging with the Bedouins, he'd had plenty of one-night stands with the types of women who liked bikers. Most of them were either crazy or drug addicts.

He didn't permit himself to think about Fig, who was way above his class.

Josh went to Facebook. There were numerous blues pages: Blues You Can Use, The Blues, Rhythm and Blues, B.B. King, Albert King, Muddy Waters, Lightnin' Hopkins and on and on. Three were closed to the public. Josh went to Blues You Can Use, open to the public with 263 members. There were plugs for podcasts discussing various artists, a picture of a Robert Johnson stained glass window and much heated debate on the music's relevance, health and provenance.

Being a whiz kid, Kofsky could create fake FB pages and bounce them around the world so that nobody could track their origin.

Again Josh felt frustrated by his lack of technical knowledge. The modern detective did most of his work online. Josh planned to take a course on internet searches from the Professional Association of Wisconsin Licensed Investigators in the fall.

There were also a dozen blues discussion groups in other forums, including Yahoo.

Josh methodically visited the open groups to no avail. He just wasn't smart enough to read between the lines. He joined the three open groups. It was just past six and still bright out when he heard the rumble of V-twins.

SHOOT-OUT ON PTARMIGAN

JOSH COULDN'T BELIEVE IT. HOW COULD THEY be so stupid? Josh had no intention of confronting them. He got up, went into the living room and peered through the partially closed blinds. There were three Insane Assholes in his driveway plus Buddha, their leader, riding up on his lawn and looking even less tranquil than before. Across the street Dave Lowry stood with his hands on his hips at the top of his magisterial driveway while his two schnauzers, George and Gracie, constrained by the Invisible Fence, stood at the property line and barked.

The Assholes unassed. As Josh continued to watch through the blinds, Buddha reached into his black leather saddlebag and took out a pipe, which he began to thwack into his palm. Following his lead, the other three unsheathed. One held a chain. One slipped on a pair of brass knuckles. One had a baseball bat.

"HEY DUMBFUCK!" Buddha bellowed from the front stoop. "GET YOUR ASS OUT HERE AND TAKE YOUR MEDICINE."

He heard a crash and knew they'd kicked over his ride, a capital offense among bikers. He thought about the arsenal in the basement, but as a convicted felon he was barred by state law from owning firearms. Josh moved to the side and saw three Insane Assholes go to work on his bike with their weapons. They were jacked up on something, and Josh didn't know if he could take all three, even with the bō staff mounted above the picture window.

One of them picked up a rock from the side of his driveway. Josh moved back just in time as the rock smashed through his picture window, fouled the blinds and fell with a thump on the sofa.

Wailing sirens announced the arrival of four screaming, flashing MPD cars, which screeched to a stop in front of his house. Out piled eight officers with their guns drawn. They immediately spread out in a broad semi-circle, all their guns trained on the goons in the yard.

"POLICE. PUT DOWN YOUR WEAPONS. GET DOWN ON THE GROUND WITH YOUR HANDS BEHIND YOUR HEADS."

What happened next seemed hallucinatory against the elegant shade and cultivated green of the neighborhood. Two Assholes reached behind them and drew automatic weapons. The cops either ducked behind their rides or fell flat to the ground and opened fire, unleashing a fusillade that seemed to go on and on but actually lasted four seconds.

"CEASE FIRING! CEASE FIRING!" a cop yelled. An eerie silence fell on the neighborhood. Josh felt as if he'd just smoked some dynamite shit. His head throbbed and his skull felt like a vacuum. Even though he was shielded by the walls of his house, the sound had been deafening. For long seconds gun haze drifted in the evening air. Then, one by one, the cops rose and closed on the four figures lying in Josh's yard, two hands on every pistol.

Josh realized he wasn't breathing. He consciously rolled his shoulders and drew the air deep into his guts, waiting for the next move. He knew cops.

They stood by his front door with their guns drawn.

"WHO'S IN THE HOUSE?" the same cop yelled, partly because he'd deafened himself during the shoot-out.

Josh used the bō staff to ease open the front door, which wasn't locked. He stayed back.

"JOSH PRATT, OFFICER! I'M UNARMED."

"Come out of the house, Pratt," the cop said. Josh realized it was Don Fortier, whom he'd met.

Josh gently pushed the screen door open and came out holding his hands in plain view. More cops had arrived and were setting up roadblocks and yellow tape.

Great.

One cop pulled a bullhorn and addressed the street. "PLEASE REMAIN INSIDE UNTIL WE GIVE YOU THE ALL-CLEAR."

Josh saw faces pressed against windows across the street.

Lowry still stood at the top of his driveway but no longer with his hands on his hips.

"What happened?" Fortier said. He was a wiry little guy with a military haircut.

Josh brought Fortier up to speed on the Assholes since their encounter last week. All four were pronounced dead at the scene. No police sustained any injuries, although one Asshole had got off a couple shots.

He looked at his bike. They'd knocked out the headlight and taillights, and shivved both tires. With police help he got it upright and wheeled it into his garage onto the hydraulic lift. He was too exhausted to work on it.

It was three hours before they removed the blockade and tape from one of Madison's wealthiest enclaves. Had it happened on the East Side, the tape would have been up for days. It was after nine by the time they finally withdrew, and only then under pressure from a city councilman who lived there.

It wasn't just Ptarmigan that had been affected, it was the little side roads and dead ends that crept into the countryside like mangrove roots. Palmside Way. Applewood Court. Bluff Lane. A map of the neighborhood looked like a circuit schematic.

Josh was persona non grata in his own neighborhood.

SELASSIE POSSE

THE PHONE BEGAN RINGING AT NINE TWENTY. Josh turned it off and cleaned up the shattered glass in his living room. A fresh night breeze streamed in through the broken window, and he lay on the sofa with a lamp on, reading.

So there we was in P's crow's nest chillin', Dom Perignon in the bucket, barbecue ribs, cornbread, collard greens and chitlins courtesy Bro' Lamereaux's Louisiana Kitchen, speakers punchin' out "Superfly" when one of P's girls pops up outta the stairwell like a prairie dog. And she don't look happy.

"P!" she said.

P looked up from where he sprawled with Angela and Shyneeka. "Whassup?"

"The Jamaicans are here! They beat Tiny unconscious!"

Then we heard the screams from the dance floor and we looked over the rim to where six dreadlocked motherfuckers was roaming P's floor smashing tables, smashing faces, robbing people and waving guns.

"Those fuckin' Jamaicans!" P shouted and went for the little automatic in his pocket.

I looked down and saw the Jamaicans were packing big semi-autos. "P," I said, "that .25 ain't gonna cut it. What else you got?"

"Come with me!" he said, leading the way down a short hall to his private office. Inside he locked the door and went to the gun safe in the corner. There were no windows in his office, but some TV monitors flickered black-and-white feed from the floor. I wondered how much time we had before the pigs arrived.

If they arrived.

All we knew, the pigs set us up. They didn't like P and they didn't like me. The Jamaicans had moved to the Bronx last year dealing coke and weed. Their territory came right up to Gangster #1's territory, and P's Place was on the border. We'd do better looking to Gangster #1 for help than the pigs.

Downstairs erupted in shots fired. A lot of P's customers walked around strapped and it sounded like the Jamaicans had run into resistance.

The pigs weren't coming anyway. P dialed open the safe and pulled out two pump-action sawed-off twelves, handing me one and a box of cartridges. "Try not to kill any customers," he said.

We nervously loaded the guns, looked through the peephole.

They hadn't made it to the second floor yet, they were still fighting with customers. We hustled back out to the crow's nest from which we had a clear view of the whole floor, but the buckshot spread might do more harm than good.

"Take this!" P shouted, tossing me a Colt .45. This was more like it! I'd spent plenty of time at my cousin's farm in Georgia practicing on Dixie bottles. I lined up on a Jamaican wearing an ocean blue wife beater beating a man with a chair. I squeezed and watched as the Jamaican's head exploded.

The Jamaicans had misjudged resistance and were on the run, leaving three dead including the one I'd shot. P and I went downstairs to help the wounded and learn what happened.

"I heard them motherfuckers talkin'," said a waitress named Yolanda. "They said this was a message from Junior."

"Junior, huh?" P said and spat on the floor.

Junior was the head Jamaican. Called theyselves the Selassie Posse after Haile Selassie, the Ethiopian emperor whom the Rastafarians worship.

That whom popped Josh right out of the narrative. He dove back in.

We spent the rest of the night cleaning up the joint and patching P's customers. The Jamaicans had killed Artimus Johnson when he pulled his old mule gun. We laid him out on the bar and drank to what a stud he'd been and did a few lines and were still cleaning up the place when the sun rose.

Pigs never showed.

Nobody cares what happens in Niggertown. Round eight I give one of the girls a C-note and send her to Bushnell's for coffee and doughnuts. I'd been up for 36 hours but I wasn't tired, not with the magic fairy dust coursing through my veins.

Gangster #1 showed at eleven with his niggas Pluto and Varese. Gangster #1's real name was Maurice Hughes. He was built like a fire hydrant with a black dome could blind you under the right light, wearing a custom Italian suit and snap-brimmed fedora, black shirt, red silk tie. He looked at P and me with his bulldog eyes and said, "This ain't gonna stand. P, I'm real sorry these sad-ass motherfuckas got up in your face like this. They know you's under my protection and I'm not gonna rest until I run their asses out of Harlem."

P and Gangster #1 did the slow shake. P was fierce. "I 'preciate your help, Maurice, but it was my joint they fucked up. If anyone gon' fuck up that motherfuckin' Junior it be me. Ahm go with you."

Gangster #1 put a hand on P's shoulder. "Yo my brother. We thicker 'n blood." He looked at me. "What about you, Shred? You comin'?"

"I wouldn't miss it," I said.

Just then Shyneeka comes up to us with a scared expression on her face.

"Hey Shyneeka, girl," P say. "What up?"

She looked at me and I got a chill feeling in my soul.

"Shred, there's a message for you on P's answering machine. I think you need to hear it."

CHAPTER

22

WHAT WILL THE NEIGHBORS THINK?

WHEN JOSH WOKE, THE COPS WERE PICKING bullets out of the walls. They had to recover every bullet and each officer had to write a report on why he'd fired. They'd struck the front of the house at least twelve times, nothing Josh couldn't fix with a little paint and spackle.

"Always buy the cheapest house in an expensive neighborhood," his friend Danny Bloom had advised. Danny was the one got him out of prison. The maniac Moon had killed Danny.

Josh felt disapproval and downright loathing of some neighbors as they slowly passed the police vehicles in their BMWs, Lexuses and Mercedes on their way to banks, universities, insurance companies and investment firms. Well fuck 'em. He was there first. That was his ace card. No matter how they bitched and moaned about his stupid little ranch house, HE WAS THERE FIRST. He'd bought the place with proceeds he'd collected from an insurance company when a little old lady had T-boned him at an intersection.

Bloom had helped with that too.

Josh missed Danny. The dope-smoking criminal attorney had been funny and generous.

Josh raised the Road King on the lift and rummaged through his vast collection of junk for replacement parts. There was no saving those tires—he'd have to pick up a new pair at Motorcycle Performance on University Boulevard.

He measured his picture window, phoned Replacement Glass and drove to a nearby Home Depot in his old Honda for plywood, which he had to strap to the roof. Fortunately the Honda had a roof rack that had been on the car when he bought it. On the way back he stopped at Dunkin' Donuts and picked up a copy of *The Wisconsin State Journal.*

SHOOT-OUT ON WEST SIDE LEAVES FOUR DEAD screamed the headline in 46-point type.

When he arrived home there were two news vans parked in front of his house and a cluster of news hounds waiting for him in the yard. A news babe stuck a mike in his face.

"Mr. Pratt, I'm Katy Varner of WMAD News. Can you tell us why this happened?"

Josh faced the camera. "They were seeking payback because I evicted them from a tavern last week. I would like to apologize to my neighbors for this disturbance and assure them that nothing of the sort will ever happen again."

She had more questions but Josh fled inside.

It took him an hour to fit the plywood exactly to the frame using his circular saw and workbench. When he was finished he went out front. The news crews were still there, now joined by several more. Ignoring them, he stood in the middle of his yard and surveyed his handiwork.

Great.

With the plywood in place and holes where the cops had dug out the bullets, his home looked like inner-city Detroit. All it needed was the cinder block Camaro he'd sold to appease his neighbors.

He went inside, made coffee, took his doughnuts out on the deck and opened the paper.

A shoot-out in an upscale neighborhood on Madison's far West Side left four dead. Responding to a 911 call yesterday at approximately 6:15 p.m., Madison police arrived at the scene on Ptarmigan Road to find members of the Insane A**holes Motorcycle Club disturbing the peace in the yard of Josh Pratt.

Police Chief Dave Matthews said 10 officers responded to the call and when members of the motorcycle club drew their weapons, his men opened fire. The resulting shoot-out ended with all four members dead of multiple gunshot wounds. Prior to the police arrival, the gang members had thrown a rock through Pratt's living room window and vandalized his motorcycle.

Pratt gained notoriety last year during an armed assault on the Richard Munz family in Rock County that ended in Munz's death, as well as the death of security guards Rob Stuart and Lee Foucalt, Cass Rubio, and that of their killer, Eugene Moon.

Police Detective Heinz Calloway told WSJ that the West Side incident is not the result of increased gang activity and that there is no danger to the general public.

It was past eleven when Josh went inside and got his phone off its charger in the office. He had twenty-four messages, most of them from journalists and TV types. Calloway had phoned an hour earlier.

"Call me," Calloway had said.

Josh did. It was a half hour before the detective called back.

"Milwaukee police arrested a guy yesterday, name of Davante Daniels. He's got 'Shred Husl' inked across his chest."

DAVANTE

THE MILWAUKEE PD WOULD NOT NORMALLY permit a private investigator to observe an interrogation but Calloway insisted. Milwaukee Police HQ on State Street was an eight-story concrete monolith like something out of a Fritz Lang film. Calloway and Josh checked in, got passes on lanyards and went to the second floor, Felony Division, where Davante Daniels waited at a bolted-down table in an interrogation room. Josh looked at the booking photo of the young man without a shirt. SHRED HUSL was inked across his abs in Gothic script.

They showed Josh a video of Daniels walking up to a white septuagenarian at a mall and sucker-punching him on the side of the head from behind. The video included the laughter of Daniels's friend who had filmed it and posted it to Facebook. The friend also was in custody.

Through the one-way glass Josh saw a dark-skinned young man with a fadeaway, cut arms protruding from an Affliction T-shirt, wearing two-hundred-dollar sneakers without shoelaces. A cop switched on the sound as Calloway entered the room accompanied by a black MPD sergeant.

"Detective Calloway's gonna ask you a few questions," the sergeant said.

Daniels leaned back with a big FUCK YOU on his face. "Where my PD?" he said.

"He'll be here shortly. In the meantime if you cooperate it will help your case. You have a lengthy record."

"Whatch'all want to know?" Daniels said.

"You got 'Shred Husl' inked on your chest," Calloway said. "Who is he?"

Daniels shrugged. "Fuck if I know. I just like the sound."

"Well why don't you have 'booty' or 'pussy' inked across your chest? You like the sound of that, don't you?"

Daniels looked confused and angry. "It's just somethin' I saw on a wall, okay? Shred Husl. He like the voice of the underclass. The disenfranchised." Said with lip-smacking exactitude.

Calloway consulted his notes. "You drown that white boy from Marquette in the river?"

Daniels gaped at him. "What?"

"You know who I'm talking about. They found 'Shred Husl' spray-painted on a wall near the body. Was that you?"

"What the fuck you talking about? Where my lawyer? I ain't sayin' shit until I get my lawyer!"

The sergeant whacked Daniels across the back of the head hard enough to send him slamming into the table. "It would behoove you to cooperate with Detective Calloway. The District Attorney is not sympathetic to your situation."

"Who's Shred Husl?" Calloway said.

Daniels rubbed the back of his head. "He an old-time pimp and hustla. He stuck it to the pigs!"

"Did you know he was the hero of a series of novels?"

Daniels looked as if he'd been confronted by a space alien. "A what?"

"Who is Curtis Mack?" Calloway said.

"I ain't never heard that name," Daniels said.

"Who told you about Shred Husl?" Calloway said.

"I ain't no snitch."

"Look, Davante. It ain't no crime to mention a literary figure. We just want to know how you found out about him, and don't tell me you got it from some graffiti!"

"Davante knows all about graffiti," the sergeant said. "He was busted four years ago for vandalizing a school."

"They're going to make an example out of you," Calloway said. "They don't want the knockout game in Milwaukee. It's bad for business. The mayor doesn't like it. With your record you're looking at a minimum twelve years."

"I mighta heard it on the corner."

"Oh come on," Calloway said. "You can do better than that. You want a cup of coffee?"

"Got any Red Bull?"

"I'll get you a Red Bull," the sergeant said, signaling to be let out. The door buzzed and he exited. Calloway just stood there with his arms crossed staring at Daniels. After a minute Daniels began to fidget. Calloway was a statue. Daniels rearranged his legs, crossed this way, uncrossed the other way.

The sergeant re-entered the observation room. His name was Hawkins.

"Mighta been Jerell."

"Jerell Moore. A real prize," Hawkins said in a subdued voice.

"Jerell who?" Calloway said.

"Jerell Moore," Daniels said. "He always talkin' that revolutionary shit, how we gon' overthrow the white power structure and take what's ours. You know how dat go."

"No I don't know how that goes. Tell me."

"He tied into BPSN. They a gang down in Chicago."

Calloway made careful notes even though the whole thing was recorded.

"And where can I find this Jerell?"

"He like to hang at Brother Mel's. Sometime call hisself Shred Husl."

Calloway signaled to be let out.

"Hey!" Daniels said. "You gon' put a word in for me with the DA?"

Calloway pointed a finger at him. "You bet."

BREAK ROOM

CALLOWAY, JOSH, HAWKINS AND TWO DETECTIVES moved into the break room, which overlooked State Street and contained a room-length counter with a sink, refrigerator and microwave, and two cheap Formica-topped cafeteria tables surrounded by folding chairs. A big bulletin board on one wall was plastered with notices, pictures of missing persons and pets, and clipped cartoons.

Calloway and Josh sat opposite Hawkins. Calloway opened his laptop. "You know Jerell?"

Hawkins pecked at his own laptop. "Head of the Jet Brodies gang. They deal in blow and guns and may be connected to BPSN."

"What's that?" Josh said.

"The modern equivalent of the Blackstone Rangers," Calloway said. "Your original Chicago street gang. Now they're all Muslim, calling for jihad. FBI's been watching them longer than you've been alive."

"Plus which," Hawkins said, "they're connected to the Latin Kings, the Five Percenters and Los Zetas, and all the black separatist movements."

"So maybe they hate Whitey," Calloway said. "They see their opportunities and they take 'em. But somebody's got to be guiding them. How do they do that?"

One of the other cops, a big Latino with a black mustache, ORTIZ on his shirt, said, "Aren't you the guy whose house those bikers shot in Madison?"

Josh nodded.

"What the fuck, man!" Ortiz said. "It's the Wild West out there!"

Everybody laughed, even Josh. "Those guys were too fucking stupid to understand they'd crossed a line."

Calloway shook his head, grinning. "Some neighborhoods it doesn't pay to act like an insane asshole."

Hoots, guffaws.

"I saw your house on TV," Ortiz said. "No offense, but it wasn't exactly Mar-a-Lago."

"Josh bought the place before the neighborhood grew up around him," Calloway explained. "It's kinda like a time warp."

Josh wanted to ask about Moore but it wasn't his place. Calloway did it for him.

"This Jerell Moore available?"

Hawkins pecked at his machine. "He's wanted on several outstanding warrants—guns and drugs. You can put in a request to the FBI Gang Task Force."

"You mentioned a drowning from several years ago," Ortiz said. "What's this about?"

Josh put his hands on the table. "I've been hired by the family of a recent drowning victim in Madison to look into it. The coroner ruled it an accident but the family thinks otherwise. There may be a connection to the so-called Smiley Face Killings."

Ortiz snorted. "That's bunk. The Feds said so."

Josh shrugged. "Maybe."

"Anyway," Calloway said, "we'd appreciate it if you'd give us a head's-up if Moore should appear."

"We can do that," Hawkins said. "You'd probably have better luck with the FBI."

"Yeah right," Calloway said, and they all laughed.

CHAPTER

25

UPSET NEIGHBORS

AT HOME JOSH RESEARCHED JERELL MOORE, Jet Brodies and BPSN. More radical Muslim-oriented members later formed El Rukn, which preached the usual Muslim jive.

BPSN hated Whitey, but they didn't give off that psychopathic vibe Josh got every time he looked at that smiley face. Maybe Moore admired Curtis Mack's novels and used Shred Husl the way kids talk about Spider-Man or Batman. A phrase, an idiom that sweeps through a sub-culture until it either withers or crawls its way into the dictionary.

Shred—to rip it up, tear it up, do it up brown.

Husl—the early bird gets the worm.

Daniels was too stupid to drive to Madison and pull off a murder.

Josh turned away from the computer and heard how quiet it was, only the thrum of his hard drive and the chirping of crickets through the screen window. Whereas before it had been a peaceful quiet, now it was ominous because of the shoot-out. He'd pissed in the punch bowl, shat on the carpet.

Even though he was there first, the surrounding millionaires had regarded him with bemused contempt. Now he was a menace. He had no intention of moving. He was there first! On the other hand he didn't know what he'd do if someone offered him a million dollars.

He pushed back, made a sandwich and settled in front of his flat-screen TV in the living room, now in perpetual twilight due to the blocked-off window, and switched on the five o'clock news. The County Commissioners were reviewing the Newton Corporation's proposal to build an upscale housing development in Fitchburg. Then the program cut to the big news.

"In a moment, WMAD reporter Katy Varner will have the neighbors' reactions to Thursday's West Side shoot-out, which left four members of a motorcycle gang dead."

Dread descended on Josh like a shroud. He sat immobile through commercials for a used-car place, ambulance chasers and a public service spot urging him to be a Big Brother.

The blow-dried news announcer returned. "And now, a field report from our own Katy Varner as she interviews residents of Ptarmigan Street, where Thursday's shoot-out occurred."

The pert, brunette news babe with the turned-up nose had appeared in front of Josh's house while the police were picking bullets out of the wall.

"This was the scene Friday morning on the West Side's normally quiet Ptarmigan Street, following a shoot-out between gang members and the police that left four bikers dead. Their name is Insane—and I can't say the last word but you all know it. We spoke to Phil Bass, who has lived on Ptarmigan Street for a year."

Scene shift to Phil Bass on the stoop of his neo-Georgian Revival 6,000-square-foot manse. Bass was a pink-faced fiftysomething in a pale yellow knit shirt that stretched taut across his belly. He was executive vice president of sales for Wisconsin Healers Group, a non-profit insurance company.

Non-profit my ass, Josh thought.

"Mr. Bass, do you know Josh Pratt?"

"We've never met but I've seen him riding up and down this street on his motorcycle. I didn't know he was a private investigator."

"Were you home when the shoot-out occurred?"

"Yes. I'd just arrived home from work and I was in my den when I heard a series of shots. At first I thought it was just kids celebrating the Fourth of July. When I realized what it really was, I took my wife and kids into the basement."

"Didn't you hear the police sirens?"

"I guess. They really didn't register. You always hear sirens."

"And what was your reaction?"

"Well at first I was frightened, then I was concerned and now I'm angry. We're all hard-working families on this street. We moved out here for the quiet and the security. We never expected a motorcycle gang shoot-out."

Josh turned it off.

Fuck Phil Bass.

Maybe Josh should have spoken to the news babe. But no, Josh was not a talker, and froze up whenever someone pointed a lens or a microphone at him. He went into the garage, put on Bartemius Johnson's *Nothin' but the Blues* and went to work on his bike. He glanced at the basket case Harley, a hardtail frame, an engine resting on a workbench, various parts strewn about the garage, and thought it might be quicker to throw that together, but the idea of riding a hardtail again made him queasy. With any luck he'd have the Road King back on the road in twenty-four hours.

He looked at his watch. It was too late to get tires.

Josh knocked off at nine, went into his bedroom, took off his jeans and shirt and sat on the bed. He looked at *Tear the Roof Off the Sucker* lying facedown on his bed stand. A wave of weariness washed over him and he went to bed.

CHAPTER 26

I WAS HERE FIRST

KNOCKING AT THE DOOR WOKE HIM UP. HE looked at his watch. It was just past eight. Swinging his legs out of bed, Josh pulled on his jeans and padded through the dark house to the front door. He opened the door and there she was, the irrepressible Katy Varner, with her producer, cameraman and van.

Josh was about to shut the door, but the expression on Katy's face stopped him. She looked so hopeful.

Josh put a hand up in front of his eyes. "Come on, guys. I'm sure most of your viewers can sympathize with the fact that you got me out of bed on a Saturday morning."

"Mr. Pratt, I'd like just a moment of your time. You haven't said anything regarding the shoot-out and your neighbors are concerned."

Josh rubbed his eyes. "Give me ten minutes to shower."

He showered, thought about shaving. Fuck it.

When he emerged, Katy was directing her cameraman, who was shooting footage of the bullet holes. Josh wore a clean Harley T-shirt.

"Mr. Pratt, why did this happen?"

"The deceased gentlemen were snorting lines of meth off the table of a tavern where I was working security, and I had to ask them to leave. They were looking for payback. For me doing my job."

"Your neighbors are now concerned that your presence constitutes some kind of threat. Would you care to comment?"

Danny Bloom had taught Josh to look straight at the camera and not to move. "These guys were degenerate junkies. I've never run into such lowlifes before. What happened here was a once-in-a-lifetime freak occurrence that could never happen again in a million years. I have nothing but respect for my neighbors, and I promise to do all that is within my power to prevent any other lowlifes from entering this neighborhood.

"Mine was the first house on the block. There was nobody else near me when I moved out here five years ago."

Katy had another question.

Josh smiled. "That's all I have to say."

He began to back into his house. Katy pulled off her headset and mike and handed them to the cameraman as she came close so only Josh could hear. She handed him her card.

"Call me sometime. I'd like to know you better."

"Thank you," Josh said, taking the card, backing into his house and shutting the door behind him.

She was extremely attractive and had the added cachet of local celebrity. But Josh was a simple man and right now he had his sights set on a different woman. While putting the card in his card book with all the others, he heard his cell phone ring from the bedroom.

It was Calloway. "Drowning victim in Boston. BU's star quarterback found in the Charles River this morning by joggers."

"Smiley face?" Josh said.

"They're checking the area now. This ain't on the news yet—we got a bulletin."

"Do the Feds believe it's a conspiracy?"

"No. I messaged the UPN to send me any info on similar killings."

"UPN?" Josh asked.

"United Police Network. You got anything?"

"No sir. I will tell you when I do."

Mounting tires on wheels was a complex task most people left to their dealers, but Josh had his own wheel-mounting hardware from Harbor Freight, the biker's favorite store. It took him an hour to detach the wheels from his Road King and remove the tires, which he loaded into the back of the stealth Honda and drove to Motorcycle Performance. Forty-five minutes later he was back with a pair of Metzelers. Playing "Midnight Son" through his Bose, Josh spooned the tires onto the wheels, balanced them and remounted them on the chassis. He reconnected the belt drive.

By then it was one. He slapped pale bologna on white bread, slathered it with mayonnaise and ate it on the back deck. He went online and googled "star BU quarterback drowns in Charles."

The Boston Herald online had it. Patrick Unger was the son of Charles Unger, a silk stocking Boston attorney who lived in Newton. Patrick was the youngest of three children and had been attending BU on the full football scholarship they award to players they want badly enough, regardless of ability to pay. He had been a tall, handsome, charming young man, excellent GPA, his whole life before him.

"Preliminary reports indicate that Unger drowned following a night of drinking but an autopsy, due tomorrow, may shed further light on the tragedy."

There was no mention of gang graffiti.

The doorbell rang. The window company had arrived to install the new picture window. While that went on, Josh retreated to the garage and began choosing replacement parts for the Road King. He figured he had the makings of four complete motorcycles in his two-car garage, and his eye was on a Yamaha 500 single he planned to turn into a cafe racer. At a break between songs on Otis Rush's "Not Enough Comin' In," he heard his cell phone play "Lucille."

"Pratt."

"Josh, it's Sandy Meyer. Aaron phoned me last night."

CABO

JOSH WAITED UNTIL THE MEN HAD INSTALLED the new window, paid them and drove to Sandy's condo in Middleton on the west end of Lake Mendota. He kicked out in the parking lot of The Rusty Scupper, a seafood-oriented restaurant adjacent to the Middleton boat ramp, and went up the stairs to the artfully weathered condos, built in the seventies.

Sandy lived in a ground-floor unit with a patio overlooking the pool and a slice of the lake between buildings. She buzzed him in.

"I was asleep when he called but I saved the message. Would you like a cup of coffee?"

"Sure," Josh said. She made him a cup and they went out on the patio and sat in plastic chairs. She pulled out her cell phone.

"He sounded drunk," she said, cueing up the message.

Sound from the checkbook-sized device was surprisingly loud and clear. Ambient conversation and glass clinking—Kofsky had been in a bar.

"Hey babe," Kofsky said in that loose way of drunks. "Sorry I bailed on you like that. I got a lot of shit on my plate right now but I wanted to tell you that I'm thinking of you and I miss you and maybe you'd want to come down here and join me."

Someone said something to him and he spat back rapid-fire Spanish.

"Sorry 'bout that. Anyhoo, thinking of you. Give me a call when you get a chance."

A guitar played a blues lick.

"Gotta go—it's about to get loud!"

The guitarist bit into the blues and the call ended.

"What?" Sandy said, looking at Josh's face.

"That's Bartemius Johnson. He moved to Cabo ten years ago."

"Who?"

"Bartemius Johnson the blues player. Kofsky was in his club."

"Oh that's right!" Sandy said. "He took me there the last time I was down. Yeah, that's probably where he's hangin'."

"Well shit."

"What's the problem?" Sandy said.

"Now I have to go to Cabo."

Sandy transferred the saved message to Josh's phone so he could play it for Fleiss. Josh rode downtown to Fleiss's

offices and used Fleiss's company credit card to book a
one-way ticket to Cabo. He didn't know how long he'd be
there or if he'd be able to persuade Kofsky to return with
him. Delivering notice of a lawsuit in Mexico was legally
worthless.

He rode home, dug out his passport and threw some
clothes and *Tear the Roof Off the Sucker* in an overnight bag.
He only had the passport because Fleiss insisted. He'd never
used it. He phoned Louise Lowry.

"Louise, I'm going to be out of town for a few days.
Would you pick up my mail and keep an eye out?"

"Of course. Where are you going?"

"Cabo. Omma have to skip your cookout."

"Oh, Dave and I were down there five years ago," Louise
said. "Vacation?"

"Work. Maybe a little blues if I have the time. You have
a key to my place, right?"

"You bet."

"Thanks, Louise."

He went online, and was in luck. Rolf Gomez, his travel
agent, was online, too. They texted back and forth for a half
hour.

He phoned Fig Newton.

"I just wanted you to know," he said, "I have to fly to
Mexico on business. I should be back in two days."

"Mexico? What for?"

"Oh it's boring shit. I'm gonna try to convince this guy
to come back with me."

"Sounds like fun. Call me when you get back."

His flight was at 5:00 p.m. He called Union Cab and arranged for a pickup at four. The cab was on time, green, a Chevy Volt. The driver had wire-rimmed glasses, a tie-dyed shirt and a long ponytail.

"Airport please," Josh said from the back seat.

They pulled silently out.

"Hey you're the guy had that shoot-out on his front lawn," the driver said. "What was that all about?"

"Just some disgruntled bar patrons."

The driver could tell from Josh's tone that was the end of the conversation. He punched a button on the dash and the Grateful Dead sang "Dire Wolf."

The flight to O'Hare took forty minutes. Josh grabbed his bag and raced through the endless terminal, just making his direct-to-Cabo flight on Southwest. He sat next to a kid plugged into his iPod, focused on killing zombies on his notebook. Josh pulled out his book.

CHAPTER
28

KOFSKY

"P," YOLANDA SAID ON THE PLAYBACK, "PLEASE tell Shred that I'm in Baxter, North Carolina. This cop stopped me as I was driving through, said I had a broken headlight. Now he says I was resisting arrest! Shred needs to come down here..."

"HEY!" a pig grunted in a voice I knew. "Who said you could make a phone call?"

The call ended with a dial tone.

I saw red and white. Of all the burgs in all the states between Harlem and Atlanta, she had to go through Baxter. My heart raced like a Top Fuel dragster. I had to go down there and get her out.

But first I had to talk to Tyrone.

I raced home to my crib on West 157th Street, parked out front, paid Jimmy John Jackson a five to watch my whip. I took the stairs two at a time, banged into my crib and went straight to Yolanda's red leather address book which she kept right by the yellow princess phone. And sure enough. There on the day she left was Tyrone's phone number.

It was two o'clock when I phoned.

Woman picked it up. "Hello."

"Ma'am," I said, "this is Shred Husl in Harlem. My girl Yolanda was supposed to pick up her cousin Tyrone. Is Tyrone there?"

"No he isn't here right now. He's workin' at the lumberyard. He'll be home 'round five. You want me to have him call you?"

"Yes please. It's very important."

"Everything all right?" she said.

"You Tyrone's mom?" I said.

"Oh excuse me. I should have introduced myself. Yes I'm Tyrone's mother, Alice, and of course I know my niece Yolanda. Is she all right?"

"Not sure. She phoned me from Baxter, North Carolina. Said she was in jail for a busted taillight."

"Oh my," Alice said.

"Don't you worry none," I said. "I'll take care of it."

I was torn between the desire to take right off and wait for Tyrone's call. If Yolanda was stuck in jail in Baxter she wasn't going anywhere. I smoked half a pack of Pall Malls before Tyrone called. When the phone rang I snatched it up.

"Tyrone?" I barked.

"This is Tyrone," he said in a soft voice. "Mama tells me you called."

"Have you heard from Yolanda?"

"Not since she phoned me Friday morning and said she was coming down. Said she'd be here by dinnertime. I phoned her but I didn't get an answer."

"Says she got arrested in Baxter, South Carolina. I met the chief before. Biggest ofay cracker peckerwood I ever seen. I'm heading down there, see if I can bust her out."

"You want any help?" he said in a soft voice.

"Naw, Cuz, I'm just givin' you a head's-up. Might be a while before she gets down your way."

"Okay," he said softly, and hung up.

I've always been a solitary cat. Never ran with no gang, learned to do shit on my own. And that's just how I planned to get Yolanda out of the Baxter County jail. One thing for sure—all niggers look alike to a cracker like Billings. So the first thing I did was to shave my righteous 'fro. Time I was done my bathroom looked like a poodle exploded. I dug out some old gray dungarees and a pair of flat glass specs and put 'em on. I looked like a Stepin Fetchit motherfucker you wouldn't give a second glance.

I wasn't planning no James Bond shit, but I had to be there when the shit went down. Next thing I did was call my Jew lawyer, Murray Fine. I wanted to try the easy way first.

After a short wait Murray come on the line. "Shred, baby! What I can do you for?"

"Murray, my girlfriend Yolanda got herself arrested down in Baxter, South Carolina. Wantchoo to go down there and get her out."

"What for?"

"Fuck if I know."

"Maybe you better come down here," Murray said.

"I'm on my way."

Josh drifted off and the next thing he knew, the flight attendant was shaking him gently by the shoulder. "Mr. Pratt, we're landing. Please bring your table and seatback to a full upright position."

It was ten thirty by the time he got through customs in Mexico. The driver spoke English and suggested the Marietta, a genteel hotel several blocks from the beach on Alikan. Kofsky's condo was over near the Sheraton but Bart's Blues Club was on Ninos Heroes, not far from Cabo Wabo. Sammy Hagar, a huge blues fan, could often be found at Bart's Blues.

Josh checked into his room and walked the five blocks to Bart's Blues. The streets smelled of diesel fumes, the Sea of Cortez and roasting pork. It was eleven thirty and the street in front was alive with tourists and gamblers. Josh paid his five bucks and went inside. The club was dark, vast and smelled of cigarettes, gin and marijuana. A horseshoe-shaped bar protruded from one wall, with the stage straight back from the entrance. There was no one on the stage as the PA pumped Buddy Guy.

Josh worked his way through lissome Latin beauties and swarthy mustachioed men in colorful Hawaiian shirts to the bar, where he ordered a Dos Equis. Josh turned around and faced the room as the musicians returned to the stage to shouts and applause. Bartemius Johnson was a towering black man with a skull of gray hair. His three sidemen—drums, electric guitar and keyboards—were young and white.

Johnson launched into a fast blues shuffle that had patrons up and out of their seats instantly. Josh watched a middle-aged guy with a spreading paunch, a halo of curly hair, glasses, shorts, huaraches and a Muddy Waters T-shirt bopping to the music at the edge of the dance floor.

Josh waited for the song to end before he approached.

"Aaron Kofsky?" he said.

The man looked at him in shock.

CHAPTER

29

DEAL

THEY TOOK THEIR DRINKS TO THE INNER
courtyard, where the music was piped through a PA system,
and sat at a picnic table.

"Your partners want you back."

"So? Who are you? Interpol? You don't have any juris-
diction down here."

"I'm just a private investigator, Mr. Kofsky. I have no
authority. So far your partners have kept your disappearance
a secret from the Defense Department. What do you suppose will happen if Defense wants you back?"

Kofsky laughed. "Those clowns? They couldn't find their
asses with both hands. Where's Ed Snowden?"

"Sandy's a nice lady. She misses you."

Kofsky looked wistful as he downed a slug. He pulled a
fat doobie from his breast pocket and lit it with a Bic. "Yeah,
what else?"

He inhaled, held it and exhaled, filling the courtyard with aromatic marijuana smoke. He held the joint out to Josh, who shook his head.

"You don't come back, they'll report you. Your partners aren't exactly nobodies. If they get you declared an international fugitive and put a bounty on your head, then someone not as nice as me comes for you."

"Like Dog the Bounty Hunter?" Kofsky sneered.

"Worse than that," Josh said.

"So let me get this straight," Kofsky said. "You got no warrant, you got no power. You just want me to return to Wisconsin."

"That's right. But suppose I got something you might want."

Kofsky stared at Josh as if he were purple toad. "Like what?"

"Like your hard drive of kiddie porn."

A sick look stole over Kofsky's face. He turned ashen. "Shit."

"That was very foolish, Aaron, to leave that lying around."

"I left town so fast I forgot about that."

"How much of the money is left?"

Kofsky looked at him sideways. Josh leaned in.

"Tell me."

"A half mil."

"Why'd you do it?"

"Honest to God I'm not sure. I was feeling desperate, hemmed in. There was so much fucking pressure all the time!

We promised to deliver by May 15 but we missed the deadline! I thought I could make more money gambling but all I've done is lose."

"You sure you didn't come down here just to fuck young girls?"

At least Kofsky had the decency to look ashamed.

"Tell me there are no tapes of you out there somewhere having sex with minors."

"No! I swear! I just like to look."

"Well listen—you don't want to be a fucking fugitive. Come back with me, return the money. I don't usually say this, but are you Christian?"

"I'm Jewish," Kofsky said.

"You ever think of getting straight with God?"

Kofsky's mouth dropped like he'd just observed a talking dog. "Are you serious?"

"It works for me. Come back with me and I'll destroy that hard drive. Nobody will know. Refuse and I hand it over to your partners. Your parents will know, everybody will know. They'll show your face to fifty million people."

Kofsky buried his head in his hands. "Aw, Jesus."

"You help me, I help you. Now there is something you can do for me."

Kofsky looked at him expectantly. "What?"

"Ever hear of the Smiley Face Killings?"

Kofsky pursed his lips and looked at the ceiling. "Seems to me I have. What about them?"

"White jocks drowning coast to coast. In each case a smiley face found nearby. This would have to be centrally directed, would it not?"

"One would think so," Kofsky agreed.

"Well how would you get the word out? Suppose they are using closed forums?"

"Darknet."

"Yeah?"

Kofsky nodded. "How else? Lotta people using darknet. It's ideal for organized crime as well as terrorist activities, which is why we got this Defense Department contract."

"Could you find a darknet system for me? Could you find whoever it is that's directing this nationwide stealth jihad against college jocks?"

"Maybe. We're working on an algorithm that tracks certain key words or phrases. Allah Akbar, jihad, the Great Satan, etc."

"Well that's the deal then. You come back, face the music, help me with this thing and that hard drive never existed."

"Okay," Kofsky said, slowly nodding his head, "but let me ask you something. If you're such a good Christian, how do you reconcile that with destroying evidence of my little hobby?"

Josh put a hand on Kofsky's shoulder. "Omma be watching you, hoss."

HOME AGAIN

THEY MADE THE 7:00 A.M. MONDAY FLIGHT. Kofsky used his personal credit card to buy them both first-class tickets. Josh phoned Fleiss from the airport. As soon as he sat Kofsky pulled out his iPod and laptop, plugged in and dropped out just like some zombie kid. Very faintly, Josh heard Queen singing "We Are the Champions" through the iPod.

Josh pulled out his book.

Fine's office on 96th Street was about what you'd expect from a Jew lawyer. Red shag carpeting, and also what you might expect from a lawyer in his line of work—copies of Oui and Hustler on the reception table, and a secretary with Dagmars like a '55 Caddy. Miss Tits waved me right in where Fine sat in a high-backed leather chair like some kinda pharaoh beneath a framed painting of Felix Frankfurter.

Fine got up and came around his desk to give me a hug and the soul dap as best he could. He wore a powder blue leisure suit, a black shirt and a bolo tie with a ruby the size of a robin's egg.

"Shred, baby! What the fuck happened? You look like the janitor at a lunatic asylum!"

"I changed my look. You check into that little problem?"

Fine went back behind his desk, sank down, opened a drawer and pulled out a bottle of Jack. He placed two shot glasses on his green felt desk top, poured a couple fingers in each and slid one across the table. I picked it up.

"Yeah and there's good news and bad news. What do you want first?"

"Bad news, baby. I always take the bad news first."

"This cat, the chief, Carl Billings, is rotten. He's been on Sam Schuster's payroll for years and he's got a reputation as a violent nigger-hater from way back."

"Carl, huh?" I said. "Figures. What's the good news?"

"He'll do anything for money. You can probably buy her off."

"That the way I see it too."

Fine pulled out a mirror, an amber vial and an ivory-handled straight razor from his top desk drawer and laid out a couple lines. He used a cut straw from McDonald's to hoover a line, slid the mirror over to me.

"Ah—AHH!" he declared. "Breakfast of champions."

I told him about my encounter with Billings.

"You're lucky he didn't search that car. So what's the plan, Trouble Man?"

"That dumb cracker won't remember me, not the way I look now. They won't figure me for money. I'll just bail her out."

"Okay, here's the deal," Fine said, laying out another line. "I don't hear from you in twenty-four, I'll come down myself."

"He hates Jews too."

Fine grinned and spread his arms. "Doesn't everybody?"

I left Fine and drove to Patterson to see my man Floyd about a used car. Floyd had a '64 Ford Falcon looked like roadkill.

"Just came in last night. Ain't had a chance to do a thorough look-over but she runs good."

I handed over the keys to my Caddy. "Don't you sell my whip, you hear me Floyd?"

Floyd just grinned. "You ain't back in a week, she gone."

"You don't got title!"

"I don't need title."

And so, under an overcast sky, I turned the grille toward South Carolina and gave her the gas.

The stewardess shaking his shoulder woke Josh when they were about to land. It was 2:00 p.m. CST. He and Kofsky raced through O'Hare to catch their American Express Eagle hop to Madison, where they were met by Fleiss, who drove them to his office in his Escalade.

Fleiss ushered them into his conference room, where Marcia had coffee and doughnuts. Fleiss thumped Josh on the back.

"Marcia, get the partners on the line," Fleiss said. He turned to Josh. "I can't believe you did it! How'd you do it?"

Josh shrugged. "He missed Wisconsin."

Fleiss sat at the end and squared the old-fashioned office phone before him. "Mr. Kofsky, I'm going to inform your partners that you're back."

Kofsky sat at the opposite end of the table with a doughnut. "Go ahead."

Fleiss put it on speakerphone. "James, Tom, Ernie, are we all on?"

Three men answered.

Fleiss turned to Kofsky and raised his eyebrows.

"Hi, guys," Kofsky said. "I'm back. Sorry for the scare. I just had to get away for a little while."

"You bring back the money?" one of them said.

"Most of it," Kofsky said.

"Welcome back, Aaron," said another. "Can we all get together at five at the office?"

They agreed to get together.

On the way out Josh said to Kofsky, "When can we get together on that other matter?"

"Give me a few days to sort things out and get back on track. I'll have to do it from the office. That's where the hardware is."

"Your partners won't mind?"

"They won't even know."

BAIL MONEY

JOSH TOOK A TAXI AND GOT HOME AT FOUR. Louise Lowry had left his mail neatly piled on the coffee table in the dining room. Utility bills, *The Horse*, and a *J&P Cycles* catalog. Josh checked his e-mail and found a message from Fig asking if he'd like to go for a ride. He called her, got voicemail and said, "Sure."

Josh wondered if Kofsky had contacted Sandy Meyer, but it wasn't his business. He phoned Heinz Calloway.

"Calloway," the big man answered. Josh heard shouts.

"What's going on?"

"I'm out here at Belmar Hills. Some fool shot a dog. What do you want?"

"Know where I can find Jerell Moore?"

"You got to be shitting me. He ain't gonna talk to you."

"He might."

"Lemme call you back."

Josh went to his garage, cranked up some Winter Brothers and went to work replacing the broken bulbs and lenses on the Road King. By the time Calloway phoned, it was rideable.

"Moore and his crew hang at Brother Mel's Lounge on East Sunset in Waukesha. Usually hits that place after midnight with some of his boys. Right now he's driving a '99 Lexus, license plate HBR 135."

"Thanks, Heinz."

"You look at his rap sheet?"

"No," Josh said.

"Assault, possession with intent and he's a suspect in at least two unsolved murders."

"I'll be careful."

"Listen. I got a courtesy call from the Quad Cities Gang Task Force. There's a rumor going around that the Insane Assholes are looking for payback. I passed that on to the West Side station, thought you should know."

"Thanks again, Heinz. They'd have to be pretty stupid to try something now."

"They are pretty stupid."

They ended the call. Josh didn't know what precautious he should take. The West Side cops were buzzing like a hive on alert. Rat bikers had little chance of penetrating the upper-middle-class neighborhood to get to Ptarmigan Road.

Fig phoned. They agreed to meet at the Hubbard Avenue Diner at eight in the morning. Josh went online to check on the latest drowning victim. They called it an accident.

Josh rode to a Burger King on the Beltline and had a burger and fries for dinner, rode home and put the bike away. He looked at the holes in his front facade. He'd better get those fixed quick or sure as shit one of his neighbors would launch a complaint with the city.

It was still light out so he went out front, spackled and sanded, spraying his handiwork with a pale gray shade of Krylon that almost matched the original paint. So what if it looked a little scabby? A touch of Appalachia was just what his diversity-craving neighbors needed. Maybe he would add a lawn gnome.

It was dark by the time he knocked off. Josh took a shower and retired to his bedroom with the novel.

I drove all day and hit Charlotte just past nine, pulled into the Lamplighter Motel on Gregory Street. I'd stayed at the Lamplighter before. It was run by and for black folks and there was a good rib joint across the street.

The old bald waiter see me reading my W.E.B. DuBois. "That's the rare truth, brother," he said to me.

"Yeah," I said chewing on a rib. "This cat know all about Jim Crow."

So one thing leads to another and we start shootin' the shit. I tell him where I'm headed and he pulls back like he sees a spider.

"Baxter? That's peckerwood heaven. They throw a brother in jail just for walking on the sidewalk."

"I don't got no choice, see. They done arrested my woman."

The brother leans in so no one can overhear. "That chief of police is a stone racist and dirtier'n a pig in shit. This some kind of shake-down scam he runnin'."

"Don't I know it," I said. "He shook me down a month ago. I got lucky. He cut me loose after palming my C-note."

"You packin'?" the waiter said softly.

"Oh yeah."

"You be careful."

I left a ten-buck tip and went to bed, dreaming I was on a chain gang and that the head cracker was Billings, face like a clenched fist. Got up, shit, shaved, showered, had breakfast at Waffle Hut and hit the road in that old white Falcon that looked like a bar of soap. Probably bust me for drivin' a white car.

I hit Baxter at eleven, drove five miles under the limit right down Main Street until I come to the City/County Building where the jail was at. I parked in front of a Woolworth's a block up and walked, keeping my head down and carrying a clipboard. Man in coveralls and a clipboard can go anywhere.

Push my way into the police beneath a humming AC that drips water on my head. Inside two crackers are yukkin' it up, one on this side the counter, one on the other. Both blue suits. Big map of the county on the wall behind them. Open box of pizza on the counter, half gone, pineapple, ham and bacon, of course, from Fabroni's. My stomach rumbled. They shut up soon's I entered, looked at me like I was some kind of vermin. The one on this side got a gut like a medicine ball straining at his blue shirt. He turns around, puts his elbows on the counter and sucks a toothpick.

One behind the desk some Ichabod Crane-lookin' mother-fucker with an Adam's apple the size of a softball.

"He'p you?" he says not looking at me.

"Yes sir. You got a Yolanda Washington in here?"

"Maybe."

Medicine ball chuckled.

"Like to bail her out," I said.

"Oh you would, would you? You got some kinda ID, boy?"

I kept my head down and showed him my fake driver's license in the name of Leon Ward.

"You got any warrants out on you, Leon? You wanted for anything, like maybe theft or public drunkenness?"

This wasn't about me. He was just humiliating me for sport. I kept my head down. "No sir."

"Well lemme check here." And he went through a door into a back office leaving me with Medicine Ball. Medicine Ball whistled "Dixie," staring at me, but I kept my head down. Ichabod Crane comes back grunting to himself, lays some papers on the counter and says, "Says here Mizz Washington didn't have proper license and registration. Says here that vehicle is registered to someone else."

"I'm sure it's just a misunderstanding, officer," I said, pulling out a vinyl billfold with the corner of a C-note peeking out like a glimpse of a pretty girl's slip.

"How much you got there, Rastus?" he said.

I pulled it all out. Four C-notes—more 'n these crackers see in a month. "Four hundred. That's all I got."

His crab-like hand snatched it up. "Well we're gonna let y'all go with a warning this time, boy. And her car stays impounded. You want that, you got to deal with the impound people. Now you wait here. Don'tchoo go anywhere now."

Medicine Ball was smirking so hard he couldn't whistle "Dixie."

Ichabod picked up his desk phone and spoke to somebody in back. Five minutes later a matron the size of a John Deere tractor brought Yolanda out. Yolanda looked exhausted and dirty but she held on to her shit. Soon as they let her out from behind the counter she said, "Let's get out of here, Shred."

"Shred?" Medicine Ball says. "I thought you said your name was Leon."

"Shred's just my nickname," I said, heart beatin' faster than a ragtime player's metronome.

"Go on," the desk sergeant said. "Get the fuck outta here afore I change my mind."

RIDE

FIG PULLED UP IN FRONT OF THE HUBBARD Avenue Diner on her red Hawk GT and joined Josh at a booth. They ordered coffee and breakfast.

"Where did you want to ride?" Josh said.

"I have some secret roads out south of Spring Green I'll show you."

"Did you hear about that drowning in Boston?"

Fig nodded grimly. "Did they find the happy face?"

"If they have, they're not announcing."

"Why don't they take this shit seriously?" Fig said.

Josh poked at a waffle. "I don't know."

They headed west on county roads, Fig wearing blue jeans, a pink tank top and her pink Hello Kitty backpack. The road turned twisty. Josh struggled to keep the pink backpack in sight. The massive Road King was no match for the tiny Hawk, but whenever she disappeared from view he'd find her waiting for him at a farm pull-off or an intersection.

South of Spring Green it was pure magic, endless winding roads through valleys and forests carved by glacial melt. Whipping through sun-dappled forest smelling the fresh air with a touch of manure, Josh forgot all about time until at last Fig pulled up at a county park, got off her bike and removed her helmet, laughing.

"Wheeeeeeeee!" she said.

Josh kicked out and got off. "I can't keep up with you."

"You could if you rode something smaller."

"Maybe I should get a scooter."

Fig laughed. "Can't see it."

They stood side by side looking at the rolling hills.

"Would you like to hear some blues Friday?" Josh said at last.

"Like who?"

"I know this old white dude, John Davis, plays blues like he was born on the Delta."

"You know," Fig said, "you can't swing a dead cat up here without hitting four old white dues who play the blues. Where?"

"He's playing the club in Middleton. I could pick you up. I have a car."

"What time?"

"He starts at nine."

"Bring your bike," Fig said. "Let's head back."

She waved to him when he pulled off toward Ptarmigan.

He got home, looked at his house in the afternoon light. Not too shabby, if you didn't look at any of the other houses.

Josh smoked a joint and took a nap, waking at seven. No point looking for Jerell before midnight. Josh figured he'd have more cred if he showed on his bike. He watched TV until ten thirty. He took the interstate and wore a white cotton sweatshirt to make himself as visible as possible, pulling into Waukesha at eleven thirty. He'd Google-Mapped Brother Mel's and knew the location by heart, pulled into a 7-Eleven a block up the street, gassed up and bought a gas store hot dog for a buck. He was the only white guy in the joint but nobody gave him any shit.

He stood out front eating his hot dog and watched a white Lexus sedan cruise past and turn into Brother Mel's parking lot. Josh wanted a drink, badly. But he had to keep a clear head. Milwaukee was one of, if not *the*, most segregated cities in the country. This was black Milwaukee and he stood out like a cockroach on rye. One false move and he could end up dead in an alley, and the cops wouldn't even know who he was when they showed up—if they showed up—because BPSN would strip him of every identifying object including his hands and face.

Black criminal organizations and biker gangs rarely crossed paths. Each kept to its own turf, although Mexican gangs had been fighting bikers over the southwest meth trade for years. Josh got on his bike, rolled down the street into the parking lot and pulled into an empty space. There were six other cars in the lot, including Jerell's Lexus—two low riders, a 350Z, a Mercedes 350SL and an old Bronco.

Josh heard Young Jeezy blasting through the walls. He peeled off his sweatshirt, took what he needed from his tank bag, breathed in and out a couple of times, squared his shoulders and pushed in through the glass door.

The music didn't stop but everything else did. To his left was a chrome and glass bar with neon lighting surrounding the mirror and bottles. The bartender, who looked like a dum-dum bullet, stared at him with an open mouth. Five people at the bar turned on their stools to look. Booths along the right wall were partly occupied. Josh figured, correctly, that Jerell and posse would occupy the back booth. All conversation ceased as Josh walked toward the back clutching his package.

He reached the back booth—a banquette capable of seating seven, strewn with plates of picked-through ribs. He recognized Jerell in the back center from his mug shot—a thirtysomething playa with wide-set eyes, a fadeaway, high cheekbones, diamond stud, two guys on each side. They all looked at Josh like he was a cop. The music stopped. In the silence that followed the only sound was a muffled, "What the fuck?" from the bar.

"What are you," Jerell said, "some kind of bad motherfucker?"

Josh tossed the book on the table. Jerell picked it up and his face broke into a broad grin.

"Sit down, my man! Lonnie, make room. Tyler, move your ass."

POOR WHITE TRASH

JERELL HELD THE COPY OF *TEAR THE ROOF OFF The Sucker*. "I been lookin' for this book for years. You want to sell it?"

"I'm not finished. When I'm finished I'll give it to you."

Jerell snapped his fingers. "Lonnie, get him a beer and a Jack. You want a line?"

"Better not," Josh said. "I'm on a bike."

"So what's your name and what you want?"

"Josh Pratt. Want to talk to you about Shred Husl. I'm a private investigator working on a case, college athlete drowned in Madison."

Jerell leaned back and looked down his nose. "I don't know nothin' 'bout that. Wait a minute. Wait a minute. You the cat that had that shoot-out last week, the one with the four dead bikers. What's their name?"

"Insane Assholes," Tyler piped up. He was a pipe cleaner thin gangbanger the color of coal with a gold hoop in one ear.

Jerell cracked up. "Fuck yeah! Insane Assholes! Gotta love them white folk. What they want? You smoke any?"

Josh told Jerell about his beef with the Assholes. "Now my neighbors are mad because they think I'm a crime magnet."

"MMM, mmm, mmm," Jerell said. "Why white folks always gotta be lookin' down on someone? They ain't no niggers around they look down on you, 'cause you poor white trash."

"Just the way they are, I guess," Josh said.

"Why you axin' me 'bout some murder in Madison?"

"Heard you call yourself Shred Husl."

Jerell cracked up, slapping the table with his palm. "That's right! I do! Been reading Curtis Mack since I was in high school. Had a righteous teacher turned me on to him, Donald Goines, and Chester Himes. Thinkin' 'bout financing a Shred Husl movie. We even had Wesley Snipes interested, before he gone to prison on a bullshit federal beef. Also, we never could find Curtis Mack."

"They lock a brother up for doing well," Tyrone said.

Jerell took a rib and handed it to a German Shepherd under the table. "Here you go, Miss Lollipop. Miss Lollipop just had a litter. You need a dog?"

Josh looked under the table. Miss Lollipop lolled on her side suckling five pups on a blanket. A water dish sat between Jerell's feet.

"What I want to know," Josh said, "is there someone telling non-white gangs to sandbag drunk college athletes on their way home and leaving smiley face graffiti on the walls?"

Jerell leaned back and essayed a million-dollar smile. A half-carat ruby gleamed from one of his eyeteeth. "Why would I tell you? You think we're snuffing white college kids on somebody's say-so?"

"It occurred to me."

Jerell looked around at his posse, grinning. "Can you believe the balls on this cracker? 'Cause I call myself Shred Husl? I got lotsa names. And I don't leave calling cards."

"You know Davante Daniels?"

Lonnie set a beer and a shot in front of Josh. One beer, one shot. He could handle it. He tossed the shot and drank half the beer. Now he started thinking about a line.

"Nope," Jerell said. "Who he?"

"Some lowlife got picked up last week for assault. He had 'Shred Husl' inked on his chest."

Jerell looked around, grinning, stripped off his black-and-gold Dethrone T, revealing a constellation of ink on his dark chest, including SHRED HUSL, BLACKSTONE P. NATION and a portrait of Marcus Garvey. "You ain't no lily-white palimpsest yourself, are you Josh Pratt?"

"I got ink."

"Let me see."

Josh peeled off his Sturgis T, revealing the black, green, gold, red and blue dragon that wrapped around his torso. Jerell whistled.

"Motherfucker," Lonnie said.

"Money," Tyrell said.

"What about them Norteños?" Lonnie said. He was the size of a refrigerator and wore a black beret.

"What about the Norteños?" Josh said.

"They in Madison, they always talkin' 'bout goin' down on campus and bustin' up white college kids."

"How do you know that?" Josh asked. Latino and black gangs seldom mixed except when they were fighting.

"Heard 'em talkin' trash at that Pitbull concert," Lonnie said. He affected a broad accent. "'Eyyyy, ese! I sure fucked up some Anglos down by the lake!'"

"Got any names?" Josh said.

"Don't do names," Lonnie said.

Josh took out his card and handed it to Jerell. "You ever need an investigator, give me a call."

Laughing, Jerell put the card in his wallet. "I sure will! Fuck I will!"

Josh looked at Lonnie, who was blocking his way.

"Let the man out," Jerell said. "You sure you don't want a line?"

Josh hesitated. "Better not."

Lonnie slid out and let Josh pass.

CHAPTER 34

NORTEÑOS

JOSH WAS HOME BY TWO, TRIED TO SLEEP, mind like a hamster in a wheel. The Norteños were among a half dozen Latino gangs that had taken root in Madison over the years, and had connections to several drug cartels. They were in the business of making money, not snuffing white college kids.

Suppose it was an amazing coincidence, all these college athletes drowning while staggering home drunk from bars? All those happy faces?

Josh didn't believe it. His gut said there was some design at work here. He finally drifted off as the sun rose, and slept until eleven. He slept poorly and woke up cranky, forced himself to run five miles beneath a lowering sky, showered, and went into his office to research Hispanic gangs in Madison. The Norteños were mostly concentrated in an area just off the South Beltline near Marlborough Park, having displaced the black gangs who had migrated west to the Elver Park area.

Might be worth his while to wander around the neighborhood looking for graffiti, although he doubted any Chicano would embrace a black icon like Shred Husl.

He phoned Aaron Kofsky, who agreed to meet him at Dovetail at four in Middleton. He rode to Marlborough Park, where about a dozen Hispanic and black kids were playing basketball on a concrete court. Josh kicked out and got off, noting that some of the kids appeared to be full-grown adults. There was graffiti on the backboards and any flat surface—trash cans, the walls of a maintenance hut. No Shred Husl or smiley face. He got some hard looks but that was it.

Dovetail occupied a Bauhaus-like structure on Deming Way in Middleton. Josh unassed in the motorcycles-only parking lot next to a fully faired Kawasaki and a Sportster. Inside the foyer a young woman in tortoiseshell glasses, her blond hair cut to the nub, looked up from behind a curving oak counter.

"You must be Mr. Pratt. Here." She handed him a laminated visitor's pass on a lanyard. "Aaron says go straight back and turn left. He's in the Batcave." The halls were dark, hushed and carpeted. Josh went through the door with the bat symbol taped to it. The room was lined with monitors, routers, hard drives and keyboards, lit by the monitors and hidden lights behind the floorboards. Kofsky sat in a black mesh chair in front of a large monitor that displayed scrolls of numbers.

"What are we looking for?" he said.

"Hidden forums that contain the terms 'Shred Husl' or the smiley face symbol, particularly those with crosses for eyes." Josh grabbed a slip of paper out of a trash can and drew the smiley face. "Like this."

Kofsky glanced at the drawing and pecked at his keyboard. "Best way is to use the Onion Router. This is an excellent opportunity to test our program."

Kofsky's Dovetail home page dissolved, replaced by a gray screen scrolling white numbers with a domain name that seemed random but ended in "/onion." Kofsky poked again and a search engine appeared. He entered "Shred Husl." Within seconds two domain names popped up.

"The first is in Brazil," Kofsky said. "Shredhusllives."

"How can you tell?"

"By the domain name. The second is in Belarus." Kofsky placed the cursor over Shredhusllives and clicked. A lurid illustration appeared—a tall, thin black man in a trench coat and wide-brimmed lavender hat with a .45 in one hand, clutching a sinewy black beauty in the other. It was designed as a movie poster, SHRED HUSL, starring Shank Lodestar, Monica DuPrix and Kelvin Little, written and directed by Manklin True.

Josh pulled out his pad and started writing.

"You don't have to do that," Kofsky said. "I'll forward the domain name. You have anti-corruption software, right?"

"Webroot."

"You want me to send you this? Your call. You don't know what it'll bring."

"Maybe I'd better just write it down."

"Suit yourself," Kofsky said. He moved on to the next domain. A crude home page appeared with grainy pictures of black men hanging from trees, the Ku Klux Klan, a smiling Dick Cheney, Cyrillic script. And a smiley face with crosses for eyes.

Josh stared intently. "What language is that?"

"I'm not sure. Probably Russian, although it could be Belarusian."

"Do you know what it says?"

"Do I speak Russian?"

"That's it," Josh said. "That's got to be it."

Kofsky moved the cursor. "Look at these sub-headings. This means 'map,' I think." He clicked on it. A map of the U.S. appeared with tiny yellow smiley faces scattered from coast to coast, including Madison, LaCrosse and Boston.

"This is it," Josh hissed. "This is how they get the word out. But how is some black gangbanger going to understand Russian?"

Kofsky clicked on the smiley face symbol. And there it was.

MANIFESTO

BLACK FOLKS' HATRED OF WHITE PEOPLE IS NOT in the least "pathological," but a healthy human reaction to oppression, insult, and terror.

The whole world knows the Nazis murdered millions of Jews and can suspect that the remaining Jews are having some emotional reaction to that fact. Brothers, on the other hand, are either ignored or thought to be so subhuman that they have no feelings when one of their number is killed because he was a black man. Probably no week goes by in the United States that some brother is not severely beaten, and the news is reported in the black press.

Every week or maybe twice a week almost the entire black population of the United States suffers an emotional recoil from some insult coming from the voice or pen of a leading white man.

The surviving Jews had one, big, soul-wracking "incident" that wrenched them back to group identification. The surviving black folks experience constant jolts that almost never let them forget for even an hour that they are black.

You see them everywhere—sneering, entitled, privileged white crackers who have never known hardship, never known the daily struggle of simply trying to get enough to eat, let alone a job. They don't worry about redlining or discrimination. They got white privilege. Their path was laid out for them from the moment they were born—go to a nice white school in the suburbs, play varsity football, try out for the debate team, go to a popular, mostly white school that showers them with adoration, lauds their every achievement and we all know that 90 percent of those white crackers couldn't compete with any pick-up football or basketball game in the 'hood.

This country was founded by white people for white people and built on the backs of black people. Were they to turn over all their worldly goods to us, it would still not be enough. The White People's United States of Amerikkka can never repay the debt it owes to black people who built this country under the eyes of the overseer and the lash of the whip.

The black people of this country are treated worse than Jews under Nazi Germany. We are only 13 percent of the population yet we comprise 56 percent of the prison population! Ward Churchill was right when he condemned the "Little Eichmanns" in the World Trade Center. Every day white Americans make decisions that adversely affect our black youth. Whom should we blame? We know whom to blame.

The White power structure.

All those pretty boys born with silver spoons up their asses, particularly those from wealthy families who attend prep schools and go to college. We've all experienced the humiliation and physical violence of the By God Self-Important Jock in high school. They called you a nigger. They called you a queer. They gave you noogies, titty twisters, and snapped their towels at you in phys. ed. leaving red marks.

You know them by their Porsches, Mustangs and Subarus.

You know them by their fraternities, baggy shorts, flip-flops and blond hair.

You know them by their institutional racism.

What do we do about it?

WE RESIST!

How do we resist?

I will tell you how we resist. We take their sons as they have taken ours for centuries. We take those sons of privilege, follow them from the bars where they denigrate women and anyone who isn't like them, we drag them into the water and we drown them.

Leave this symbol nearby so that others may know.

WE ARE THE RESISTANCE.

WE WILL NOT REST UNTIL WE HAVE TORN DOWN THE WHITE POWER STRUCTURE AND RE-PLACED IT WITH A RAINBOW COALITION OF THE BLACK, THE BROWN, THE YELLOW, THE RED IN AN EGALITARIAN SOCIALIST WORKERS PARADISE!

CHAPTER 36

PETTYJOHN

"HOLY SHIT," KOFSKY SAID. "I FEEL UNCLEAN."

"Scary, isn't it?" Josh said. "So where did it originate?"

Kofsky stared at the screen. "That's the problem. Whoever did this ran it through a network of zombies to end up in Belarus. Tracing it to a specific location where it originated is almost impossible."

"Can you send this to the FBI?"

Kofsky made a pained expression. "Our contract with the Defense Department precludes sharing any information with any outside agencies."

"But technically, this has nothing to do with your contract."

"Yes it does. I used the software we developed under contract. Any breach of security not only renders the contract void, it violates the National Security Act."

"I didn't sign any contract."

"Yeah but if you send it in they're going to wonder how you found it and some men will come to your door."

"That's ridiculous!" Josh said. "Law enforcement agencies need to know what's going on." He took out his pad and copied down the darknet domain, a series of seemingly random letters and numbers. "I'll tell them I just stumbled onto it."

"That won't work," Kofsky said. "They'll find out in a heartbeat that you were hired to bring me back."

"But all these gangs, they know about it. How did they find out? Someone must have contacted them."

"Look," Kofsky said. "If you can find a credible way to pin this intelligence on the gangs, do it. Just leave me out of it."

There was a knock at the door and a young woman stuck her head in. "Aaron, you're wanted in the boardroom."

Kofsky stood. "Gotta go. We got a deal, right?"

"Yeah," Josh said.

They had a deal. In prison, child rapists were low man on the totem pole. They had a very hard time. Josh himself had participated in rough justice payback in his first few months, before he got together with Dorgan. It wasn't just the manifesto that made him feel dirty. It was hiding Kofsky's secrets.

Josh rode home, went online and reviewed Afro-American studies course offerings in the online catalog. Maurice Pettyjohn was a professor in the department specializing in pop culture. His class was called Pimps, Players, and Private Eyes: Race Through the Prism of Black Hard-Boiled Crime."

Curtis Mack was key. Josh heard the same voice in the Smiley Face Manifesto as in *Tear the Roof off the Sucker*. He called Professor Pettyjohn and made an appointment to see him at 4:00 p.m. Afro-American studies was located in the Helen C. White Hall next to the Student Union.

Back to campus. At four o'clock Josh knocked on the open door of Pettyjohn's office on the fourth floor with a view of Lake Mendota. A small, neat black man wearing camo cargo pants, glasses and a black beret pushed himself back from his desk and stood.

"Come in, Mr. Pratt. How can I help you?"

They shook hands. The room was decorated with framed movie posters: *Shaft, Truck Turner, Superfly*. Pettyjohn and Josh sat.

"Professor, I'm trying to track down Curtis Mack."

Pettyjohn smiled. "Ah, Curtis Mack! As mysterious as B. Traven! I remember stumbling across his books as a teenager in East Chicago. *Take It to the Max*. Man I was hooked. Here was a cat who saw pop culture through the prism of a tough, inner-city black, a knight errant, what Raymond called a man of honor.

"'A detective in this kind of story must be such a man. He is the hero; he is everything. He must be a complete man and a common man and yet an unusual man. He must be, to use a rather weathered phrase, a man of honor—by instinct, by inevitability, without thought of it, and certainly without saying it. He must be the best man in his world and a good enough man for any world.'"

Josh pulled his dog-eared copy of *Tear the Roof Off the Sucker* from his backpack and laid it on Pettyjohn's desk. Pettyjohn picked it up with reverence.

"And here it is. Mack's first book. Do you know how long I've been looking for a copy? I don't suppose I could borrow this when you're finished? It's the one Mack I've never read."

"Sure, as soon as I get it back from another guy I promised it to. What do you know about Mack?"

"Tell me why you want to know."

Josh told him about Stan Newton, the Smiley Face Killings and Shred Husl. When he was finished Pettyjohn stared at him wide-eyed through his horn-rimmed glasses.

"I wish I could say that's crazy but I've heard too many other tenured people say more or less the same thing."

"Like who?"

The corner of Pettyjohn's mouth turned up. "You'll have to find that on your own. It won't be hard. These people aren't exactly shy."

"Are you not telling me because you're a tenured radical?"

Pettyjohn laughed. "Some of my best friends are white."

"Why do you suppose Curtis Mack has never come forward?"

"Because it's most likely a pseudonym and whoever wrote those books wishes to remain anonymous."

"But why?" Josh said. "Now is their time. Everything old is new again. Now's the time to cash in."

"Perhaps they're ashamed. Perhaps they're dead."

"I was afraid of that," Josh said.

"Believe me, nothing would please me more than meeting the author of those books. I can't tell you what it meant to me, discovering Curtis Mack when I was a teenager. If I were ever able to track him down I'd write his biography. I've looked into Curtis Mack. He's a mystery. We know next to nothing about Onyx Press. Their physical address was a block in South Chicago since demolished. It was believed they circulated their books by working as news jobbers and sneaking the books into the shipments."

"But what happens when the retail outlet unpacks them and realizes they didn't order them?"

"In the sixties and seventies most purveyors of paperbacks weren't too solid on inventory control. Many of them were sketchy operations. The Mafia has used news outlets to launder money for years."

Josh thanked Pettyjohn and stood.

"Can I borrow that book when you're through?" Pettyjohn said.

"Tell me who's talking about killing white college athletes."

Pettyjohn smiled and cocked his head. "See you around."

THE COLLECTIVE

JOSH SPENT WEDNESDAY FAMILIARIZING HIMSELF with the darknet. It was scary, an invisible world lurking just out of the lights. It reminded Josh too much of tripping on acid when he thought he could see infinite parallel worlds stretching off into space, even when he closed his eyes. He'd become convinced he'd never sleep again. A brother Bedouin stopped him just before he was going to gouge his tripping eyes out with a knife.

Many darknet sites had fiendish malware security devised to destroy the hard drives of unauthorized users. Josh had to shut down several times to avoid losing all his files. Thereafter he used the computer at the public library until an officious librarian—one of those guys who had majored in library science—caught him and threw him out.

What Josh found was frightening. So many of the sites were dedicated to hate. White supremacist sites that Hitler would have loved. White power sites reviling American blacks and vice versa. Internecine warfare among members of the LGBT community. Lipstick lesbians vs. dykes. Transvestites vs. transgendered. Half the world engaged in subrosa battle. If you knew how to do it you could bring the war right into your home, as many had. Some of the discussion groups made Al Qaeda seem a model of probity. It made the sectarian violence of Twitter look like Parliament.

He knocked off at five and took a beer out on the back deck. His phone rang the same stupid jingle it had rung when he got it, because he wasn't clever enough to download a custom ring tone or song, or he would have chosen something by Stevie Ray Vaughan.

"Pratt," he answered.

"Mr. Pratt, this is Walter at the Little Read Book store. Remember you asked if I had anything else by Curtis Mack?"

"That's right, Walter. What did you find?"

"Well you won't believe this but I was going through some back issues of Takeover, which was a radical monthly they used to publish forty years ago, and I found an article by Curtis Mack."

"How late you open?"

"I'm here until seven."

"Okay," Josh said. "I'll be right down."

A half hour later he entered the shop. Two customers, both young men, both with Mohawks like cockatoos, browsed through the comics. Walter laid the ancient yellowed newspaper triumphantly on the counter as Josh approached.

The hand-set broadside looked like it had been thrown together in the back of a shotgun shack and printed with a mimeograph. TAKEOVER, screamed the title in big black letters. The cover stories were about how to hide your stash from the pigs, a review of a Joan Baez concert and a cartoon about the military/industrial complex.

"It's on page three," Walter said.

Josh opened the paper. "How to Off Pigs" by Curtis Mack started at the top. "What do you want for it?" Josh said.

"You can have it," Walter said. "It was just taking up room."

"Thanks, man." Josh tucked the paper beneath his arm. "Were you around in the sixties when this was coming out?"

"You bet. I went to the UW. I have a degree in Eastern philosophy."

Walt reminded Josh of his cab driver. He checked the paper's masthead. "Did you know the editor, Mark Beale?"

"I met him at the Mifflin Street block party. He was way out there, you know? Living la vida loca, dressing like a revolutionary, into survival before it was cool. You could find Beale at the forefront of any demonstration, and in those days there were a lot of demonstrations. I was even there when the pigs gassed the Dow Protest. There's a movie about it called The War at Home. He's in it I think."

"Do you have a copy?"

Walter beamed, reached under the counter and held up a DVD. "Does the pope shit in the woods?"

"Do you know where I can find Beale?"

Walter shook his head. "Haven't a clue. Back in the day he lived at some hippie commune near Richland Center."

"Any idea what they called themselves?"

Walter scratched his head, causing dandruff to rain on his shoulders. "I think they called themselves the Collective. Yeah, that was it. The Collective."

Josh thanked Walter and insisted on giving him $20 for the paper and DVD. He raced home with his booty, went online and looked for the Collective. There were at least a dozen communes by that name but only one in Wisconsin. He found an article in the October 22, 1971, issue of *The Wisconsin State Journal*, "Commune to Close Amid Drug Charges."

The Collective, a farming commune outside Richland Center with close ties to the Socialist Workers Party, was raided yesterday morning by state, county and local authorities acting on a tip. Police officers found more than 400 marijuana plants under cultivation and took five commune members into custody.

Robert McIntyre, a Richland Center farmer who rented the farm to the Collective, said he was as surprised as anyone, and that the commune was two months in arrears on their rent. Police have yet to release the names of those arrested.

Police also confiscated 200 tablets of acid, several ounces of methamphetamine, $4,000 in cash and several weapons, including a sawed-off shotgun.

Josh used county plat maps to locate Robert McIntyre's farm, then checked the Richland Center white pages. Finding McIntyre's listing, he phoned. It rang five times before a woman answered with a quaver in her voice.

"Hello, this is Alma."

"Ma'am, this is Josh Pratt in Madison. I'm trying to locate Robert McIntyre."

"Robert died eighteen years ago, Mr. Pratt. What is this about?"

"Am I speaking with Mrs. McIntyre?"

"Yes you are," she said.

"Ma'am, I'm a private detective working on a case that concerns the so-called Collective, a commune that rented your property in the sixties and seventies."

A harsh laugh. "Those hippies. They're long gone."

"Yes, I understand that, but I wonder if I could come out there and ask you some questions."

"Josh Pratt, you say? Give me your number and I'll call you back."

"Thank you, Mrs. McIntyre."

THE CORRECTIVE

MRS. MCINTYRE CALLED BACK AN HOUR LATER. "I guess it would be all right. You know how to get here?"

"Yes, ma'am. When would be convenient?"

"Well I'm not doing anything this afternoon."

Josh checked his watch. "How about two?"

"Two would be fine."

Josh searched for Mark Beale but the old revolutionary had left no footprint. Josh wondered if he was still alive. He stopped at Woodman's, gassed up and bought a pound of Jamaican coffee for Mrs. McIntyre. He'd printed out the Google Map of her farm and stuck it in the window of his tank bag. It was twelve thirty when he left Madison, and a quarter to two when he pulled off Derry Road onto the dirt road leading to McIntyre's farm. He never would have found it without the map. It was located in a little valley tucked among the forested hills of western Wisconsin, miles from its nearest neighbor.

A small rural cemetery lay across the street.

The farmhouse was a traditional Midwest dowager, two stories with a steep roof and a broad front porch. A ten-year-old Buick sat in the yard. Mrs. McIntyre came out as Josh got off his bike, a stooped babushka with a straw hat accompanied by a fat old black Lab.

Josh went up two steps to the porch. "Thank you for seeing me, Mrs. McIntyre. I brought you some coffee."

"That's very sweet of you, young man. Would you like some iced tea?"

"Sure."

While Mrs. McIntyre went back in the house Josh sat in an Adirondack chair and petted the old dog. Mrs. McIntyre returned a minute later with two glasses of iced tea.

"Did you know Mark Beale?" Josh said.

"Yes I knew Mr. Beale. He seemed like a very sincere, polite young man. He was the only one of that gang of hippies that ever bothered to thank us, even after we shared our vegetable garden with them. I asked him why they didn't grow their own vegetables and he told me most of them were lucky if they could tie their shoes. A bunch of wannabe revolutionaries playing at dropping out, or whatever it was they did. The only thing they grew was marijuana.

"We'd often hear loud music from over there and my late husband, God bless his soul, said they were doing all sorts of drugs and having orgies. Can you imagine?"

"Did you know Curtis Mack?"

Mrs. McIntyre slowly shook her head gazing off into the distance. She had the complexion of a porcelain doll covered with cracks so fine you could only see them close up. "No, I tried to have as little dealings with them as possible."

"Do you still own the property?"

"Oh yes. We rent it to the Millers, who grow sorghum there now."

"What about the farmhouse where they lived? Is that still there?"

"It is, but nobody's used it for years. It's all boarded up. There's still junk left over there from after the arrest."

"Would it be all right if I took a look?"

"Certainly. What is it you're looking for?"

Josh told her about the case.

"Oh my," she said when he was finished. "That's just terrible. I try to avoid the news these days. It's mostly bad."

"You're wise. Do you have internet?"

"No, although my son and daughter keep trying to give me a computer. I'm too old for that nonsense! I still have a rotary phone. My idea of fun is listening to the big bands with Virgil here." She leaned over to pet the old dog, which thumped its tail against the wooden floor.

Josh finished his iced tea, thanked her again and gave her his card. She peered at it through her pince-nez. "Oh my. I've never met a private detective before."

"Call me if there's anything I can do for you."

"Listen, you have to look sharp to find the entrance to the farm. It's straight back from us." She gestured broadly through the house. "Go down Derry, take a left on AB, and about a half mile down take another left onto George Road. It's on the left about a quarter mile up. There's an old gray mailbox just opposite."

Josh went out, got the map out of his tank bag and went back into the house. "Would you mark where that is?" he said, handing Mrs. McIntyre a pen. She made a big 'X' on the map to the west.

Josh passed signs for Renk Seed and Select Sires. He found the mailbox, which bore only a number. A chain-link fence stretched across the dirt road entrance, secured to steel fence posts that also anchored a barbed-wire fence. There was no lock on the chain. Josh got off, let down the chain, rolled his bike through and put it up again. The air was redolent of hay and manure.

The farmhouse at the end of the dirt road looked like something out of *The Grapes of Wrath*, a falling-down, one-story building with add-ons. A strong wind would blow it away. The windows were boarded up with plywood, and even here the graffiti vandals had made their mark, only instead of gang signs and bright plumage letters, there was the Blue Oyster Cult symbol, silly love notes and idiots' initials. Behind the farmhouse Josh saw a barn, and fifty yards behind that a garage with vines growing up over the door.

The once-white house was now a splotchy gray. Josh walked around to the back entrance off the kitchen, up three sagging wood steps. The screen door had long since been torn off its hinges. The wood door was sufficiently warped to leave a half inch of space at the top. As he watched, a lazy yellow jacket entered through the crack.

Fuck.

Josh hated yellow jackets. The door opened inward with a horrendous shriek against the yellowed linoleum floor. Enough light streamed in through chinks in the door and windows that Josh could see the threadbare kitchen, a stove the only remaining appliance. A calendar on the wall was open to September 1972. It showed a bucolic valley in autumn, brilliant yellows, oranges and greens. It could have been taken nearby.

Josh opened a warped cabinet drawer and found a pile of mouse droppings. The house stank faintly of animal feces and age. He went back outside, retrieved a flashlight from his tank bag and returned, going through an arched entry into the living room. The hardwood floor was buckling and there was a big pile of shredding from a cushioned sofa that looked like a bacteria colony. On the wall, a framed, faded *Easy Rider* poster.

The dining alcove was stripped bare, and a half bath lacked both sink and toilet. Pointing the flashlight down, Josh entered a hall with four doors. The first was a full bath. Only the bathtub remained, stained a foul green as if it had been used for a witches' brew.

Josh heard ominous buzzing and looked up. A wasp's nest the size of a bowling bag jutted from a ceiling corner. Josh carefully backed out of the room.

The next room was a small bedroom containing only a frame and a box spring with holes chewed in it. The closet held nothing but wire hangers. Likewise the next room. The master bedroom was in back, distinguishable by its size and larger closet. A king-size bed frame sat on the dust-covered floor, along with the scat of wild animals. An old fiberboard bureau was pushed against the wall.

Josh checked the closet. On the floor lay a warped pair of Earth shoes that looked like they'd been through a volcano. Josh methodically opened the bureau drawers, revealing more mouse droppings and a couple of mismatched buttons. The bottom drawer stubbornly resisted his efforts until he stooped and pulled with both hands. The door popped all the way out, setting Josh on his ass. Something squeaked and scurried away.

There, in the space between the drawer and the floor was an old, string-tied manila envelope. Josh pulled it out, unwrapped the string. It was filled with photographs. He went into the sunlight, sat on the back stoop and pulled them out.

SITTIN' IN THE TRAP

MOST WERE IN BLACK AND WHITE ALTHOUGH some were in faded color and some were Polaroids. They were impossibly young, impossibly rural, like they were posing for the cover of a Byrds or Seatrain album. The men wore overalls and stuck straw between their teeth. The women wore shapeless granny dresses, some of which failed to conceal curves, or in some cases, bodies like Case tractors.

A short mesomorph with long, wavy blond hair was at the center of many of them, often wearing a Che Guevara T-shirt. In one he stood alone posing with a copy of *Takeover*, showing a headline in 36-point type: YIPPIES TRASH CHICAGO. Josh couldn't read the story but assumed it was about the 1968 Democratic Convention.

Mark Beale. Had to be. Josh went through the photos again and there was one of Beale cutting the string on a stack of newspapers. It looked like it had been taken in the newspaper offices, with a long stapler, a paper cutter and an old Underwood on the desk behind him and a Rigid Tool calendar on the wall.

There was an eight-by-eleven black-and-white glossy of the whole clan, about two dozen, lined up in front of the house in happier days. Two planters hung from the eaves. The tribe sat, crouched and stood clutching babies, dogs and cats wearing their granny dresses and glasses, their Osh Kosh coveralls, farm boots. One boob even clutched a pitchfork like in "American Gothic." It was a multi-racial group with two young black men, one tall, skinny with muttonchops, the other stocky and wearing a tri-color knit cap, and there was a stout, cheerful-looking black woman in coveralls and glasses. In the back row a tall young man with a big chin and a grin stood with his arm around a young woman. Neither age nor dress could hide her beauty. She was raven-tressed with a perfect heart-shaped face and dark eyebrows. The man wore wire-rimmed glasses, which reflected the sun, hiding his eyes.

Josh looked at the old red barn across the yard. He stood, put the manila envelope in his tank bag and returned to the barn. It was cooler inside, smelling of hay and machine oil, motes of dust dancing in shafts of sunlight. A Mahindra tractor rested just inside the door along with various attachments. The old horse stalls still held hay, although there was animal scat everywhere. A handful of old farm tools—a pitchfork, a scythe and shovels—hung from pegs on the wall. The pitchfork looked like the one in the photo.

In the back a door led to a large room the width of the barn and a ladder leading up to a loft. As Josh entered the back room a group of starlings piled out a broken window like a gray cloud. Piles of moldering newsprint sat on the floor distorted by water, turning to dust. An antique Underwood typewriter sat on a room-length table beneath a window next to a poster of Kent State showing a young woman wailing over the body of a fallen comrade.

The *Takeover* offices.

The table had been cobbled together by amateurs with mismatched boards held together by nails instead of screws. Two rust-discolored steel file cabinets lurked beneath the desk. Josh had to use a hoe to pry them open. Inside most of the papers had suffered from water and animal damage. Mice had chewed through several files. The few intact files contained news clippings about Vietnam, the Black Panthers, the Weather Underground and Global Resistance. The article about Global Resistance was bylined Curtis Mack.

Beneath the desk were some warped albums from unknown bands. Josh pulled one out: Jam Factory on Epic, *Sittin' in the Trap*. The water-damaged cardboard sleeve showed a pencil drawing of some alien creature with a globe on its head. He slid the record out. It was in remarkably good shape. He couldn't say why but he tucked it under his arm. On the wall were tacked, faded posters of Che, Angela Davis, The Black Panthers and *Putney Swope.*

A glass-paned door opened into more barnyard and a garage-sized woodshed. Josh opened the door and stepped out. Crickets were sawing away, making that summertime noise. No unnatural sound intruded. The old farm was peaceful but forlorn, maybe even a touch sinister.

Josh saw the old, listing garage across the field now rich with sorghum, and walked toward it, careful not to trample the crop. The double-wide doors were held shut with a big padlock. The doors had remained sealed for decades, permitting creeping charlie and other vines to grow right to the roof. There was one window on the side. Josh tried to peer in but it was dark inside and the window was filthy both inside and out. He walked all around the building. The rear door was securely locked.

He retraced his steps to the barn, entering through the *Takeover* offices. He saw the paper cutter. He saw the Rigid Tool calendar.

Josh found nothing else of interest and was about to leave when he paused at the base of the ladder leading to the loft. The loft was of different wood than the barn and bore the signs of amateurs—poorly joined boards, and nails. Two six-by-six wood columns rose from the wood floor to support the deck.

Leaning the record carefully against a column, Josh climbed the ladder, the heat rising with him. Up top was a flat loft with a bug-infested queen-size mattress on the floor and a pile of old boxes stacked three deep and a banded steamer trunk. All the boxes at floor level had holes chewed in the corners.

The heavy old steamer trunk stood near the edge, forming a partial wall for the bed.

Josh opened the flaps of one of the boxes, revealing chipped china plates wrapped in newspaper, as if this were some grand heirloom they were saving. Other boxes contained mismatched silverware, clothes, an *Encyclopedia Britannica*, old science fiction paperbacks and underwear. None of it was in good shape. Josh tried to open the steamer trunk but it was held shut by an old padlock. The trunk itself was in decent condition and probably could have brought money at a pawnshop or an antique store.

On the back wall lovers and artists had carved their names and initials. The peace symbol. "Make love not war." "You're either part of the solution or part of the problem." "By any means necessary." "Jack and Diane." "Curtis and Stacy."

He left the barn, put the record in his saddlebag and headed back to Madison.

BEALE

Josh got home at six, went inside, took the record out of its sleeve and put it on his old Harman Kardon turntable. He turned on the amp, dropped the needle and listened to the pop and hiss of days long past until the song started. Jam Factory was a ferocious six-man jazz/rock group with sax and trumpet that played in the manner of Chicago. Not later Chicago, but the first two albums.

He had Dorgan to thank for that too. They'd spent endless hours in the chaplain's office listening to music Josh had missed—born too late or simply not interested. He'd been aware of the Beatles and the Rolling Stones of course but missed the great music explosion of the seventies and eighties. Dorgan introduced him to the Yardbirds, Cream and of course Muddy Waters, Otis Spann, Buddy Guy, Son Seals and Otis Rush. There was something about the blues that appealed to all bikers.

If you didn't like the blues you had a hole in your soul.

Most American popular music, and jazz, was based on the blues.

He cranked it and boogied into the kitchen, where he popped a Marie Callender chicken pot pie in the microwave. He didn't remember buying it but was happy it was there. When he boogied back into the living room he noticed that his phone had lit up. Mrs. McIntyre had called. He called her back.

"I don't know what I was thinking! I went in the house and right there on the credenza was a bowl of Christmas cards that's been sitting there for years. And then I remembered several years back Mark Beale sent us a Christmas card! I was very surprised to get it because I always assumed he was not a Christian man. And I was happy to be proved wrong."

"Did it have a return address, ma'am?"

"Yes," Mrs. McIntyre said, slowing down to read. "Whispering Pines Retirement Home, 216 Westphalian Rd., Verona, 53593."

Josh wrote it down. "Thank you, ma'am."

The microwave beeped. His food was done but he was too excited to eat. He looked up Whispering Pines in the phone book and called.

"Whispering Pines," a woman answered.

"Hello, do you have a resident named Mark Beale?"

"Yes, Mr. Beale lives here. To what does this pertain?"

"I'm a friend of his old landlord Shirley McIntyre, and I promised her I'd stop in and see how Mark was doing."

"Well I can't tell you not to come but Mr. Beale is not well. Several years ago he was diagnosed with Alzheimer's and it's gotten progressively worse."

"How late are you open?"

"Visiting hours end at 9:00 p.m."

Josh grabbed the Takeover and the photos and saddled up. Forty minutes later he pulled into the turnaround beneath the Whispering Pines' porte cochere and left his bike on the concrete apron out of the way of pedestrians. The receptionist, an older woman with blue hair, looked at him in alarm. He smiled to ease her fears.

"Can I help you?" she said.

"Yes ma'am. I'm here to visit Mark Beale."

"Are you a relative?"

"Just a friend."

"What sort of friend?"

"My father went to school with him," Josh lied.

She looked at him dubiously. "Mr. Beale is in room 219. Whom should I say is calling?"

"Josh Pratt."

Josh headed for the stairs as she picked up the phone. He hoped she wasn't calling the police. He heard the phone ringing when he reached the second floor and followed it to the end of the corridor. The door stood open. Josh entered and saw an old man slumped in an overstuffed chair, ignoring the ringing phone, staring at an old cathode-ray-style television watching *Dancing With the Stars*. Josh recognized Steven Seagal twirling a tiny ballerina.

"Mr. Beale?" Josh said.

No reaction. Josh moved around to where Beale could see him, but the man's vision remained fixed on the screen. He was old, plump and shapeless in baggy sweats, his feet on an ottoman incongruously clad in bunny slippers. The room contained a hospital bed, a cantilevered rolling table and a bureau, and was decorated with generic landscape prints.

"Mr. Beale?" Josh said again.

The rheumy blue eyes flicked toward him. "Huh?"

"Mr. Beale, my name is Josh Pratt. I'm a private investigator working on a case. I wonder if you'd mind answering a few questions."

Unkempt white hair framed the plump cheeks and receding chin covered in gray stubble. The aged Michael Pollard. "What?"

Josh held up the Takeover. "You were editor and publisher, right?"

The old man reached for the newspaper and held it in front of him. "Oh yeah. I remember this one."

"Do you remember Curtis Mack?"

A look of consternation stole over Beale's face. "Mack? Oh sure. Crazy motherfucker."

"Was Mr. Mack white or black?"

"Why, he was black of course."

"Did Mack live with you at the Collective?"

Beale's eyes unfocused as an internal struggle took place.

"Why do you want to know?"

"Sir, I'm working on a case involving the death of a UW athlete. It's possible Mack was involved. Do you remember him? What was he like?"

"Mack? Superfly. Hair out to here. Drove a custom Eldorado. Very flashy dresser, good dancer, a motormouth."

Josh pulled out the black-and-white photo and handed it to Beale, who stared at it for long seconds. "Mack had the most beautiful girlfriend."

"Is she in this picture?"

Beale pointed at the dark-haired girl next to the man in the granny glasses. "Stacy Pembroke. A real heartbreaker."

"Who's that guy next to her?"

Beale stared at the photo, pulled it close to his nose. "Shit. Can't remember. Can't remember shit. It's hell getting old."

Josh wrote "Stacy Pembroke" down. "Do you know if Stacy's still alive?"

Beale shrugged. "It was so long ago. I do remember the pigs showing up one night looking for her. Her parents sicced 'em on us. That was a real hassle."

"What can you tell me about Miss Pembroke? Where was she from? Was she a UW student?"

"She might have been. So many people coming and going. It was the sixties, you know? We were all hippies—free love, free food. We welcomed any wandering vagabond into our tribe. She came from some small town up north as I recall."

"Have you kept in touch with any of the people from the Collective?"

"No. After the pigs busted me for acid in '73 I got sent up for twenty-two months. My PD was shit."

"What did you do after you got out?"

"Worked as a printer. Got phased out in the eighties. Been on disability ever since."

Josh felt a pang of sympathy for the aging revolutionary. The fires had gone out, leaving an empty husk. He laid his card on the table.

"Is Mack in this photo?"

There were only two black guys. "I don't see him," Beale said.

"There's my card, Mr. Beale. Please call me if you can think of anything else or if there's anything I can do for you."

Beale's eyes returned to the TV. "I would give my left nut for some decent windowpane."

On the way out, Josh asked the receptionist, "What does it cost to live here?"

She handed him a brochure.

JACKALOPE JONES

FRIDAY COULDN'T ARRIVE SOON ENOUGH. Josh wanted to take Fig to dinner but she wasn't biting. "Just pick me up at nine."

The last light was fading in the west as Josh pulled up at the foot of the steps leading to Fig's bungalow. He kicked out, climbed the steps and knocked. A piebald cat leaped onto her porch and twined around Josh's ankles. The door opened.

"Come on in," Fig said. "I'll be ready in a minute."

The cat came in with him. The room featured hilariously mismatched furniture—a Queen Anne sofa, a beanbag chair, a round oak dining table, an odd collection of kitchen chairs. Southwestern-style rugs on the hardwood floor and a mutt of unknown provenance on the rug thumping his tail against the hardwood floor.

"That's Mr. Schermerhorn," Fig said from a back room.

"He's very friendly." She pointed to the cat. "That's Squish-burton."

Josh stooped to pet. "I've been thinking of getting a dog."

"Really? Well I hope you'll adopt one from the pound instead of paying hundreds of dollars for a purebred."

"That's the plan."

Fig danced into the living room wearing jeans, a black T-shirt and a denim jacket, a simple strand of pearls around her neck. "Let's go!"

Fig got on the pillion and wrapped her arms around Josh's waist. The Club was hopping when they arrived. Located next to a cemetery, the Club was built in a 170-year-old barn that had been renovated and added on to until it consisted of a series of mismatched segments. The parking lot was jammed and most of the curbside parking was gone, but there was always room for cycles. Josh found a spot with six other chops right in front. He looked at the license plates. He always looked at the license plates. Two of the bikes were from Iowa.

"That's Jackalope's bike," Josh said pointing to a Fat Bob with apes.

"Who's Jackalope?" Fig said.

Josh grinned. "Wait 'til you meet him."

Josh paid their five-buck cover charge, got stamped and went into the big room in back with a stage and a wrap-around balcony containing booths. Three big, loud, beefy Bedouins had commandeered a table in the corner. As Josh and Fig entered, a big, rangy man with a mullet wearing a flash-covered leather vest stood and waved.

"YO CHAINSAW! OVER HERE!"

Fig looked at Josh. "Chainsaw?"

"It's a long story." He led her by the hand up to the table where the boys had pushed back and added two chairs.

The big guy with the mullet stood. "Man, I can't believe that bullshit went down at your place!"

"Wild shit, man!" said a man shaped like a haystack. "Why didn't you waste those Insane Assholes yourself?"

"I'm not allowed to have guns, boys. This is Fig. Fig, this mullet-headed fool is Tim, the fat one's Bad Bob and the dude with the perfect hole smack in the center of his forehead is Jackalope Jones."

Jackalope stood, took Fig's hand and bent to kiss it like a continental fop.

"I've heard of you!" Fig said.

Jackalope looked up. He was a wiry dude in his mid-forties wearing a denim vest with flash, a white Sturgis-T, starting to bald. He had another, smaller hole directly above the big one, at his hairline.

"They tell you why they call me Jackalope?"

"No," Fig said, bemused. Josh held the chair for her and sat beside her.

Tim, Bad Bob and Jackalope all started to talk at once. Josh slammed his palm on the table and they stopped, startled.

Josh pointed to Jackalope. "Let Jackalope tell it."

"I used to be plain Jack Jones," Jackalope said.

"You always liked jackalopes," Tim said.

"That's true," Jackalope said. "But that's not how I got my name. Couple years ago we were riding up near Menom-onie, who was it, Tim? You, Bad Bob, Josh, the Big Kahuna and Orpheus."

"Anybody remember that skank Orpheus brought along?" Bad Bob said.

"Shut the fuck up, Bob!" Jackalope said. "I'm trying to tell a story here! Anyhow it's like 10:00 p.m. in July, we're riding along this snakey-ass country road and I'm in the lead. I come around a corner and there's a fucking eight-point buck standing in the middle of the road. I hit it! I hit it in such a way that its horn went in here," he pointed to the hole in the middle of his forehead, "and came out here."

He pointed to the smaller hole at the hairline.

"So all these fucks pile off their bikes, grab hold of the buck and slash it to death with their buck knives, right? Then Josh takes a saw out of his saddlebag and he saws the fucking antler off the deer, leaving it in my head until they can get me to a hospital. And Bad Bob says..."

"You look like a fuckin' jackalope!" Bad Bob, Tim and Josh all said.

Fig laughed.

"The EMTs and county cops were stunned by the amount of blood," Tim said.

"And I survived none the worse for wear," Jackalope finished grandly.

YIN AND YANG OF FIN AND FANG

JOHN DAVIS CAME OUT AND PLUGGED IN. With his long gray hair and beard he looked like an Old Testament prophet and he played like one too, wringing apocalyptic blues phrases from his ancient Les Paul on "Dust My Broom" with a drummer, bass player, keyboards and sax. The sax player was old, fat, bald with a long pony-tail, and played like a demon, bringing an R&B/Apollo-like vibe. The bass player, a thin old black man, sat on a stool playing an electric bass, stone-faced. The only part of him that moved was his fingers as he sent forth a bassline that rhythmically ripped the rug out from under everyone in the room.

Fig grabbed Josh's hand. "Let's dance!"

"Argggh!" Josh wailed but was powerless to resist. He waved goodbye to the boys and saw envy in their eyes. She dragged him through crowded tables to the dance floor, a throbbing mosh pit. Josh hated to dance, wasn't good at it, but would do virtually anything to get in Fig's pants. He'd had many a discussion with the Bedouins theorizing that the only reason men danced was to get laid, unless they were gay. Rudolf Nureyev? Gay. Alvin Ailey? Queerer than Peewee's Playhouse. They spun next to two guys dancing.

Fig bumped into one, turned to apologize and made a guffaw face.

"Avery!"

"Fig!"

Avery Waldrop saw Josh. "Josh! Hey you two. This is my friend Brad Truscewicz."

Truscewicz, dark-haired and olive-complected, displayed Freddie Mercury teeth. "Hi!"

"Fig's one of my advisees," Waldrop explained.

"I hope you don't give her any bad advice!" Truscewicz said. "Does he give you bad advice, dear?"

"Not so far," Fig said.

"We have a booth," Truscewicz said. "Come on over! Have a drink with us."

They followed Waldrop and Truscewicz up three steps to a booth in the back held down by two women, one with a shaved head, her arm around the other, who wore a short cap of red frizz. Both were heavily inked. Waldrop introduced Josh and Fig, who slid in next to the women.

The one with the shaved head was Sal; the frizzy one was Valerie.

"Nice ink," Sal said.

"Thanks," Josh said.

Truscewicz pointed a finger at him. "You were at that absolutely grisly faculty party at Brett's place last week, weren't you?"

Josh nodded. Fig squeezed his knee under the table.

"I wasn't there long," Josh said.

Truscewicz stuck a pinky in his mouth. "Oh my Gawd. The yin and yang of fin and fang! You know that girl Audrey, from Greenpeace?"

"What a pill," Sal said. "Her and her constant sniffles. She's addicted to antihistamines. And the feed bag."

"Tell me about it!" Truscewicz said. "She brings her fucking kitten to the party..."

"I'm surprised she didn't bring a baby harp seal," Sal said.

"She brings her fucking kitty to the party and gets in Norm Orstein's face. Norm is head of PETA Wisconsin."

"As well as Distinguished Professor of Jargon and Psychobabble..."

"So Audrey practically shoves her kitten in Norm's face, he reels back 'cause he doesn't want his eyes scratched out and she says, 'How do you justify asking for donations when you're euthanizing hundreds of dogs and cats every day!' And it's true. PETA slaughters millions. They should change their name to PGA. People Gassing Animals."

"Wait," Fig said. "Why is Audrey there?"

"Oh she's a student, Fig," Truscewicz said. "Been one for lo, these fourteen years. Working on her doctorate in environmental studies. She was on some boat in the Antarctic Ocean when they tried to intercept a Japanese fishing trawler. Nearly died. Now she's full scholarship, goes to every faculty party she can. I don't know if you notice but she carries this big feed bag around, ostensibly it's for the kitten, whose name is Quagel, by the way, but it's filled with plastic Ziploc bags and when no one's looking, she goes to the buffet and—zzzzzzzzipp! Into the purse it goes. A girl's gotta eat."

Everyone laughed. Truscewicz turned to Josh. "After you left, that bitch Yvonne got into it with Sal over, what was it, free-trade coffee?"

Sal nodded. "I told her I couldn't be troubled to check the lineage on every cup of coffee, and she called me a typical white racist exploiter."

"Then she accused Sal of hating unions," Valerie said.

Truscewicz's mouth made a big oval.

Sal sighed. "Because I crossed that ridiculous picket line to get a Big Mac."

"And that was *before* Jeffrey Harold Wolfe IV arrived," Waldrop said.

"He'd *shit* if he heard you call him that!" Truscewicz said.

"Is that his real name?" Fig said with a half guffaw.

Truscewicz held a finger to his lips. "Mustn't tell! Very hush hush! Our Jeffrey is a man of the *people*. No one has worked harder to obliterate his upper-class roots."

Sal laughed and slapped her knee. Josh grinned although he knew not why.

"Stan used to butt heads with that guy all the time," Fig said.

"Who you talking about?" Josh said.

"Professor Wolfe, Stan's Politics in Multi-Cultural Societies teacher."

OH WHAT A NIGHT

JOSH LAY IN FIG'S BED WITH HER ARM ACROSS his chest as she gently snored. He could see the moon through her open window. He couldn't believe his luck!

Fig was the first woman Josh had had who was a higher class than he. Oh, he knew America was supposed to be a classless society, but nobody was fooled. People still judged your status by your looks, how well you were doing, how well you were known, how much you made.

Maybe she was slumming. He'd seen it before. But he didn't care.

Josh was afraid to move lest he wake the sleeping princess.

Excitement coursed through his veins like nitrous oxide. Not just the great girl in bed with him, but the case. Things were starting to happen and now he had a direction. He lay there fitfully, afraid to move until the sun poked through the window and Fig opened her eyes.

She rolled over on her back and groaned. "What time is it?"

"It's 5:00 a.m."

"Oooohhh," she moaned. "Why did I get up so early?"

Josh sat on the edge of the bed. "Go back to sleep!"

She scrunched over and put her arms around his waist. "Don't go."

He leaned over and kissed the top of her head. "Got to. Can I cook you dinner tonight?"

"You cook?" she said.

"Nothing fancy."

"What time?"

"Six."

"Okay," she said. "I'd love to see your place! It might be as famous as the OK Corral, or Dien Bien Phu!"

"Ha," Josh said.

He got up, visited the john, splashed water on his face, got dressed and headed home. He arrived at six, put on a pot of coffee and ran while it brewed. When he returned he showered, got his coffee and went into the office. He googled Jeffrey Harold Wolfe IV.

Jeffrey Harold Wolfe IV is an American socio/political theorist and a former leader in the counterculture movement that opposed U.S. involvement in the Vietnam War. He is known for his 1970s radical activism as well as his current work in political theory and his controversial style of instruction. In 1972 he co-founded Global Resistance, a self-described communist revolutionary group that conducted a campaign of bombing public buildings (including police stations, the U.S. Capitol Building, and the Pentagon) during the 1970s in response to U.S. involvement in the Vietnam War.

Wolfe is the third of three children born to robotics pioneer Jeffrey Harold Wolfe III, whose inventions can be found in most major automobile plants. Wolfe III has long been a target of organized labor, which maintains that his automated assembly line has brought the loss of jobs and contributed to the waning of UAW power. Wolfe IV has repeatedly denounced his father.

He is a professor in the College of Sociology at the University of Wisconsin, formerly holding the titles of Distinguished Professor of Sociology and Senior University Scholar. During the 2008 presidential campaign, a controversy arose over his contacts with then-candidate Michael Romero. He is married to Nedra Keppler-Wolfe, who was also a leader in the Global Resistance.

There was a picture. It was the Silva Thins man. Wolfe was scheduled to address a meeting of the Dane County 4H Club at the Dane County Coliseum next Thursday.

Josh never thought about Vietnam. He'd been born too late. He did remember once his father deliberately not washing or shaving for two weeks prior to his mandated Selective Service physical, then stuffing himself with laxatives. The old man came home with a grin on his face and pumping his fist, then went on a three-day bender that ended up with his being charged with vagrancy and public drunkenness.

Josh had been in prison when 9/11 happened. Many black inmates who had turned to Islam cheered at the tiny TV in the break room when the Twin Towers fell. Josh kept his mouth shut although he was no great patriot. Chaplain Dorgan encouraged him to read, which is how he filled his days. He read voraciously, playing catch-up for virtually no formal education. He read several histories of the world, including Will and Ariel Durant's *The Story of Civilization*, Tacitus's *Annals of Imperial Rome* and *The Last Lion*.

Coming from the streets and a hardscrabble background, Josh had a healthy skepticism and did not expect life to be easy. He had known deep in his gut from a very young age that he was on his own and couldn't count on the kindness of strangers or the government to support him or make him happy. In Josh's opinion, you were a fool to look for an outside source for your happiness.

He didn't think God intended people to be unhappy. Josh had known a vague dissatisfaction for some time and now he named it. He'd been lonely. Maybe that was over. Maybe Fig was the One. This after listening to endless club and prison discussions that man was not meant to be monogamous.

He put on the Beach Boys' Pet Sounds and cued up "That's Not Me." He had Dorgan to thank for that too.

At ten he phoned Kofsky at Dovetail.

"What?" Kofsky said. He seemed busy.

"Would the hard drive of whoever is sending out the happy face message contain proof that he did it?"

"Yeah, but how you gonna find the hard drive? Listen, I gotta go. We're on deadline here."

Josh thanked him and hung up.

OUT OF THE FRYING PAN

WHISPERING PINES COST $115,000 ANNUALLY. Not something a failed printer could afford. Josh was hopeful Kofsky could find out who was paying Beale's tab. He went to Woodman's and bought rib eyes, potatoes, salad fixings and what the clerk assured him was a first-rate Merlot. He was no great chef but he could grill a steak and bake a potato. He put on Son Seals's *Midnight Son* and went into a frenzy of cleaning, vacuuming, dusting and washing windows and countertops until he dripped with sweat.

He showered and picked up the book.

Now it's true I vowed not to give Billings one red cent, and technically I hadn't. But still, that four bills weighed on me. I wanted it back, plus a lot more. I just didn't know how to do it. We got in my piece of shit Ford Falcon and headed north. I was passing the last McDonald's when I heard the cop car whoop and saw the strobing lights in my rearview.

"I don't fucking believe it," I said.

Yolanda turned in her seat and looked back. "It's that fucking pig! The one who busted me."

I thought about running for it but no way could my weak ass ride outrun the pig's Mopar. I pulled over and said to Yolanda, "Time to play house nigger."

She rolled her eyes. Cracker Billings got out the driver's side, Medicine Ball the shotgun seat, both with their hands on the butts of their pistols.

Billings comes up to my open window. "You got a busted taillight, bwah!"

He looked right through me. Didn't remember me from the other night 'cause all niggers look alike, right?

"I'm sorry, officer, I was not aware. Thank you for bringing that to my attention."

"Get out the car, bwah. You too, sister."

We got out keeping our hands where they could see 'em.

"This bwah just bailed her outta jail," Medicine Ball said. His name was Cummings.

I was ready to fork over the five hundred I had stashed in my sock, already thinking who I could get to help me wipe out this hornet's nest of pigs.

"Come on back here, bwah. Want to show you somethin'."

I followed Billings to the back of the Falcon. He took out his baton and smashed the left rear taillight. "You see? You creating a public hazard, bwah!"

I shuffled and looked down. "I'm sorry, officer. How much is the fine?"

"How much you got?"

I stooped and both them fat pigs pulled their guns quicker than a ho suckin' up a line. I put my hands out.

"Officers, I'm just reaching into my sock for some money I keep there."

I pulled the five hundred and fanned it. "This is all I got. Ain't got gas money you take it all."

"You got enough in the tank to get your asses outta town," Billings said, snapping up those five C-notes like a fat boy at a buffet. "Mebbe you better open that trunk too."

I got the key and opened the trunk. There was a bunch of old clothes back there and a spare tire. Cummings paws through the rags and pulls out a sawed-off shotgun.

"Well lookee here! This here's an illegal weapon!"

Right then I cursed Floyd and all his descendants, selling me a short he hadn't checked out.

"Put your hands behind your back!" Billings snapped.

"You in a heap o' trouble, bwah!" Cummings crowed. "You too, sister."

They shoved us hard up against the Falcon and cranked the cuffs to cut off the blood. They shoved us in the back of their cruiser, which stank of vomit and urine. They drove us back to jail and booked us in, not bothering with a matron this time. Cummings eyed Yolanda., "You ain't bad lookin' for a shine."

A little while after that I heard Yolanda screaming and I knew I would have to kill a whole bunch of crackers.

Josh looked up. It was five o'clock. She would be there in an hour! He put on a fresh pair of jeans, anointed his body with half a bottle of Axe, pulled on an Indian (the motorcycle) T-shirt and went into the kitchen to make the salads.

Women liked salads. You could feed them almost anything if you put it in a salad. He put Buddy Guy, Basie, Smokey Robinson and the Tempts on his six-disc CD changer, and as Buddy's electric peals filled the room he heard the sound of a motorcycle out front.

Josh opened the front door to see Fig get off her Hawk, take off her helmet and shake her hair out. He would rerun it a thousand times in his head. That girl. That hair. She came to the door grinning and melted into him. Without speaking they went into the bedroom and tumbled onto the bed like puppies.

A half hour later he uncorked the Merlot, poured a half inch into a glass and handed it to Fig the way he'd seen it done on *The Blacklist*.

Fig held it to her nose and inhaled mightily, deliberately causing her sinuses to palpitate like a card in a bicycle wheel.

"SNORRRRRRRRRK!"

Frank Zappa would be proud. She tossed back the wine, threw herself to the floor and writhed spastically, ululating like an Afghan war widow and waving four limbs in the air. She got up on her elbows and grinned.

"That's how a true connoisseur tastes wine," she said. "What's a connoisseur? One who is especially competent to pass judgment! What are we having?"

"Steak, potato, salad."

"Didja ever stop to think that cowboy chow was also chowboy cow?"

"How so?" Josh said.

Fig sat with her legs out. "Cowboys love beef!"

Laughing, Josh helped her up off the floor.

"Let's go light the grill."

CHAPTER 45

STEAK

WHILE JOSH GRILLED THE STEAKS, FIG CAME out with a glass of wine and the book.

"What's this you're reading?" she said.

"The name Shred Husl was found near several of the drowning victims," Josh said. "The hero of that book is Shred Husl."

Fig sat in a lawn chair and looked at the back cover. "'In a white man's world the black man knows his place,'" she read in a stentorian voice. "'And if he doesn't, a man with a badge, a shotgun and a club will show it to him in a New York minute. But one man isn't afraid to stand up to the crackers, the crooked cops, the corrupt politicians and the White Power Structure. Shred Husl is that man!'

"Wow. This is an old book." She checked the copyright. "Forty years! Where'd you get it?"

"The Little Read Book store. I know it's old," Josh said.

"But the graffiti is recent. The Milwaukee PD arrested a dude with 'Shred Husl' tatted on his chest and that led to another dude who's in a gang."

"Do you have any proof?"

"That a gang did it? Not yet."

"What?" she said.

"It's just a hunch."

"Tell me," she said.

"I think this Professor Wolfe may be involved."

She guffawed. "Jeffrey Wolfe? He's a clown! He's a domestic terrorist! He tried to bomb the Pentagon! I looked it up. Seriously? He's just a hothead who has no business in higher education. He's lucky he wasn't found guilty of terrorism."

"Someone capable of bombing police stations is capable of murder, don't you think?"

"I would think he's got too much to lose. Look how far he's come—from wanted outlaw to tenured professor. I see him on TV all the time. He's one of those go-to guys for a reliably left-wing opinion. Why would he risk giving that all up, and for what?"

"I'd like to talk to him."

A guffaw, with lower lip pulled up over the teeth. "This I'd like to see."

"Chances are he had nothing to do with it. I'd just like to talk to him."

"Rotsa ruck."

"Have you ever met him?"

"No."

"You know that guy who was going into the party while we were leaving? Who drove up in a Porsche?"

Fig's forehead wrinkled. "I think so."

"That was him."

"Figures."

"How do you like your steak?" Josh said.

"Medium rare. I want the dudes who actually did it, if they did it. I want the ones who dragged my brother into the lake and held him down."

Josh grunted. That would be hard, unless the mastermind knew his minions. Was he ordering certain individuals to kill certain individuals? Josh had searched for a pattern among the victims, but aside from the obvious characteristics, nothing.

But what about their teachers and advisers? With over fifteen victims going back ten years, that was quite a cast. Nevertheless it was worth looking into. Jeffrey Wolfe wasn't the only tenured radical. Josh also needed to take a closer look at what Wolfe had said. Like those guys wishing death on all NRA members. Sure it was a free country and all that and the First Amendment. But sometimes people get a little crazy and say exactly what's on their minds.

"Earth to Josh," Fig intoned in a low voice. "Earth to Josh."

"Huh? Oh! Sorry! Ahmina put the steaks on."

"Ahmina watch," Fig said unfolding from the sofa, following him from the kitchen out onto the back deck, where he had a basic Weber going with charcoal.

Josh's neighbor in the back was having a party. They heard the chatter and laughter, saw the people in bright party dress standing and sitting on the neighbor's expansive multi-deck back patio, more square feet than Josh's first floor.

"Don't you have a bill for me?" Fig said.

He did, but he was reluctant to bring it up, considering the way things were going. True to their word the partners had delivered a cashier's check for ten grand, which Josh had deposited in his savings account. "I'll write one up."

"Do it right now. I'll write you a check."

"You sure?"

Fig opened her pink Hello Kitty backpack and took out her checkbook. Josh went into his office and added up the hours and expenses. His only expenses had been gas money, which was negligible, but he still had a bill for eight hundred dollars. He printed it out and gave it to Fig, who wrote him a check on the spot and put her checkbook away.

"How are your neighbors reacting to the shoot-out?" Fig said.

"The silence is unnerving," Josh said. "They're holding secret meetings. They're raising funds. If they offer me a mil I'm outta here."

"Seriously?"

Josh shrugged, flipping steaks. "I doubt it. That was a once-in-a-lifetime event. I'm sure they realize that."

"And those dickheads—who are they again?"

"Insane Assholes."

"Yeah. Are they still after you?"

"I doubt it. Every Asshole I pissed off is dead. Police are all over this neighborhood. It's like our own little Beverly Hills."

"Why do they call you Chainsaw?" she said.

Josh grimaced. He wasn't proud of it. "We were fighting another gang and I used a chainsaw. They charged me with atrocious assault."

"Did you kill him?" she said, all wide-eyed innocence.

"No. I just maimed him."

Fig brought the salads out and they ate on the deck, listening to the laughter and murmur of conversation through the trees.

"Want to go for a ride tomorrow?" Josh said.

"Can't. Promised Pops I'd help with his garden. Then we're having dinner."

"You and Pops get along?"

"I'm his little princess."

"Does he know you hired me?"

"No."

LUD

FIG PULLED UP ON THE REDBRICK TURNAROUND in front of her father's Zebrawood estate shortly after one in the afternoon, took off her helmet and shook out her hair. She wore a Shoe Box tank top and a sports bra so Lud wouldn't give her the snake eye. She went into the vast vestibule with its stained glass skylight and boomed, "Daddy! I'm home!"

"In here!" Lud bellowed from the kitchen. She found him over the sink washing tomatoes from the garden. Lud was six two, bald with a fringe of white around the ears and a thick mustache. He wore a T-shirt and shorts and hugged her hard.

"How's my little princess?"

"Great! What are we doing today?"

"Weeding. That recent rain brought the spores. It's a full-time job just keeping that garden in shape."

"Why don't you hire a gardener, Daddy?"

"I prefer to do it myself. With your help of course."

They grabbed a couple of waters, went out through the sliding door in the rec room to the half-acre backyard with its neatly laid-out vegetable garden. Tomatoes on wire ziggurats, beans on poles, broccoli, succotash, squash and peas. Lud handed Fig a weed prong and they went to work from opposite ends, uprooting weeds and tossing them in a pile.

"How's Grace?" Fig said. Grace was her mother, who had divorced her dad ten years ago over his affairs.

"She's in a tailspin. She hit the bottle right after Stan's funeral, and I don't think she's come up for air since."

Grace lived in a condo in Whitefish Bay on a very generous divorce settlement.

"Oh dear. Maybe I should go see her."

"That's up to you." Lud and Grace didn't get along.

Fig was on her knees digging out a tenacious weed with a huge taproot. "I hired a private investigator."

"Huh?" Lud said.

"To look into Stan's death. I don't believe he drowned accidentally."

Lud rocked back on his haunches. "You know, I don't either. I was thinking of hiring someone myself. I'm glad you went ahead. Who is it?"

"Guy named Josh Pratt."

"Josh Pratt, Josh Pratt. Why do I know that name?"

"He was involved in that shoot-out last week. The four bikers?"

Lud got to his feet and put his hand on his hips. "You're shitting me. That dude's a biker! He's got a criminal record!"

"The governor expunged his record. He told me all about it. He's a born-again Christian, Daddy. He's a good man."

"Why, with all the reputable agencies in the state, would you hire a guy like that?"

"He was recommended to me by Detective Calloway of the Madison PD."

"Has he found anything?"

Fig yanked the weed like a dentist pulling a molar with pliers. "He thinks someone is directing gangbangers to drag drunk white college athletes into the water and make it look like an accident. Then they leave a smiley face nearby."

"The police said that has no basis in fact," Lud said.

Fig stood with her weed. "Think, Daddy. There have been fifteen cases of white college athletes found drowned in the past ten years, most with smiley faces nearby."

Lud shrugged. "How do you prove something like that?"

"Josh is working on it," Fig said.

In a feat of father-daughter precognition, Lud looked at her accusingly. "Are you seeing this guy?"

"Daddy, I'm twenty-five years old. I can see who I like."

"Jesus. I should be grateful he's not some faggot-haired metrosexual."

Fig laughed, a sound that never failed to make Lud smile. "You should meet him."

"Yes, I should," Lud concurred. "Why don't you set it up?"

CHAPTER 47

STACY

JOSH ARRIVED AT THE OFFICE OF THE REGISTRAR at nine Monday morning. The dot Indian female grad student looked up from her computer and smiled. "How can I help you?"

"Ma'am, I would like to know if Stacy Pembroke registered for the fall 1971 class here at the university."

The woman parted her lips. "Nineteen seventy-one? That was before computerized records and before I was born!"

"Well they must keep such records somewhere. Where would that be?"

She held up a finger. "Hang on." She picked up a phone and spoke. She put the phone on her shoulder and said, "They're kicking me down the road."

Two phone consultations later she hung up and said, "The university maintains its old paper files in the basement of the State Historical Society, which is across the street from the Student Union near the library."

"Thank you, ma'am, I know where it is."

Josh rode his bike back to campus and found that all the bike slots across from the Union were taken by crotch rockets, so he wheeled up onto Library Mall and kicked out at the base of the Historical Society stairs. He took an eight-by-eleven card from his saddlebag and tucked it into the seat. It said: "Engineering Open House This Friday!" He found it useful for parking around campus.

Inside he asked the elderly clerk behind the counter about 1971 fall registrations.

"May I see your student ID?" the old man said. With his floppy white hair, pince-nez and thin scrawny neck, he reminded Josh of Bob Cratchit.

Josh took out his state license. "Sir, I'm a private investigator working on a case."

The old man looked up with rheumy gray eyes. "Like Sam Spade, huh?"

"Yes sir."

"Do you even know who Sam Spade is?" the geezer said.

"The stuff that dreams are made of."

Geezer didn't bat an eye. "Down to the basement, File Room C, you'll see the records are arranged chronologically. Let us know if you need any help."

"Thank you." Josh turned to go.

"Wait a minute," the old man said. Josh stopped.

"Suppose I wanted to hire you. Where could I find you?"

Josh gave him one of his cards. "I don't know when I'll be free. Is it something urgent?"

The old man barked mirthlessly. "No, no it's not urgent."

Josh took the broad marble stairs to the basement, which smelled richly of dust and old books. File Room C was off a main corridor, a twenty-by-forty-foot storeroom with marble floors and a ten-foot ceiling. Metal shelving lined three walls and marched down the center of the room in ranks. Stools with wheels waited at either end. Hanging files were stored in industrial cardboard boxes with index cards giving the classes and years at the end. Josh was glad he'd brought along a pocket flashlight, as the dust-covered lights in the ceiling gave off only a pale glow.

He worked his way down the wall to get a feel, then zeroed in on his corridor. He used the wheeled stool to reach the higher files, carrying them to the front of the room, setting them on an oak table while he methodically checked them. Some idiot had misfiled numerous entries. It took Josh two and a half hours to finally find her.

Stacy Pembroke had registered in the UW's College of Liberal Arts for the fall semester, 1971. Josh took out his pen and pad and wrote down, "Daughter of Carl and Meredith Pembroke, of 519 Box Elder St., Beaver Dam, Wisconsin."

A small faded color picture was attached to her registration papers, the impossibly happy face of a smiling young woman on the cusp of a great adventure. If it was her freshman year, she would have graduated in 1975. It took Josh another hour to locate the files listing the graduates, and then there were over twelve thousand. As far as Josh could tell, she had not graduated. Not that year.

Her papers listed her immediate family including a younger brother, Seth Pembroke, attending Beaver Dam High as a senior. He heard a sudden snarl and an animal squeal and looked up to see a tabby slink between the shelves with a still-twitching mouse in her jaws.

"Good job," Josh said, putting the lid back on the box.

BEATDOWN

THERE WAS ONLY ONE SETH PEMBROKE ON Facebook and he lived in Minneapolis. Josh saw that Seth had attended the University of Wisconsin, and sent him a friend request and a message: "Sir. I am a private investigator. I would like to talk to you about your sister Stacy."

Seth worked at Manic Media, a P.R. and web-design firm, was married to the lovely Greta with two boys, aged fifteen and eighteen. Josh was astonished by the info people put on the web. He'd joined Facebook reluctantly because other investigators taught him it was an invaluable resource.

And so it was. He dropped over to Dovetail, where Kofsky was in a meeting.

"Would you like to play video games while you're waiting?" the pretty young receptionist asked.

"No thanks." Josh smiled. "I brought a book."

Cummings and Billings came for me at nine. Sound barely penetrated their bunker-like jail, only the occasional squawk of loud voices from the front, and Yolanda's whimpering through a vent connecting the men's and women's sections.

Cummings and Billings—two red-necked bulls slapping their billies into their palms.

"Come to teach you a lesson, bwah!" Cummings sneered with a face like a half ham.

"What's a pretty little dinge like her see in a loser like you?" Billings added.

And then he peered at me. I kept my head down.

"I know you?"

"No suh," I said, pouring it on like some field nigger.

Billings pulled out his keys and unlocked the door to my cell. I figured I'd have one shot, kick him in the nuts and grab his club. Weren't wearin' no guns.

"I got to thinkin'," Billings said, "where does this nigger come up with five C-notes? We both know you didn't earn it. Is it drug money? Pimpin'? Maybe you runnin' some back-alley blackjack or some such shit. Point is, I'll bet maybe you come up with some more."

I kept my head down. "No suh. That was all de money I hab in de world."

Billings smiled at Cummings. "Smart, ain't he? Puttin' on that dumb act."

WHAM! Without warning Billings smashed his club into my knee. I curled up on the piss-stained floor gasping for breath and seeing only a terrible blinding white.

Then they were both in the cell—two white buffalo working me over like Max Roach on the drums. They used their oak clubs and steel-toed boots. I curled into the fetal position and crabbed under the steel bunk platform, and they stood there kicking at me like kids stamping on a rat.

I felt a finger snap under Cummings' size-16 boot. Blood ran from a cut on my skull. The bunk was too shallow for me to find any real protection and their boots kept finding their marks. I watched blood flow to the drain in the center of the concrete floor.

"No more, massuh! No more!" I cried out like a little bitch. "I know where dere's lotsa money right here in town!"

The blows stopped.

"Well why don'tchoo shinny on out from under there and show us," Billings said.

"I know just where it be at! I show you on dat map you got out front!"

"Get your ass up, bwah," Cummings said, stepping back.

I used the bunk to pull myself upright, acting the beat house nigger the whole time. They'd worked me over pretty good. I didn't know what I was going to do—didn't have a plan but I knew if I did nothing they'd most likely beat me to death and dump me in a ditch somewhere. I was hoping to lull them into a false sense of security and then go for one of their guns. How I was going to do this with a broken finger I hadn't figured out yet. Use my other hand I guess.

With Cummings's ham-like hand heavy on my shoulder they marched me out of the holding cell back out to the front, where a silver-haired grandma was sitting at the front counter. Her eyes went wide when they dragged me out. It was raining.

"Lyle," she says to Billings, "he's bleeding all over the floor!"

"Don't you worry about it none, Irma. He's gonna clean up after himself just as soon as he tells us where the money is, ain't that right, bwah?"

"Yassuh," I said with my head down.

"Where'd this money come from?" Cummings said.

"Ah, you know," I said. "Hos, drugs and gambling."

Good enough. They marched me right up to that big map of the county and Billings said, "Where is it? And don't you fuckin' lie to us, bwah, or you wish you'd never been born."

I raised my head and looked at the map. It had the police station marked with a little red pin.

The front door swung open and a kid slouched in wearing an XXXL Oakland Raiders hooded jersey with the hood up.

"The fuck you doin', bwah?" Billings roared at the newcomer. "You trackin' rain all over my jailhouse floor?"

"What's up, Josh?" Kofsky said.

Josh closed the book and stood. Kofsky wore shorts and a Hellboy T-shirt. His calves were thick as fence posts. Josh followed him back to his corner office overlooking an office park with a reflecting pool and a fountain. The corner office was decorated with pop culture artifacts—X-Men action figures, Godzilla, film noir posters. Kofsky sat behind a gunmetal-gray desk and gestured Josh to the sofa.

"What can I do for you?"

"Gotta guy who may be involved. He's a UW professor. Is there any way you could break into his computer and see if he's talking smack about white college athletes?"

"What, you mean his e-mail and such? Probably. But that's a federal crime."

"Okay forget that. Suppose I wanted to find out who was paying someone's bills at a retirement home. Could you find that for me?"

Kofsky folded his hands and had a silly little grin on his face. "What's this about?"

"A case."

"All right. Give me the particulars."

Josh wrote down "Mark Beale" and "Whispering Pines."

JAILBREAK

JOSH WAS IN HIS OFFICE WHEN SETH PEMBROKE called.

"Pratt," Josh said.

"Mr. Pratt, this is Seth Pembroke. You sent me a message regarding my sister."

"Yes, Mr. Pembroke. Thank you for getting back to me. As I mentioned, I'm a private investigator working on a case which may involve your sister. Do you know how I can get in touch with her?"

"My sister has been missing for forty years," Pembroke said.

"Can you tell me the circumstances under which she went missing?"

Pembroke inhaled, obviously troubled. "Are you in Madison?"

"Yes sir."

"I'd rather do this in person. I'm going to be in Madison tomorrow for an event at Monona Terrace. You know it?"

"The Frank Lloyd Wright building."

"Yes. I will meet you on the deck overlooking Lake Monona at one. Is that convenient?"

"Thank you sir. I'll see you there."

Josh did not know why the girl in the picture haunted him so, but she did. She'd had the same effect on Beale, he could tell. Who was Stacy Pembroke? What was in that trunk in the loft?

Josh saddled up, deposited his check in the First National Bank of Wisconsin and got a sandwich at Woodman's. When he got home he hauled out the hose and sprinkler and watered his front lawn lest the neighbors complain. He wanted to be a good neighbor but he also wanted to be left alone. Crabgrass, weeds and overgrowth didn't bother him like it bothered his neighbors. He was willing to be reasonable short of hiring someone else to do the yardwork.

Maybe he could get Fig to help. He called her, left a message.

He showered, ate his sandwich, checked his e-mail, thought about getting a dog. He'd have to train that fucker to stay in the yard or sure as shit the neighbors would have it impounded. And the barking. The barking from his neighbors' dogs was already irritating. There wasn't a house on the street didn't have at least one dog.

At dusk he curled up on his sofa with the book.

The kid's hands hung out of the voluminous sleeves but you didn't have to look at the skin to know he was a brother. No white boy would dress like that. Billings and Cummings acted like the kid's very presence was an affront. Cummings rounded on him like a pit bull on a Chihuahua.

"Man asked you a question, bwah. What the fuck do you want?"

The kid's right Adidas Jabbar semaphored into Cummings's crotch like a sharp salute, causing the pig to grunt and double over, eyes bulging. The kid stepped back, spun on his right leg and pistoned his left foot into Cummings's gut with a spinning reverse kick.

Billings went for his gun but I grabbed his thick wrist in both hands as the kid dashed forward and delivered another stunning kick to the big cop's groin. The kid reached inside his jersey and withdrew black nunchaku, which he used like Ty Cobb's bat, rendering Billings unconscious before he hit the ground. He spun and laid one on Cummings, who lay on the ground groaning.

The kid flipped back his hood revealing an impossibly young, smooth, handsome face that had not yet begun to sprout hair. "I'm Tyrone, Yolanda's cousin. Where is she?"

"Come on!" I said, stooping for the key ring on Cummings's belt. "She's in back. We've got to make tracks, son!"

The little old lady tried to squeeze beneath the desk.

I pointed at her. "You stay right there you won't get hurt."

Lightning flashed through the windows. Seconds later thunder rumbled the ground. We raced back through the corridors to the women's section, where Yolanda lay on her bunk with an arm thrown over her bruised face, her shirt carelessly pulled out of her pants. She looked up as I inserted the key.

"Shred! Thank God! Get me out of here!"

Then she saw Tyrone.

"Tyrone! What are you doing here?"

"He's gettin' us out of jail, girl," I said, swinging the door open. Yolanda leaned on my arm as we made our way back to the front, where Cummings was out cold and Billings was groaning and twitching. I checked the key ring and saw the familiar pentagon-shaped Chrysler key. I paused just long enough to go through the pigs' wallets and retrieve the money they'd taken from me plus whatever else was in there. Thought about taking their credit cards but decided against it. Tyrone grabbed their guns and their cuffs, cuffed them together and took Cummings's keys.

It was raining like a motherfucker when we got outside. We piled into the chief's car, I hit the siren and the lights and we wailed out of crackertown like a bat out of hell. There was a twelve-gauge shotgun sticking out of the passenger side floor.

Yolanda threw her arms around my neck. "They raped me, baby. They raped me good. I want them dead!"

I couldn't let my emotions get the better of me, not at ninety miles per hour on rain-slick streets. "They'll die. I promise you that."

Tyrone sat in the back playing with the pigs' service revolvers.

"How'd you find us, Cuz? What made you do that?" I said.

"When I didn't hear from you yesterday I thought I'd better come on up and see for myself," he said quietly. "I took the bus."

"Man, that was some Super Fly shit you laid on them pigs. Where'd you learn to fight like that?"

"I been practicing karate and kung fu since I was six years old," he said.

"How old are you, Cuz?"

"I'm twenty-two."

"You look like you're fifteen," I said.

Tyrone laughed. "I make my youth work for me."

"You sure do," Yolanda said. "You're my hero, Tyrone! You saved us!"

"What about me?" I said. "I come down here to bail you outta jail, get the shit kicked outta me, what thanks do I get?"

Yolanda ran a hand along my thigh. "I be thankin' you later, Shred. You know that."

I was kind of relieved that she hadn't gone all to pieces like some white girl might, but Yolanda's upbringing had been none too gentle. In fact, one of her worthless no-good uncles had raped her when she was seventeen and I would have tracked him down and killed him if he hadn't already died from a heroin overdose.

The headlights caught a sign—twenty-two miles to Monroe. Once we crossed that state line we were in the clear. Ain't no one gonna mess with a cop car rolling full-tilt boogie down the road.

That's when the flashing lights appeared in the rearview.

Josh laid the book down and went to bed.

SETH

JOSH RODE DOWNTOWN ON WEDNESDAY AND left his bike in a corner of Fleiss's parking lot, a short walk from the Capitol Square and Monona Terrace. The city fathers had whooped it up over Monona Terrace, which opened in 1997. Although the terrace used Wright's exterior plan and Taliesin architects, it conveniently ignored one of Wright's prime dictums: never cut a city off from its waterfront. But the road and rail lines had been there far longer than the terrace. All the terrace did was to cover the road with a cantilevered design. You only saw the rail lines if you looked straight down.

Josh bought a coffee from a kiosk on the square and carried it over to the terrace, looking down at the customized bricks. They'd raised money by selling bricks that you could personalize with your own message, so long as it didn't offend anyone. Most of them were just the names of the donors.

He was early so he went to the east rail and looked out on Lake Monona, where a dozen white sails were flitting.

At five after one his phone rang.

"This is Pratt."

"Pratt, it's Pembroke. I'm wearing a gray suit. Where are you?"

Josh looked up and saw a tall man on his phone in a gray suit. Josh raised his hand and waved. "Over here."

Pembroke was a serious-looking man in white shirt and red tie, thinning hair on a big square head. They shook hands.

"What's this about my sister?"

Pratt brought him up to speed on the Newton investigation. They stood side by side at the rail looking out on the lake.

"Stacy was always a dreamer, a New Age hippie child. I used to tease her about it mercilessly, but we were all excited when she went to the university here. She dropped out after the first semester, saying she'd gone to live on a commune with some guy. She never would tell us the guy's name. She came home once in February with a black eye. Claimed she'd fallen down some stairs but we all suspected her boyfriend did it. If my father hadn't been so completely absorbed in saving his business from a hostile takeover, he would have found that son of a bitch and beat the hell out of him. I wanted to, but it was my senior year in high school. I was class president and quarterback of the football team. We should have done something. It makes me sick every time I think about it.

"I'll never forget the night it all blew up. We hadn't heard from her in a week. My folks were frantic. They called that commune and a cop answered. Said they were conducting a raid. Our father went down there the next day but there was no sign of Stacy. He filed a missing person's report. Nothing ever came of it."

Josh pulled out the group photo he'd found and handed it to Pembroke. "Do you recognize your sister?"

Pembroke instantly pointed to Stacy, held the photo close to his face. "So this is the guy."

"We don't know for sure, but they seem close."

"Damn. You can't get a good look at him because of those shades. Any idea who he is?"

Josh was torn. On the one hand he had a very good idea. On the other he didn't want Pembroke rushing in like a bull in a china shop. "That's what I intend to find out. Anything you can tell me about Stacy would help. What classes she was taking, friends and addresses, that sort of thing. This guy she was seeing. Did she say anything about him?"

Pembroke seemed to wither as he rested his forearms on the rail. "She called him wise and beautiful with a unique philosophy. Made me think of Charles Manson."

"Was she political?"

"She was a typical hippie-dippy of the times. Love, peace, happiness. She didn't dwell on the bad stuff. She didn't rail about racism or capitalism but she was always one to smooth things over. She'd rather die than offend anyone. I suspect that in her heart she was a typical liberal who believed in all that kumbaya nonsense, but she was my sister and I loved her."

"Are your parents still alive?"

"No. Mom died six years ago. It's just me now. Unless Stacy's alive, which I doubt."

Josh knew this was a terrible thing for a man to admit. Not knowing, not having closure could be maddening. "May I have your card?"

They exchanged cards.

"If you find something, will you let me know?" Pembroke said. "If it's a matter of money..."

"Of course I'll let you know, and you don't have to pay me."

Pembroke looked at his watch. "I have to get back to my meeting. Trying to figure out how to sell something nobody wants or needs."

Josh watched him walk across the plaza like a defeated man.

OFF THE PIG!

JOSH WENT UP TO SEE FLEISS, WHO WAS IN court, so he shot the shit with Marcia, who flirted outrageously and offered to fix Josh up.

"I'm seeing someone," Josh said.

Marcia's eyes went round and that gossip smirk crept onto her lips. "Who? Dish, boy, dish!"

"Nobody you know, a young lady who rides a motorcycle."

Marcia vogued with the Klingon sign. "I can just see her—dyed pink Mohawk, enough piercings to hang an art gallery, inked all over, especially her ass."

Josh laughed. "You nailed it!"

"Where'd you meet her? At a biker rally?"

"Marcia, you know me too well."

Josh stopped at Woodman's—again—and bought a frozen pizza and a bag of apples for dinner. Even as he stood in line he cursed himself for having the attention span of a fruit fly, stopping at the grocery store every day, buying his groceries day by day because it never occurred to him to sit down and make a plan or a list.

But of course he'd have to drive a car if he did that. What else did he have to do? It wasn't as if he were a brain surgeon. He was lucky he was out of prison and not on welfare or drugs. He'd stopped beating himself up by the time he got to the cashier, a young man with a quarter-sized disk inserted in each earlobe.

When he got home he phoned Fig to see if she'd join him, and went to her voicemail. He baked the pizza and sat in the living room eating while watching Ultimate Fighting on television. The fighters ended in a clinch on the ground and rolled around like mating earthworms. Josh turned if off and picked up the book.

The pigs were ten feet off our rear bumper whooping and flashing like drunk frat boys. Their pigmobile had a speaker mounted on the bar.

"THIS IS THE POLICE! PULL OVER!"

Tyrone cranked down his window and seized one of the police revolvers in both hands.

I said to Yolanda, "Yolanda, babe, grab that shotgun and hand it to Tyrone."

She yanked it free like a foot from a boot and passed it back to Tyrone, who broke it open, revealing a shell in each barrel. Yolanda rooted around in the wheel well and came up with a box of twelve-gauge shells, which she passed back.

There were two pigs in that car 'cause the pig in the shotgun seat lowered his window and the twin barrels of a shotgun appeared. They fired first. There was a loud popping sound and the rear quarter of the car sounded like a tin roof in a hailstorm. The rear window shattered, sending pieces of broken glass like shredded ice behind us. Tyrone leveled the barrel on the windowsill and squeezed the trigger.

The pigmobile's windshield shattered, the driver cried out and the car began to fishtail. It skidded in a complete circle and rolled off the road into a ditch.

"Someone must have come in right after we left," I said. I wished I had the map of South Carolina I'd left in the Falcon. But I didn't. We were on a state highway barreling toward North Carolina, flying blind. I thought about turning off onto one of the numerous side roads disappearing in the rain and hills, but without knowing where I was going that was out. All I could do was hold the pedal to the metal and try to make it to that state line before the pigs tumbled to us and set up a roadblock. It was ten minutes since we'd left the jail. On a night like this how many pigs could they spare to stop a couple of jailbirds?

Another flashing bar appeared in my rearview. And another.

What the fuck?! It was raining pigs!

Yolanda and Tyrone saw them.

"Ain't they got nothin' better to do?" Yolanda said.

"They never do," I said. "They'd rather hassle a black man than fuck."

I looked down at the speedo and we were going 120 with plenty left in the Dodge's 426 hemi, but with rain-slick roads I could feel the tires barely holding on. One little mistake, we could all end up with our heads wrapped around a tree. There was nothing to do but to press blindly on through the pouring rain, visibility no more than thirty feet, with two screaming pigmobiles on our ass.

Tyrone reset the gun on the rear of the back seats aiming straight back at the lead pigmobile. It was a tight, winding little two-lane blacktop road. He squeezed, the air popped, and the headlights on one side of the lead pigmobile went dark. The pig in the shotgun seat leaned out and fired his pistol at us one-handed.

Tyrone squeezed, popped, and the cop's pistol went flying in the wind as he cried out and yanked his arm back in the car. The second pigmobile was so mad-dog crazy to get in on the action it had pulled level with the first, racing at 120 per down the wrong side of the highway. I prayed to Haile Selassie that they'd run into a truck going the other way.

A sign flashed by. "Ten miles, Shred," Yolanda said. Ten miles in five minutes. I mashed the pedal harder and the big Mopar roared, the needle moving past 130. It felt like we were just skimming over the surface—that the slightest disturbance would send us into a spin right off the highway. Those pigs must have felt the same thing because little by little their headlights began to recede.

Nobody said a word as we hurtled through the rain-swept night, Tyrone soaked from the backlight. He broke the barrel and reloaded as the pigs continued to recede. Suddenly the surface of the road changed and Yolanda whooped.

"Welcome to North Carolina!" she said as the pigs stopped at the border and watched us go.

SPEECH

JOSH WOKE THURSDAY MORNING WITH excitement and apprehension. Jeffrey Wolfe was speaking to the local 4H clubs at the Dane County Coliseum at 3:00 p.m. At last Josh would get a look at the man. Fig didn't know and he wasn't about to tell her. The last thing he wanted was a confrontation that would tip Wolfe to the fact that he was being investigated.

Curious gaps spotted Wolfe's record. His PhD dissertation had been redacted from university records. In fact no one even knew the subject except Wolfe's mentors, a like-minded group who kept their lips buttoned. Wolfe gave speeches at fifty grand a pop. Josh wondered if Wolfe had charged the 4H clubs of Wisconsin fifty grand. He contacted the organization via e-mail and asked them.

Josh rode to the newly renovated Coliseum on Madison's South Side at two forty-five and parked his bike in a striped area reserved for motorcycles. There was no entry fee; it was National 4H Week and the organizers would take anybody they could get.

Inside the exposition hall were numerous booths representing 4H clubs from around the state. Some held livestock and were covered in hay. Others displayed grains and produce. One chose to display hand-crafted beer brewed from self-grown hops and barley.

At the opposite end of the vast oval hall a stage had been set up and folding chairs arranged in semi-circles facing the podium. There were perhaps 120 people—half kids, half adults, waiting for Professor Wolfe to speak. Josh took a seat in the front row. A speaker's podium with the Great Seal of the State of Wisconsin had been set up in front of an American flag and a Wisconsin flag.

Josh looked around. One guy at the opposite end of the first row might have been a reporter. Everybody was playing with their smartphones when Wolfe walked out in professor/hipster apparel, blue jeans, a big rodeo buckle, boots, a Cramps T-shirt and a tweed jacket. It was the dude with the Boxster, his silver hair fixed in a ponytail, wearing amber-tinted aviator shades. There was a smattering of applause. A small man in a plaid shirt and dungarees played with the microphone until it squealed.

"Welcome, 4-H-ers!" he said in a squeaky voice. "Our next speaker is a Distinguished Professor of Sociology at the University of Wisconsin, author of *Achieving Consensus, The Evil of Capitalism* and the children's best-seller *The Little Red Hen*. Please welcome Professor Jeffrey Wolfe!"

The applause was only slightly more enthusiastic as Wolfe gripped the sides of the podium with both hands and looked out.

"Hello and thank you. I'm very pleased to have been asked to speak to you, the future farmers and ranchers of America. Too often, those of us in academia forget where our bread comes from. It comes from you, the salt of the earth, the proletariat who take it upon themselves to feed the world. It comes from people who are willing to get down on their knees in the dirt and till the soil. Too often, those of us in the groves of academe look at the world theoretically and forget what really makes it run.

"I'm proud of the university's agricultural and animal husbandry programs. They are among the best in the nation, and Wisconsin is in the forefront of beef, poultry, pork, corn, soy and alfalfa producers! I see where one group is brewing their own beer. I hope you dudes are all twenty-one. A sheriff's deputy will be around to check your IDs.

"Just kidding! But seriously, let's not overlook the brewing industry. Not only do brewers provide employment for thousands, Wisconsin is in the forefront of the micro-brew revolution that is sweeping the nation. I applaud your industry and innovation!

"As you know, genetically modified organisms, both animal and vegetable, propose one of the greatest challenges we face here in the twenty-first century. Unfortunately our governor has chosen to ally himself with Monsanto and other genetic modifiers, because they put money in his pocket.

But this comes as no surprise, as the governor has always favored his cronies and campaign contributors over the common person. Please keep that in mind in the upcoming elections.

"The horrors of genetically modified foods have been well-documented. Children in Tanzania born with deformities and missing limbs after their mothers consumed genetically modified crops. The big corporations do a lot of testing in Africa because they can get away with it. They enslave people with ignorance and superstition so they can hang on to their easy money. We are no longer citizens of one country, my friends. We are citizens of the world and we ought to start acting like it.

"Which brings me to a rather sensitive subject, I'm afraid, and that is the 4H tradition of encouraging 'military clubs.' The military does one thing—it turns out professional killers. Does the world really need more killers? Who is it that sets brother against brother, nation against nation? It's capitalism, my friends!"

Josh glanced over. The man he thought was a reporter was scribbling furiously in a notepad and tending to the micro-recorder on his seat. The speaker noticed.

Wolfe walked to the stage nearest the man. "Sir, what are you doing? Are you recording this?"

The man stood. "Professor, my name is Alan Schneider. I write for Isthmus. How do you reconcile your support for farmers while your father's company, Wolfe Robotics, manufactures devices that do the work of six men? I'm talking about devices that both plant and harvest a wide variety—"

Wolfe didn't wait. "The reason I'm here, and not vice president of Wolfe Robotics, is because I rejected my father's values to embrace more humanistic ones. I decided at an early age I wanted no part of his capitalist system that chews up and spits out a piece of the earth in exchange for money."

"But Professor," the reporter said, "your salary is over two hundred thousand. You're getting fifty grand for speaking here today."

"For your information I am not charging the 4H clubs of Wisconsin. It is my privilege to address them. If you have any further questions please contact my office."

And with that Professor Wolfe walked off the stage.

RUNNING WOLFE

JOSH SPRANG UP AND RAN AFTER HIM, BUT Wolfe had exited at the far end of the stage and disappeared into the inner workings of the Coliseum by the time he got around. A man in a security uniform guarding the door went stiff when Josh appeared, so he turned around and raced back through the Coliseum toward the public exit nearest to where Wolfe had gone.

He slammed out the exit and looked to his left. Wolfe and another man were thirty yards away walking toward a black SUV. Josh ran after them. He was still twenty yards away as the first man reached the SUV and opened the rear door.

"Professor!" Josh shouted.

Wolfe paused and turned, then turned back.

"Professor! Did you know Stan Newton?"

Without looking, Wolfe shook his head and put a hand on the SUV to ease his entry.

"Did you know Stacy Pembroke?"

For an instant Wolfe went rigid like a galvanized frog's leg, then got in the SUV and slammed the door. He said something to his driver through the open window. The driver hustled around to the wheel, got in and drove off.

Josh was walking around the huge oval building toward where he'd left his bike when he heard footsteps approaching. He turned to see Schneider, the reporter, wearing a trilby and hipster glasses, chasing after him. Josh waited.

Schneider was a tall, thin individual with a sailfin-like nose and clusters of zits on both cheeks. "Excuse me! What did you ask Wolfe?"

"That's none of your business," Josh said.

The kid squinted. "Aren't you that biker dude who had the shoot-out at his house last week?"

Josh sighed and resumed walking toward his bike.

"I saw you on TV, man," the kid said. "They said you were a detective, is that right? Is this some case you're working on?"

"Y'know how you're not supposed to divulge your sources?" Josh said, still walking.

"Yeah. And I wouldn't! I mean if you had something newsworthy to tell me. Are you investigating Wolfe?"

They reached his bike. Schneider took out his phone and snapped a picture of the bike. Josh turned on him and said, "What are you doing?" and saw fear, real fear in the kid's eyes. The kid stepped back.

"I'll delete that if you like."

"I would appreciate that."

"But it's not like it's any big secret. They showed this bike on TV when those hoodlums knocked it over. Listen, let me give you my card. You need any help, you have anything to say, I'm available. Do you read *Isthmus*?"

"I only read it for the music listings," Josh said. "And you even manage to politicize those."

Schneider laughed nervously. "True dat." He took out his card and handed it to Josh, who took out his wallet.

"Can I have one of yours?" the kid said. "You never know when *Isthmus* might need a detective."

Well what the hell. He was in the Yellow Pages. Josh peeled off a card and handed it to Schneider. He headed west on the Beltline, cutting north on Midvale Boulevard and peeling off into the Westmoreland neighborhood, with its small houses on small lots, including Frank Lloyd Wright's famous Usonian House on Toepfer Avenue. Frank Lloyd Wright was all over the city. You couldn't miss him. From Monona Terrace to the Unitarian Meeting House to Herbert Jacobs House, the master had left his stamp on the whole state.

He wasn't far from Fig's house when he pulled into the driveway of a small one-story ranch house on Brierly Road. It was not a Frank Lloyd Wright. Its pale yellow paint was chipped and fading, its white curtains shut, the lawn unkempt. Josh rapped on the door. The drapes parted and a moment later the door opened, revealing a man who looked like Uncle Creepy, with a monadnock of skull poking up through a fringe of white hair. He stepped back and held the door.

"Come on in," said Mason Stock. He was a small-time dope dealer Josh knew from Bedouin days and from whom he still bought the occasional bag of weed.

The house smelled of cigarettes and marijuana, body odor, dead skin and fried grease. Mason's 72-inch flat-screen TV was frozen on *Call of Duty IV*. The game yoke sat on a discarded—or borrowed—phone company cable spool that served as a coffee table. A smoldering cigarette lay next to a dozen butts in a big amber ashtray like they used to have in Vegas. A framed poster of Arnold as the Terminator was the only decoration.

Mason retreated to his sofa, reached behind the telephone spool and pulled out what looked like an electronic hookah. He turned a dial, put the plastic tube to his mouth and exhaled, releasing a dense gray cloud.

"Want a hit?" he said, holding his breath.

"No thanks, man," Josh said, knowing he was probably going to get a contact high just being in the room.

"Whaddaya need?" Mason said, resuming combat.

"Got any decent acid?"

"Man I got some crazy good shit friend of mine makes in Michigan. How much do you need?"

"Just one hit."

Mason looked up. "One fuckin' tab? Shit, I'll give it to ya."

"Thanks, man," Josh said. "I owe you one."

Mason was too busy shooting jihadists to answer.

MEET THE FOLK

WHEN JOSH GOT HOME, FIG'S BIKE WAS IN the driveway and Fig was sitting on his stoop poking at her iPhone. She stood and smiled like the rising sun. They clinched. They smooched.

With Josh's arms around her Fig said, "Daddy wants you to come to dinner tomorrow night."

A sliver of fear sliced into Josh's heart. He had never met the parents of any of the girls he'd dated, if you could call them dates. Some were just convenient repositories back when he was riding with the Bedouins. There had been gangbangs but the girls had been willing. Or as willing as eighteen-year-old coke and meth heads who thought biker gangs were glamorous could be.

He looked over Fig's shoulder and watched an old but well-preserved Mercedes cruise slowly by, the driver looking at house numbers.

They went inside. Fig had brought a chilled Chardonnay, which she uncorked and poured into a red Solo cup. She got Josh a beer from the fridge and opened it, and they went out on the back deck.

"Whatdja do today?" Fig said.

Josh told her about his encounter with Wolfe.

"Who's this girl?" Fig said.

"I don't know. She may have been Wolfe's girlfriend back in the day. But Beale claims he never knew Wolfe and that Curtis Mack was a black guy."

"Why do you think she's Wolfe's girlfriend?"

Josh got up, retrieved the photo from his office and showed it to her.

Fig stared at it. "Could be anybody."

"I think Beale knows more than he's saying."

"How old is he?" Fig said.

"Beale? Got to be seventy, at least."

"Well he's not going to talk. Code of silence and all that."

Josh smiled. "He might."

Fig threw her arms around him. "What?"

Josh shook his head. "Can't say."

"What if he's just senile?"

"Then I'm shit out of luck," Josh said.

Sex, dinner, a movie. They sat on the sofa opposite the flat-screen as Fig burrowed through her backpack. "I brought a movie."

"What?"

She handed him *The Band Wagon* starring Fred Astaire and Cyd Charisse.

"Never heard of it," Josh said. Fig smiled and plugged it into the slot.

When it ended Josh said, "I think that's the greatest movie ever made."

Fig was outta there at zero dark thirty to attend to her mysterious business. Josh went to bed without reading any more of the book. The sun woke him. He stretched languorously in bed before rising and running five miles.

It was Friday. Din-din with Daddy. He didn't know why it bothered him. He'd never worried much about the impression he made. Could it be he was in love with this girl? Was that possible?

How could he not? Wasn't that a source of joy and confidence? He found himself humming silly love songs. Especially that damned McCartney.

But her old man still scared the shit out of him. Had to be the class difference. Josh had spent most of his life with blue-collar stiffs, drifters, grifters, bikers and cons. He'd seldom had occasion to mix with the rich, and let's not kid ourselves, class lines in America were mostly economic.

Josh went online and researched Ludlow Newton.

Ludlow Ross Newton, Class of '70, is a Realtor and developer from Lancaster, Wisconsin. The third of three boys born to Tom and Judi Newton of Lancaster, Ludlow grew up in the Frank Lloyd Wright-designed Newton House. Ludlow originally studied architecture but switched his major to Business Administration in his second year.

He launched Newton Development in 1976 with a loan from his family and has gone on to champion the Prairie school of architecture pioneered by Wright. Newton is a Taliesin Fellow and lives in a home he designed along with the Fellowship. When University Hospital planned to demolish the Wright-designed Waring House during their mid-eighties expansion, Newton bought the property, dismantled it, tagged every piece, and rebuilt it in its entirety on a hill near Sun Prairie. Waring House is open to the public and available for private functions.
—The Wisconsin Alumni Foundation

Josh set down the computer and called Mrs. McIntyre. "Ma'am, there's a sealed steamer trunk in the barn and a locked garage out back. Do you have the keys for those?"

"No. I haven't been on that property in years."

"Do I have your permission to open those up?"

"I guess, if they're not Mr. Miller's. Let me ask him and I'll get back to you."

Josh thanked her.

At the appointed hour Josh put on clean blue jeans and a clean blue work shirt that covered his tats, and stopped at Woodman's for what the clerk assured him was a cunning Cabernet Sauvignon. Newton lived in Zebrawood, a luxury development west of Madison off Mineral Point Road. Josh turned into Newton's curving blacktop that ran under the porte cochere and parked his bike by Fig's by the double front doors. He rang the doorbell.

Seconds later, Fig opened it smiling, wearing a long-sleeved white shirt with the sleeves rolled up and khakis. She kissed him.

"Come on back. Dad's on the patio. Would you like a beer?"

Josh handed her the bottle. "Sure."

Josh walked through the long, low house and stepped down to the family room, noting the wood floor, joists, beamed ceiling and walk-in fireplace. He went through the sliding glass doors out back where Newton was fiddling with his gas barbecue not far from a gleaming blue oval-shaped pool.

Josh went up to him. "Sir, I'm Josh Pratt."

Newton gave him a firm handshake. He was about five nine, wiry, with close-cropped iron-gray hair, wearing a blue-and-yellow Hawaiian shirt with palm trees and surfboards. "Ludlow Newton. Call me Lud. Fig tells me you're a detective."

"Yes sir."

"You ever work construction?"

"Yes sir."

"It's always good to have something to fall back on."

Josh wondered if Newton was joking or admonishing him. Right now the only job he had was through Fig.

"What can you tell me about Stan?" Newton said.

Josh brought him up to speed.

Fig came out with a tray containing two beers and glasses and a glass of wine.

Newton poured his beer into the glass. "So you suspect this Wolfe character of inciting mass murder?"

"Sir, I don't know. I ask the same question you would, why would a respected academic, someone who has overcome a shady past, risk everything for a vicarious thrill?"

Newton sat in a cushioned lawn chair. "He's said a lot of inflammatory things over the years. He's an embarrassment to the university and I've told them so. His wife is even worse."

CHAPTER 55

RACISM

"BOYS!" FIG SNAPPED. "LET'S NOT TALK POLITICS."

Newton smiled self-deprecatingly. "Sorry! Sorry. Oh honey, don't let me commence! It's just that they make it so damn hard to do business!"

"Daddy's pissed because the City Planning Commission is getting in the way of his new project."

"To put it mildly," Newton said. "Well, all politics is local, isn't it?"

"The city wants Daddy to build a natural wetlands for whooping cranes on his new development."

"At a cost of $6 million," Newton said. "It's extortion."

"It's for the whooping cranes, Daddy."

"It's for the Planning Commission Chairman's worthless brother-in-law who runs some bullshit non-profit from which he draws a six-figure salary."

"No politics, Daddy!"

"Who brought up the whooping cranes?"

While Newton grilled antelope steaks, Fig set the table in the backyard.

"My daughter thinks quite a lot of you," Newton said.

"I think the same of her, sir."

"You have quite a history."

"Sir," Josh said, "the last thing I want is publicity."

"I get that impression," Newton said. "And call me Lud, wouldya? Things get slow for you, I can always use an experienced builder."

"Thank you, sir. Lud. That's good to know."

After dinner Newton brought out the single malt but Josh held up his hand.

"I have to be able to ride."

"You guys can stay here," Newton said. "You can even share the same bedroom. I won't say a thing."

Fig waved her arms. "*No, nein, nyet!* Thank you very much."

They left at nine and went to Josh's place. Afterward they lay in bed.

"Remember the faculty party?" Josh said, Fig's head in the crook of his arm.

"How could I forget?"

"Remember we saw Wolfe entering as we were leaving?"

"Yeah."

"Where was Nedra?"

Fig turned over and threw an arm across Josh's chest. "I think they have an open marriage."

"How would you know?"

Fig sat up and swung her legs out of bed. "I think I read it somewhere. I gotta go. I forgot to feed Mr. Schermerhorn. What are you doing tomorrow? Would you like to come over to my place for dinner?"

"Sure. Seven okay?"

Fig leaned down to kiss him. "See you then."

After she left, Josh went online and looked up Nedra Keppler-Wolfe.

Nedra Keppler-Wolfe was a leader of the Global Resistance, a group that was responsible for the bombing of the United States Capitol, the Pentagon and several police stations in New York, as well as a Greenwich Village townhouse in which one of the group was killed in the explosion. As a member of the Global Resistance, Keppler-Wolfe helped to create a "Declaration of a State of War Against the United States Government," and was placed on the FBI's 10 Most Wanted list, where she remained for three years. From 1991 to 2013 she was a Clinical Associate Professor of Law at the Children and Family Justice Center at the University of Wisconsin School of Law and is married to Jeffrey Wolfe IV, a co-founder of the Global Resistance, who is a tenured professor at the University of Wisconsin.

Nedra Keppler-Wolfe was born Nedra Siegel in Milwaukee, WI, and grew up in Whitefish Bay, an upper-middle-class suburb. Her father, Everett, changed the family surname to Keppler when Nedra was in high school. Her father was Jewish and her mother, Amelia (née Nordstrom), was of Swedish background and a Christian Scientist. Keppler graduated from Whitefish Bay High School, where she was a cheerleader, treasurer of the Modern Dance Club, a member of the National Honor Society and editor of the school newspaper.

Keppler became one of the leaders of the Revolutionary Youth Movement (RYM), a radical wing of Students for a Democratic Society (SDS), in the late 1960s. Keppler, with ten other SDS members associated with the RYM, issued on June 18, 1969, a sixteen-thousand-word manifesto entitled, "Death to the White Power Structure" in New Left Notes.

The manifesto concludes with, "The RYM must also lead to the effective organization needed to survive and to create another battlefield of the revolution. A revolution is a war; when the Movement in this country can defend itself militarily against total repression it will be part of the revolutionary war. This will require a cadre organization, effective secrecy, self-reliance among the cadres..." The manifesto also asserted that African-Americans were a "black colony" within a U.S. government that was doomed to overextend itself. And the RYM was needed to quicken this process. Keppler said, "The best thing that we can be doing for ourselves, as well as for the black and the revolutionary struggle, is to destroy white privilege and the white power structure."

On the UW site Josh saw that Keppler-Wolfe was hosting a White Privilege Seminar in August. "The White Privilege Conference offers a challenging, collaborative and comprehensive experience. We strive to empower and equip individuals to work for equity and justice through self- and social transformation."

Keppler-Wolfe herself taught a seminar called "Math: Domain of Old White Men," including how to make math relevant by incorporating "social justice."

The program included "Navigating Triggering Events," "White on White: Communicating about Race and White Privilege Using Critical Humility," and "Our Bodies Know the Way: Using Cellular Wisdom to Dismantle Whiteness and Live in Deep Community." There was a letter from the mayor welcoming the White Privilege Conference to Madison.

When Josh was in the joint there was no white privilege. The racial makeup was overwhelmingly black. Josh had been forced to ally himself with the Aryan Brotherhood in order to survive, but at least the Aryan Brotherhood had a respectful relationship with the black prison gangs such as United Blood Nation and the Black Guerilla Family.

He'd had frank talks about race in prison with Dorgan, the Aryan Brotherhood and many blacks. All agreed that racism was an inherent part of the human condition and stemmed from a time when there was ferocious competition for scarce resources and man was genetically inclined to stick with his own kind for survival. Racism was as natural as hunger. The trick was to recognize it and deal with it.

Josh left the internet and went to bed, too tired to read his book.

SATURDAY IN THE PARK WITH MARK

JOSH ARRIVED AT WHISPERING PINES IN HIS Honda at 10:00 a.m. Saturday. He signed in, found Mark Beale in a wheelchair on the patio and wheeled him through the retirement home, out the front door to his car, where he helped Beale into the driver's seat, collapsed the wheelchair and put it in his trunk.

"I'm taking Uncle Mark to the park," he told the receptionist.

She smiled and said, "He's lucky to have a nephew like you."

Beale was perfectly amenable. "You got any reefer?" he said as they pulled away.

"Better than that," Josh said. "I brought you a hit of windowpane."

Beale smiled like a child on Christmas morning. "Seriously? Lay it on me, brother."

Josh reached into his pocket, handed Beale the pill and a bottle of water. He pulled into the Olbrich Park parking lot, set up the wheelchair and helped Beale into it. Olbrich incorporated formal outdoor gardens, a Japanese gazebo and an indoor glass hothouse as well as paved trails. Josh slowly wheeled Beale behind the administration building out to the gardens. There were a handful of visitors, mostly seniors who volunteered to help. Josh stopped at a reflecting pond and sat on a commemorative bench while they watched the fat koi.

After a little bit Beale said, "Whoa. I can feel it!"

Josh pulled out a fat doobie, lit it and passed it to Beale. Technically it was illegal but there wasn't a cop in Madison who'd do a damned thing about it. "Remember the Collective? Wouldn't it be great if we could get everybody back together who's still alive?"

Beale inhaled deeply, held it, exhaled. "Ahhhh," he declared. "What the fuck you talking about? You weren't even born then."

Josh laughed. "I'm researching the Collective for a case."

"Who the fuck are you again?"

"Josh Pratt. I'm a private detective. I was out there last week, saw your offices."

Beale inhaled again and passed the joint back to Josh, who held it. "How'd they look?"

"Looks like they haven't been touched in forty-five years. Hopin' that windowpane might jog your memory a little bit."

"What do you want to know?"

Josh opened his backpack, took out the eight-by-ten glossy and handed it to Beale. "Can you put names to all these faces?"

Beale took the photo, held it at arm's length, brought it close to his nose, held it out again, zoomed back. "Whoa," he said. "They look alive! Do they look alive to you?"

"Yeah, man. Let's start on the left." Josh put his finger on a nondescript dude slouching in a guayabera.

"Fuck if I know. The day that was taken, there could have been people there from Kathmandu. People were always dropping in, staying a few days and taking off again. This one dude came by with a reconverted school bus painted all psychedelic, recruited any nubile young female stupid enough to believe his bullshit, went off and started a commune in Colorado. He was later busted for prostitution and drug dealing."

"Is he in this picture?"

Beale examined the photo more closely. "I don't see him. 'Course I don't remember what he looked like either. Ha!"

"What about Curtis Mack? Is he in this photo?"

Beale stared, breathing heavy. It sounded like the air exchange in a tenement. He tentatively put his finger on a slim black man wearing a puffed-out Rasta cap, with a neat Van Dyke. "This dude here might be Curtis."

"Was he writing when he was with you?"

"Oh yeah! Now I remember. He was always bangin' away on a typewriter in the office. Had to uproot him a couple times just to put the paper to bed."

They worked their way down the line with numerous digressions. Thoughts flitted through Beale's mind like larks in and out of an abandoned church. The time they smuggled in a key of Afghan hash. The time they sold their marijuana crop to some bikers from the Twin Cities. The time the cops raided them looking for underage runaways.

It took a half hour to get halfway through the lineup when Josh pointed to a mousy woman in a tie-dyed dress that came down to mid-calf.

"Nedra something," Beale said. "A real pill."

"Nedra Keppler?"

"Yeah, that's who it was."

"Do you see Jeffrey Wolfe in this picture?"

"No."

"Is Jeff Wolfe paying for you to stay at Whispering Pines?"

Beale shrugged. "Fuck no. That money comes from the Revolutionary Legal Defense Fund, a non-profit set up to take care of aging revolutionaries. Weren't for them I'd be dead."

"Did they contact you or did you contact them?"

Beale scrunched up his face. Josh wondered how much of his mind was left if he was willing to drop acid at his age. "I forget. I mighta reached out."

"How long you been there?" Josh said.

Scrunch face. "Since '98 I think. Before that I was living out of my car on the East Side. I had some people useta help me out, give me food and such. Useta school those kids on the movement. Half of 'em wearin' Che shirts don't even know who he was. 'Some guerilla, man.'"

Josh pointed to Stacy Pembroke.

"Stacy Pembroke," Beale said with relish. "Everybody wanted to get in her pants. Too bad she ended up with that fucking sell-out Fine."

"Who?"

"Murray Fine. He was in pre-law. I'm sure that fucker went on to become some fat-cat corporate lawyer. Never should have let him join."

Josh pointed to the dude in the shades hanging onto Stacy. "Is that Fine?"

"Yeah. That's him. Prick."

JUDGE FINE

ON THE WAY BACK TO VERONA, BEALE OFFERED advice through the open window. "You!" he shouted to a kid on a skateboard. "It's your life! Don't waste it getting stoned!"

Josh was glad when they hit the Beltline, where they were going too fast to be heard. It was two thirty when he returned Beale to the nursing home, still tripping. Josh had written the names of the participants on the back of the photo whenever possible. Beale was only able to identify sixteen of the twenty-four people in the photo. Some would never be identified.

Murray Fine my ass, Josh thought. It had to be Jeffrey Wolfe, aka Curtis Mack, who had created all those characters when he wrote the Shred Husl novels. But Beale claimed Wolfe had never stayed at the commune. What did Beale know? He'd dropped so much acid over the years, it was a miracle he could remember anything.

Yet, throughout the day, Beale had remained sharp as a tack.

Once home Josh went online and searched for Murray Fine. Bingo! Judge Murray Fine sat on the Ninth Circuit Court of Appeals. Before that he had been a district attorney for San Francisco, worked in private practice and received his law degree from the University of Wisconsin, Madison, in 1974. He was returning to the university in July to receive the Edward Ben Elson Distinguished Jurist Award. There would be a swank dinner at Monona Terrace.

Murray Fine was real! Josh wondered if the judge knew he had appeared in the Shred Husl novels. No question Fine and Wolfe knew each other. They had to have crossed paths at the Collective. Josh wrote Fine a letter and sent it via the Ninth Circuit's web page.

Dear Judge Fine: I am a private investigator looking into the cause of death of Stan Newton, a UW athlete who was found drowned several weeks ago. Did you know there is a Murray Fine character in the Shred Husl books by Curtis Mack? Did you know Curtis Mack? Do you know Jeffrey Wolfe IV? Did Wolfe write the Shred Husl books under an assumed name?

Josh did not expect an answer.

Mrs. McIntyre called. "Mr. Miller says he has nothing to do with either the steamer trunk in the loft or the locked garage, and you're welcome to take a look."

Josh thanked her and hung up.

He stopped at Woodman's and picked up what the clerk assured him was an ebullient Chardonnay, and a six-pack of Capital lager for himself. The wine went in a saddlebag; he bungeed the beer to the pillion. Mr. Schermerhorn was waiting when he climbed the steep stairs to Fig's joint. The old dog grinned and thumped the wooden porch. The front door was open, leaving an unlatched screen door, so he went in.

Fig called to him from the kitchen. "Hi! Make yourself at home. I got you beer."

Josh took his bottles into the kitchen and put them in the refrigerator, choosing the Odell's Fig had bought over the Capital. He kissed her, went out the back door to her small backyard and a sun-dappled patio. Mr. Schermerhorn followed him out and lay at his feet, thumping the ground. Squishburton followed, purring. They ate lasagna on the patio and made love in the bedroom. They got dressed and walked around the neighborhood filled with quaint American Craftsman-type bungalows, solar panels and vegetable gardens.

"When are you going to give me another bill?" Fig said.

"Not until I learn who killed your brother."

"Do you think you will?"

"Yes," Josh said. "I may never find the actual hoods who held him underwater but I'm going to get the guy who gave the order. I can feel it."

"Do you think it's Wolfe?"

"It's either Wolfe, his wife or Judge Murray Fine."

Fig made that overbite. "What?"

Josh filled her in on what he'd learned from Beale. "I have to go back out there tomorrow and search the trunk and the garage. Want to come?"

"Sure. We can ride!"

Later as they lay in bed she trailed her fingers across his chest. Her nails were neatly trimmed but she didn't go in for nail polish, barely used any makeup at all. "You remind me of Stan. He was good and decent too, under a rough exterior."

"I wasn't always this way."

"No? What made you change?"

Josh thought of all he'd been through. "Did a lot of soul-searching in prison. I was lucky to have Frank Dorgan as chaplain. He brought me to Christ." Josh laughed. "He brought me to blues and jazz, for that matter!"

"Do you ever talk to him?"

Josh felt guilty. He should have reached out. "No. But I will. I'll see if I can track him down."

"You never asked if I was Christian," Fig said.

"I don't care."

She did the overbite. "You don't care?"

"Don't go changing, to try and please me...You never let me down before..." Josh sang badly.

Fig laughed. "Want to watch a movie?"

"What?"

"Singin' in the Rain! You'll love it."

While they were watching the movie an old but well-preserved Mercedes cruised by the house on the street below and stopped several houses down.

CHAPTER 58

SCENIC RIDE

FIG AGREED TO MEET JOSH AT ONE FOR THE ride to Richland Center. Josh spent the morning researching the Honorable Murray Fine and learned that the judge had been involved in many controversial opinions, including one that illegal aliens were to be given driver's licenses and free medical marijuana. Not surprisingly, Fine did not respond to Josh's query.

At eleven Kofsky phoned. "Beale's bills are paid by the Revolutionary Legal Defense Fund."

"Who they?" Josh said.

"I figured you'd ask, so I'm e-mailing you a list of the board of directors. That's all I got right now."

Josh thanked him, hung up and checked his e-mail. He was not surprised to find Jeffrey Wolfe on the board. He went into the garage and got a bolt cutter, which he bungeed to the pillion on his bike. For the padlocks. He figured they'd get out there by two thirty, have a couple of hours to poke around and stop in Spring Green for dinner at the Frank Lloyd Wright-designed Riverview Terrace Cafe. He poked around on Facebook, appalled by what people said.

No one loves me. I'm unlovable. I deserve to be alone.

Two things: 1) I slept like a baby last night, in spite of not even having a bed. 2) My wife is gone for good and I will never have to see her ever again.

I want to thank all the people that have reached out to me. I would be lying if I said this wasn't incredibly difficult, and I appreciate the people reaching out. I apologize to many of you that are shocked, I think I kind of am too. Our relationship was something incredibly special, and I think more connected and intense than many marriages I've seen. I am still very much in love with Judy, and I think at this point at least, she still loves me. In lieu of a more in-depth explanation, we have come across a basic incompatibility. I hope for a new form of relationship with her, but she and I have much work to do in order to determine what our future is. Thank you again, those of you that have helped.

Dear Radar Online,

F U C K Y O U,

Nothing and I mean NOTHING on this list is even worth mentioning. I assume EVERY single married woman who has a 'take no shit' policy would react the same way in many of these situations. This article is CODE for "Angry BLACK Woman."

I'm gonna shut up for an extended period until I get things sorted in my life. If anybody has a problem with it, you know where to find me. I'm depressed, been sick for days. And no, I don't have a good opinion of myself. My life is shit and so am I. No one will miss me. But if I focus on getting my ducks in a row, I might be okay. Now, allaya, scram.

And that was hardly all of it. Josh had learned through bitter experience to keep his feelings hidden, and he couldn't imagine putting his soul on display as so many did. He wanted to warn them. People! Facebook is not your friend! All these "friends" are not your friends! See a shrink, talk to a priest, get drunk with your best friend, but for God's sake don't put it on Facebook!

The front screen door creaked open. He went to the living room and there was his golden girl bringing sunshine and the smell of flowers into the house. She made him want to sing silly love songs. He kissed her.

"You ready?"

"You bet."

Josh had made a copy of the Google Map to the Miller Farm. "Here's the route. Stick it in your tank bag."

While Fig put on her open-face helmet, Josh wheeled his Road King out of the garage and closed the door. It rumbled at the push of a button, and he and Fig headed west on Ptarmigan. It was a beautiful summer day with some clouds in the west promising rain, but not until the evening. They rode through emerald forests on sun-dappled asphalt, past grazing cows and running horses, over creeks and under chestnut trees.

Josh tried to keep Fig's pink Hello Kitty backpack in sight, but she frequently lost him in the twisties, only to wait for him laughing at the next intersection.

They had the road to themselves, hardly saw a soul for the hour and a half it took them to reach Richland Center. They rode through the city, stopping in front of the Frank Lloyd Wright-designed A.D. German Warehouse.

They parked their bikes on the opposite side of Church Street and walked up to the blocky building, which resembled Scrooge McDuck's money bin.

"German was a cement, coal and grain wholesaler," Josh said. "Wright owed him money and German figured he'd never see a dime, so he told Wright he'd accept payment in design. It was supposed to cost thirty grand, ended up costing over 125 grand by the time German went under." Josh barked in mirth. "Story of Wright's life."

"How do you know all this about Wright?" Fig said.

"Prison chaplain. He was a nut for this stuff. Gave me some books to read. Since then I've kind of been visiting all the Wright buildings I could. Gives you a different perspective on things."

"You're so brainy," Fig said.

Josh barked again. "No one's ever called me that."

They rode west past grazing cattle and busy combines. Twenty-five minutes later, they came to the chained entrance to the farm Miller rented from Mrs. McIntyre.

The chain was unlocked. Josh let it down while he and Fig rode across, then put it up again. They rolled into the packed earth in front of the barn and got off. Fig took off her helmet and shook her hair out, the sight of which Josh never tired. She took off her light leather jacket and laid it on the seat of her Hawk, wearing an Emperors of Wyoming T-shirt.

"Where to?" she said.

Josh unhooked the bolt cutter and pointed to the barn. "Let's start with the trunk."

Fig walked into the barn, stopped with her hands on her hips and looked around. As Josh stepped from light to shadow she looked back at him. Her expression morphed into shock.

Ten thousand volts ripped through Josh's frame and turned him to jelly.

CHAPTER 59

THE JESUIT

HE SWAM TOWARD THE LIGHT. NEEDLES PIERCED his back and his neck as something dragged him across the rough barn floor and then the electric deluge coursed through him and he lost consciousness. He sank into warm tar. Down, down, so far down he would never surface. Buried beneath a translucent, heavy viscosity. His limbs didn't respond. Trapped in the cage of his body.

The steady grunting of a feral hog spiraled into his brain like a dentist's drill. He felt numb with a sickness that penetrated to the bone, an acrid taste in his mouth, unable to breathe through his nose because something had smashed it flat. He tried to touch his face but his hands were strapped behind him as he sat on the ground leaning against a rough wood pillar. Someone had used his head for a piñata. He tried to move his jaw. Jagged lightning flashed and his bones clicked. Something was loose in his jaw. His left eye was swollen shut and felt blown up and artificial.

He opened his right eye. For an instant he couldn't make sense of it—a jumble of body parts lurching to that repetitive grunt. *Hunh hunh hunh.* A huge muscular man, pants around his knees, humping something. Fig. It was humping Fig. He'd tased her and now he was fucking her. Black bristles covered his back like a boar. Tribal tats covered his arms.

"No," Josh said but nothing came out. He kicked his legs feebly in frustration.

"Hey," he croaked. "STOP!"

The boar looked at him, grinning. Shaved skull shaped like a howitzer shell. The boar pulled out and stood, abandoning Fig like garbage, pulled up his pants and fastened his belt. He wore a white wife-beater revealing fully tatted blue arms. He shuffled over, leaving Fig groaning and twitching. He crouched in front of Josh.

"Know who I am?"

Josh stared at him with hatred. "You're a dead man," he said out of the right side of his face accompanied by fusillades of pain and clicking.

"I'm Wayne Culligan. You killed my brothers, Phil and Dave."

"I didn't kill them," Josh said through cracked lips. "The cops killed 'em."

"Same dif. Phil warned you. I'm the Jesuit."

Josh tried to spit but nothing came up. "So what," he said, yanking barbed wire through his jaw.

Culligan backhanded him savagely across the face with no change in expression. The explosion of pain nearly made Josh pass out. "You're wondering how I found you. It wasn't hard. You left the map to this place face up in your tank bag. Know why they call me the Jesuit?"

Josh looked down.

"They call me the Jesuit because I'm the guy that does the church's dirty work, only in this case, the church is the CIA. I'm retired now. I quit when they elected that nigger. I'm in the private sector now and I've never been busier. I cost a lot but I'm worth it. You, of course, I'm doing as a memorial to Phil and Dave. You thought they were just a couple of peckerwood bikers. They were dumb and mean but they were my brothers. They were the only family I had left.

"I know about you. Think you're hot shit. You've been in the joint. You should have known this was coming. When I'm done, nobody will know about me. They'll find your charred bodies, maybe remnants of the plastic bags I'm going to put around your heads." Culligan grabbed his crotch. "Mmm. She had a tight pussy. Now ahmina put a plastic bag over her head."

Culligan walked toward Fig, who lay moaning and twitching, and pulled an opaque black plastic bag from the pocket of his cargo pants. He knelt, jerked Fig's head up by the hair and forced the plastic bag down as she struggled feebly.

Josh spasmed, lashing out with every limb, testing his bonds, scrabbling backwards, mad with grief and rage. The pillar at his back cinched back a quarter inch. Lousy construction. It had been casually nailed to the floor with penny nails at an angle.

Culligan took out some twine and wrapped it tightly around Fig's neck. Josh scrabbled desperately, somehow getting his feet under him and inching upward. He lurched with all his might. The pillar shifted and a curtain of dust descended from the loft forming a straight line where it landed on the floor.

Culligan looked up. For a moment he just stared. Josh strained again and the pillar lurched back an inch. Another curtain of dust. Culligan sprang to his feet. Josh shoved with all his might, felt the pillar lose traction and swing up and toward the rear. He went with it backing up desperately as Culligan strode toward him. The loft groaned, shifted and, with a crack like bones breaking, spilled.

The steamer trunk shunted forward and down, the corner striking Culligan on his head. Culligan collapsed. The loft groaned like a dying ship, the hinges and joists gave way and the whole thing came down. A brick wall slammed into Josh, knocking him down and out.

He came to seconds later, blinded by the dust and the crap that lay around him. He tested his bonds. He was still tethered to the pillar but now it lay loose, pointing toward the rear of the barn. Josh scrabbled backwards in a crouch until his bonds slipped off the end. He lay on his back, drew his knees up and brought his bound wrists to his front. Culligan had used a plastic wiring harness.

He writhed in darkness, choked by the dust, working his way toward the rear of the barn. He saw light streaming in through a crack, went toward it and found the door to the back office. Choking and coughing, tears streaming from his eyes, Josh stumbled into the office in a cloud of dust. He looked around with crazy eyes and saw the old paper cutter on the desk. Josh brought the two-foot lever upright, looped his hands over the blade and sawed. The plastic snapped.

He burst through the rear door, ran limping around to the front to Fig, who lay still with the plastic bag around her neck. Josh fell to his knees, drew out his pocketknife, flipped it open and carefully cut across the front of the sack, tearing it open. Fig was blue. Josh heard a faint whining as he slipped the blade beneath the rope around her neck and cut it loose. The whining came from the back of his throat. A drop of blood fell on her pale cheek. Bending over, he tilted her head back and breathed into her lungs. One two three, breath. One two three, breath.

Fig coughed and twitched. She started to breathe. Sobbing with fear and relief, he gathered her to him. It was some moments before he looked up. The steamer trunk lay on its side, split open like the *Titanic* spilling paperback books. No Jesuit.

Josh looked around wildly. He held Fig tightly—she was so light!—and carried her back to where the loft had collapsed, forming a crude lean-to against the back wall.

He put her in a horse stall next to the collapsed loft and left her lying on a pile of horse blankets breathing shallowly but not fully awake, slipped out of the horse stall and slithered along the wall in shadow until he came to the pitchfork.

He ripped the pitchfork off the wall and whirled as the Jesuit charged grunting, thrusting the black cylinder of the Taser. Josh caught the Taser in the pitchfork tines and wrenched it free but the Jesuit kneed him in the thigh as Josh turned. Pain exploded in a cone and he lost his grip on the pitchfork. He instinctively reached for the back of the Jesuit's head and butted him in the nose, pulling himself into the butt. The impact jarred him, caused broken bones to scrape and brought tears to his eyes as it sent the Jesuit staggering back in a haze of blood.

For the first time since the collapse, Josh got a good look at him. The steamer trunk had left a dent in the side of his skull that meant brain damage, but the Jesuit came at him again, a primordial force, the savagery of the raging beast. Josh juked to the side, slamming his knee into the Jesuit's stomach. It felt like hard canvas. The Jesuit hooked Josh beneath the arm but Josh leaped and whirled backwards, striking the Jesuit in the face with his elbow. Blood exploded from the Jesuit's ruined nose.

Josh grabbed the Jesuit in a Thai clinch and kneed him twice in the groin. The Jesuit fell, groaning. Josh seized the pitchfork, held it overhead and plunged it with all his might into the Jesuit's chest. He set his foot on the Jesuit's chest, yanked the pitchfork loose and plunged it again. And again. And again.

AFTERMATH

JOSH DIDN'T CHECK TO MAKE SURE THE JESUIT was dead. He was sure of it. He'd felt the tine break through a fleshy wall of resistance, a lung or a heart. He staggered to the horse stall, kicking one of the paperbacks out of his path. *Tear the Roof Off the Sucker* by Curtis Mack.

He knelt next to Fig, who was breathing shallowly but steadily. Her face was bruised where the Jesuit had struck her, her lip split. She wore no pants. Her legs were covered in blood. Josh looked around for his cell phone, could not find it. He got up, gimped through the barn until he found Fig's backpack and ripped out her cell phone. He couldn't get a signal.

He went to the Jesuit, who lay with sightless eyes staring at the ceiling. Josh went through his pockets, pulled out a phone, which he tossed over his shoulder, and a set of keys with a Mercedes fob. He found the Mercedes sedan parked a hundred yards away behind the garage, which was behind the barn, and spewed a rooster tail of dirt and gravel driving it into the barn. He laid Fig down on the back seat, covered her with a blanket, and drove to Richland Center at 120 miles per hour, picking up an RCPD who followed him, siren wailing, lights flashing all the way to the ER entrance.

Josh braked hard directly in front of the ER and leaned on the horn. He got out. The cop squealed to a stop six inches from his back bumper. As Josh took Fig out of the back seat, the cop ran up screaming and waving his gun. Josh took Fig out of the back seat and ran with her toward the double glass sliding doors. The cop was still screaming as an orderly rushed out to meet them wheeling a gurney. As soon as Josh laid Fig on the gurney, the cop threw Josh to the concrete and landed with his knee in the small of Josh's back.

Josh didn't hear what the cop yelled, didn't fight as the cop savagely handcuffed him. By the time the cop got Josh into the back of his cruiser, two more police vehicles had arrived. They conferred along with the orderly who'd taken Fig into the ER. The three cops were arguing. One of them, not the cop who'd cuffed Josh, came over, opened the door, helped Josh out and relieved him of his wallet. He took out the driver's license.

"What happened to the young woman?" he said.

"My name is Josh Pratt," Josh said awkwardly, unable to use his mouth as he wished. Sharp pain radiated through his jaw. "The young woman has been beaten, raped and nearly suffocated. She may be suffering from internal bleeding."

The cop pulled out a little recorder and laid it on top of the vehicle. "What happened?"

Josh explained. The cop took off the cuffs. The shootout on Ptarmigan had been national news for twenty-four hours. The hothead cop refused to meet Josh's eyes, got in his car and drove away. Josh entered the ER accompanied by the other cop. A young dot Indian doctor wearing the name tag VISHNA came out.

"Are you the boyfriend?" he said.

Josh nodded.

"She has some internal bleeding. Looks like she was sodomized with some object. We're operating on her now. I don't know when she'll be out of surgery. Why don't you come with me."

A tidal wave of fatigue and pain washed over Josh, who stumbled and would have fallen if the cop hadn't caught him under the arm. First came antiseptics and bandages. Then the X-rays.

The doctor pointed to the results on a computer hanging from the ceiling. "You have a fractured jawbone and occipital ridge, and a concussion. We need to wire that jaw back together. We're also going to have to go in there and check for nerve damage to the eye." Vishna made a "V" sign with two fingers. "How many fingers do you see?"

"Fo," Josh said.

Vishanti shook his head. "Just as I thought. Do you have health insurance?"

Josh shook his head, setting off shrill alarms and causing his gorge to rise.

The doctor muttered under his breath in Hindi. "Do you have the means to pay for this operation?"

It hurt to talk. "How much?" It came out, *howuch*?

"Well I don't know exactly, but these things can run into tens of thousands of dollars. I don't understand the pricing or billing process. No doctor does. It's out of our hands. Of course we're going to operate and your ability to pay won't affect the quality of our work; I'm just telling you what to expect."

Josh wondered how much Fleiss could loan him. He could sell a couple of his bikes. That ought to bring in a few thou. He really had nothing else of value except the house itself, bought and paid for, but he'd be damned if he gave that up. It was the first home he'd ever known. As a child they'd never stayed in one place more than a few months. Duane would fuck up or fuck someone up and sooner or later the police, the deputies, the bill collectors would come and they'd pull up stakes in the middle of the night and flee like gypsies.

A dull throbbing in Josh's jaw increased. He made the thumbs-up with his hand.

In excruciating pain he filled out forms regarding assets and medical history. They wanted to know if he'd ever served time. He answered truthfully. They wanted to know if he had any guns at home. He lied. They admitted him, put him in a hospital gown and prepped him for surgery.

Dr. Vishna found Josh in pre-op. "Well it turns out that the damage to your jaw and occipital ridge is going to require more complicated surgery than we thought, so we'd like your consent to use a general anesthetic. I assure you there is no cause for concern. I know the tech and she is a thorough professional."

Josh signed the consent form. They put him on an operating gurney, wheeled him into the anesthesia room and hooked him with an IV drip and a mask that fitted over the nose and mouth. Black washed over him.

RECOVERY

HE SAW THE GLOW AND THOUGHT, *I'VE MADE it. Heaven at last.* The end of the tunnel. The glow faded, replaced by blackness, and then it reappeared with features and an electronic pulse. He came out of it in the recovery room surrounded by blinding white—the walls, the bedclothes, his nightgown. His jaw was immobilized, left eye covered with bandages and surgical tape. He felt a maddening tingling in his limbs. He tried to flex his jaw and felt nothing. It was numb. He moved his fingers. An orderly saw it and came over.

The orderly was a stocky Asian-looking man. "How you doin'?" he said, strapping an inflatable band around Josh's bicep. He pushed a button and the wrap inflated until it beeped and stopped. The tech pulled out a watch and took Josh's pulse with his index and middle fingers. He pulled out a penlight, thumbed Josh's right eye open and gazed into the void. He put the stethoscope around his neck in his ears and listened to Josh's heart.

"Thirsty?" the tech said, maneuvering a plastic cup with a bent straw, all white, to the right corner of Josh's mouth. Josh sucked greedily, feeling the cold wash down to his stomach.

"Hrrronggg ohhhhht?" Josh said.

"How long have you been out?" the tech replied. "About four hours. It's nine thirty Sunday night. Hang tight. I'll send in the doctor."

Josh moved his head but all he could see was the right side of the room—the white curtains, and through the gap another patient so covered in blinding white gauze as to be unrecognizable. The room smelled of disinfectant through his one working nostril.

He felt himself drifting off when Dr. Vishna strode briskly in, felt his wrist, stared into his right eye and listened with his stethoscope. "We wired the jaw shut and used one small titanium plate and a few screws. You'll be eating through a straw for a month, but with any luck we're looking at a complete recovery. Fortunately there was no damage to the nerve with your eye injury, and that should heal as well. You'll have a new scar to go with the rest. I have never seen someone of your health and vitality with so many scars. I may want to write a paper about it. Of course I would not do so without your permission. I am of course aware of the gunfight at your property last week. Some reporters have been snooping around. I have referred them to the police."

Dr. Vishna turned on the overhead monitor, plucked at a wireless keyboard sitting on a shelf, and an X-ray of Josh's jaw appeared. It looked like an exploded diagram of a Swiss watch. Tiny screws and plates formed an intricate constellation beneath his ghostly teeth.

Josh tried to say, "How is Fig?" but it came out unintelligible nonsense. He made a writing motion on his palm. Dr. Vishna rooted in his white lab coat and came up with a pen and pad, which he handed to Josh.

"How is Miss Newton?" he wrote.

"The operation to stop internal bleeding succeeded but she is in a coma. Right now our main concern is sepsis. We're watching her very closely. She is in a coma due to head trauma. Now it's in God's hands."

"Dog and cat," he wrote.

Vishna stared at it quizzically.

"Fig's pets," he wrote.

Dr. Vishna nodded. "Ah. It is my understanding her father went to her house. You'd have to ask him."

The cop who'd taken off the cuffs entered, followed by Detective Calloway.

"Doc says you can't talk, so we'll try to make this simple," the cop said. His badge said COLLINS; he was about thirty, with red hair and freckles on chipmunk cheeks. "Detective Calloway is here because your assault is now part of his ongoing investigation into gang activity in Dane County."

"Wayne Culligan," Calloway said. "Ran his fingerprints through the NFDB and he popped up as a diplomatic attaché of the State Department attached to the Honduran Embassy. So we reached out to State and they said no such person, and moreover, they are sending someone up here to impress upon us just how much this person doesn't exist.

"He was carrying a driver's license and two credit cards in the name of Edward Martin. The car was reported stolen in St. Louis a week ago. I asked State whether they'd ever heard of the Jesuit and they threatened me with incarceration."

Josh's good eye blinked. You don't threaten Calloway. Calloway dimmed and the tide took Josh out.

The next time he woke, the sun was shining brightly through the window and the mummy in the next compartment was gone. He reached for the plastic water container at his elbow and sucked deeply on the straw, feeling the new hardware in his jaw. His left eye had about a half inch of bandage taped to it.

A nurse came in and smiled brightly. "Mr. Pratt! How are we feeling?"

Josh held up a thumb. The nurse took his vital signs. "You know your jaw is wired together, so don't try to speak. We've got you on a morphine drip and you may activate the dose whenever you feel the need, via this button."

She placed a cylinder connected to a wire in his right hand. "However, you're limited to one hit every three hours. Let me know if this is inadequate,"

Josh grabbed the pen and pad. "How is Miss Newton?" he wrote. His handwriting looked like that of an old woman—shaky and hard to decipher.

The nurse stared at it. Josh tried to speak but he sounded like Boris Karloff in Frankenstein. The nurse figured it out.

"Oh. Miss Newton! She's in a coma. We'll just have to wait and see."

"Can I see her?" he wrote.

The nurse frowned at the note. "I'll give this to her doctor and you can discuss it with her. I'm guessing not, since she's in a coma in intensive care."

Josh grunted and strained, and as if by telepathy or mind meld the nurse intuited. "That would be Dr. Barlin. I will tell her you'd like to talk."

Josh eased himself out of the bed and realized his ribs were taped up. He was as stiff as a cardboard tube. The nurse put a hand on his shoulder and pressed him back into the bed as easily as if he were a kitten.

"Where are you going?" she said.

Josh pointed at the bathroom.

"Oh." She handed Josh a bedpan, left the enclosure and pulled the drapes shut.

CHAPTER

62

SPOOKSVILLE

THE BEDOUINS CAME BY ON TUESDAY. TIM, Bad Bob, Jackalope and Filthy Fred, all wearing their colors. They had smuggled in a flask of Johnny Walker, a nude plastic blow-up doll, a quarter-ounce baggie and some papers. Josh wondered how they expected him to light up in a hospital.

"Hey," Tim said. "Biker picks up a hitchhiker on a cool and breezy night and as they plug along, the passenger complains that he's cold. The biker pulls over, takes off his leather jacket and gives it to him, tells him to put it on backwards, better to ward off the wind. A few miles down the road, they go off the road into a ditch. After the first cops respond, others show up and one asks how the bikers are doing. 'Well,' says the cop, 'one of them was dead when we got here, and the other died while we were trying to get his head straightened out.'"

Josh stared with his single orb.

It was Wednesday before Dr. Barlin appeared. She was a short, intense Persian with jet black hair piled in a bun. Josh had taken his med tree into the john with him, and she was waiting when he came out. She watched his halting progress across the tile floor with obsidian eyes.

"What's wrong with the bedpan?" she said.

Josh eased himself back onto the bed, swung up his legs and leaned back.

"You are the boyfriend," Dr. Barlin said. It wasn't a question. "She had a ruptured spleen and has been in a coma since they brought her in. We removed the spleen. There are also other injuries. I won't lie to you, Mr. Pratt. She is in very serious condition. She's had a lot of internal bleeding."

Despair washed over Josh.

"Her father has visited. He wanted to see you but the hospital thought it would be wise to check with you first."

Josh nodded.

"Yes? It's all right for Mr. Newton to visit? I will tell him."

He was alone for a while and then Steve Fleiss came in with some motorcycle magazines and comic books. "I'da brought you some hooch but I know they got you hooked up to a morphine drip. Anything I can do? Anything I can getcha?"

Josh used sign language and his pad to explain his financial situation. Fleiss nodded.

"Let me look into that. If you're not eligible for Medicaid we'll figure out something. What's the bill?"

Josh shrugged.

"I'll check with billing. Want me to go by your place?"

Josh nodded and wrote, asking for underwear, clean jeans and shirt, a toothbrush, a razor, his phone, his charger and his book *Tear the Roof Off the Sucker*.

"On nightstand," Josh wrote.

"Got it," Fleiss said, pocketing the note. "You ever think about getting a laptop? You'd have access and it would make writing notes a hell of a lot easier."

"Not for me," Josh wrote.

"Okay. Go easy on the nurses, willya?"

Josh rolled his eye. Josh was alone. He switched on the television, which was tuned to Headline News. Unemployment, food stamp recipients and those on disability were way up. ISIS fighters poured across the Mexican border like freelancers at an open bar. A sex tape surfaced of an A-list Hollywood celebrity cavorting with two underage teens and a mule.

Josh turned it off and dozed. When he woke, a short, gray, balding man with the demeanor of an undertaker, wearing a gray two-piece suit, sat on a folding chair with a briefcase by his side staring at his electronic notepad. The man stood.

"Mr. Pratt, I'm Roland Stoeckle from the National Security Agency. We're very sorry for your troubles. They told me you couldn't speak, so please just nod or shake your head at what I'm about to say. Do you understand?"

Josh nodded, wondering where this was going.

"It is crucial, for matters of national security, that the man you killed in the barn is known as Edward Martin. Do you understand?"

Josh shook his head and took up the pad. "Everybody knows," he wrote, "I fought Culligan brothers. Insane Assholes. What's the prob?"

"Yes, we're aware of Mr. Martin's connection to the Insane Assholes. Wayne Culligan does not exist. He ceased to exist the day he signed a loyalty oath to Central Intelligence, do you see?"

Josh saw. The Jesuit was a spook, a government killer, a potential source of embarrassment to the administration. Josh stared at Stoeckle with his one good eye.

"We are prepared to cover your medical expenses and those of the young lady, which currently exceed $100,000. I only ask that you also sign a loyalty oath. There is no Jesuit, there never was any Jesuit. Do you see?"

Josh nodded once. He wasn't surprised. From beat cop to state licensing board, his encounters with governmental authority had seldom gone well. The Jesuit was dead. So be it. Josh didn't give a shit. But there was something else.

"How do you trust me?" he wrote.

"We know all about you, Mr. Pratt. Frankly, your story

beggars belief, and I for one applaud you for making a sincere change in prison. I have talked to several people whom I respect who assure me that you are trustworthy. Incidentally, I too am a Christian and a Promise Keeper. Stay strong in Christ, my brother."

They clasped hands.

Stoeckle set his briefcase on the end of the bed, opened it and took out a form, which he clipped to a board and handed to Josh. Josh read it over.

I swear (or affirm) that I do not advise, advocate or teach, and have not within the period beginning five (5) years prior to the effective date hereof, advised, advocated or taught, the overthrow by force, violence or other unlawful means, of the Government of the United States of America or of the State of Wisconsin and that I am not now and have not, within said period, been or become a member of or affiliated with any group, society, association, organization or party which advises, advocates or teaches, or has, within said period, advised, advocated or taught, the overthrow by force, violence or other unlawful means of the Government of the United States of America, or of the State of Wisconsin. I further swear (or affirm) that I will not, while I am in the service of the United States of America, advise, disclose or admit to matters of national security pertaining to the events of June 22, 2016, at the Martin farm of rural Richland County, in the State of Wisconsin.

Josh underlined "while I am in the service" and followed it with a question mark.

Stoeckle essayed a tight little smile. He looked like a guy who rationed himself to one beer on the weekends.

"Needless to say, the consequences of violating this agreement will be quite severe, do you see?"

Josh nodded.

"In order to underwrite your medical expenses, we're putting you on the payroll as a security analyst. We are offering you a one-year contract, complete with all benefits, at a salary of $112,000. Are you amenable?"

Josh thought and thought. He drew the water cup to him and sucked greedily. He picked up the pad and wrote, "Yes, but I need a favor from you. Complete dossier on Judge Murray Fine of the Ninth Circuit Court of Appeals."

CHAPTER 63

PIZZA

ZIGGY SAT OPPOSITE ME IN THE BACK BOOTH AT Mr. P's Place. After the shoot-out Mr. P. called in some favors. He'd replaced the bullet-punctured pine paneling with gold paisleys on a red velvet background. Black velvet paintings of James Brown, Sam Cooke, Malcolm X and Frederick Douglas hung on the walls framed in gold, each with its own tiny spot. Mr. P. uncovered the natural walnut flooring and had it finished to a high sheen.

Now Ziggy, two months back from 'Nam, sat opposite me wearing an olive drab pea coat, dandelion hair and beard, lean and hungry as a panther. He handed me a rectangular package under the table, wrapped in brown paper and tied with twine.

"One key C4. Whatchoo gon' do with that shit? You a playa, you ain't Derek Flint."

I handed him a fat envelope under the table. "Don't pay no never mind. That my business. I will say this. You'll hear about it and when you do, you'll be glad."

Ziggy nodded. I'd known him since he was a snot-nosed runner for the Hamilton Mob in Crown Heights, all the way up to his draft notice. Ziggy went. Ziggy learned. Ziggy smoked dope every day and participated in combat stoned. He'd been assigned to the quartermaster and kept his contacts after his discharge. Now Ziggy was a righteous Black Panther down for the struggle.

"You okay?" *I said, sliding a glass and a bottle of Jack across the table.*

Ziggy slowly uncapped the Jack and poured a couple inches. He held it in his hand and stared at it. "Some days are better than others. Some nights I wake up screaming 'cause I been in battle, and I'm covered in blood and hungry and thirsty and stinking and hurting in every fuckin' fiber of my being and I AM SO SICK TO DEATH OF KILLING..."

The cords on his neck stood out like cables on the Brooklyn Bridge. His eyes bulged like a Jap demon mask. Even though it was only four o'clock in the afternoon there were at least a half dozen patrons and they all looked over. Burnoose, P's top bouncer, caught my eye and made a gesture. I shook my head.

Ziggy suddenly realized what was happening and shut himself down. He drank the four fingers of Jack and poured four more.

"The smack over there...it was so good, and so cheap."

"You ain't still doin' that shit?" *I said.*

"Nahhh," *he said wistfully and put the envelope inside his jacket.* "This money gonna buy a lot of ammo to kill pigs."

"Then you gonna be tickled pink when you read about what omma do."

Ziggy reached inside his jacket and pulled out a cheroot-sized doobie. "Okay to light up in here?"

"Sure. Ain't nobody complain."

He lit up, inhaled and handed me the joint. It was a one-hit wonder.

"Michoacán," Ziggy said with his lungs full, sounding like he was on helium. "Brought this batch up from Mexico myself. Ain't no thang. They wave me right through."

The paisleys on the wall floated free and whirled around my head. I filled my shot glass from the bottle of Jack and slugged it back. Breakfast of champions.

"I'll take a key of that shit," I said.

"No problem. I'll bring it by your crib tonight."

"Don't do that," I said. "Bring it here. I'll be rightchere."

Ziggy took the joint back. "How your fine lady makin' out? Man, that was some cold shit went down in Bucktown."

"Yolanda's tough," I said. "She'll survive." Wasn't the first time she'd been violated, no thanks to her worthless daddy. I ever catch him, I'll cut him like a steer." She wholeheartedly approved of what I was about to do. After Ziggy left I took my package down into the basement, a cold, damp cavernous place that dated back to the nineteenth century. Beneath a bare 60-watt bulb hanging from a frayed cord I set the package on a folding card table and cut it open. It was like a lump of dough, you could mold it.

Minutes later my man Tyrone came down the stairs looking like some Oreo square in a V-neck Perry Fuckin' Como sweater, Arrow shirt and striped tie, wearing horn-rim glasses. You *wouldn't believe he could kill you with one finger. He carried a Fraboni's pizza box he'd just brought back from Spartanburg. They had franchises all over the state and North Carolina too.*

"How was the trip, Cuz?" I said. "Any problems?"

Tyrone handed me the empty box. "No sir. Used that bus time to read Cicero and Tacitus."

"That's good, Cuz," I said. "You keep reading. Anyone gonna make it out of the ghetto, it's you."

I kneaded the C4 and made a pizza.

Josh placed a Band-Aid in the book and set it on the stand as Lud Newton entered. He looked gray. It was five days after Josh's surgery and he'd learned to speak in a kind of low muffled grunt without opening his jaws. It amused him to feign speech using only his tongue and larynx.

Newton placed a hand on Josh's shoulder. "I don't blame you for any of this. I just want you to know that," he said. "She surfaced for a minute. 'Where's Josh?' she said."

Josh started to get out of the bed but Newton gently pushed him back. "You can't do anything. She's in a coma. They took out her spleen. They're transferring her to University Hospital. They say her chances of survival..."

He hiccupped, turned away and coughed into his hand. He took out a handkerchief, wiped his hands, stuffed it into his hip pocket.

"Your quick action probably saved her life. Of course if not for you, this fucking animal never would have got his hands on her, so it's a wash."

She came to me appeared in Josh's private screening room but didn't make it to the mouth. Fig had nothing to do with the Insane Assholes. That was on him. He looked away.

"I understand you're having difficulty with medical expenses..." Newton said.

Josh held up his hand, shook his head until his jaw hurt. He grabbed the pad and wrote, "Taken care of!"

"Oh?" Newton said. "Well it's none of my business. What about the investigation? I appreciate your efforts and honesty and believe you would not prolong this if you didn't think it was going anywhere. Do you have any leads?"

Josh nodded emphatically.

"Want to tell me about them?"

Josh wrote, "I'm sorry, sir. You're not the client."

Newton nodded and swiped at an eye. "All right then. See you soon."

Josh held his hand up in a "stop" gesture.

"What?" Newton said.

"Dog and cat?" Josh wrote.

"Don't worry. I've got them."

C4 WITH A DETONATOR

JOSH WAS DISCHARGED ONE WEEK AFTER THE incident. It had stormed the previous day and Monday smelled fresh and clean. Fleiss picked him up and drove him home. Fig remained in a coma. Her father spent most of his days sitting by her bed listening to the machines hum and beep.

From behind the wheel of his Chrysler 300, Fleiss said, "You want, I'll send a flatbed out to that farm and pick up your bike."

"Get Fig's too," Josh said through his wired jaw. He was understandable now that he could move his lips.

Josh's lawn was going to seed as they pulled into the driveway.

"You want me to send someone to cut your lawn?" Fleiss said.

"Sure."

Josh went straight to his office to check his e-mails while Fleiss went through the kitchen. Fleiss came into the office.

"Okay, you got enough soups and shit to get you through the day. Make up a list and I'll have someone go get it."

"I can drive," Josh said through his mangled jaw. They'd taken the bandage off his left eye and to his relief, he could still see.

"Whatevs, man. I gots to rumble. Holler if you need me."

"Thanks, Steve," Josh said.

Fleiss left.

Not surprisingly, Judge Fine still had not responded to Josh's query. The rest of the e-mails were the usual collection of chitchat, political ads and come-ons from mysterious women who had seen his portrait on Facebook and "felt we would make a good match."

The Isthmus reporter Alan Schneider had sent three messages. "Urgent we speak."

Schneider had also left several messages on Josh's phone, as had Katy Verner of WMAD and three other broadcast journalists.

He checked his news feeds but there had been no progress on the last mysterious athlete's drowning, over three weeks ago. He stripped, went out on his deck with his book and gingerly lowered himself into his hot tub.

One week later we made that drive to Baxter, Tyrone and me. Tyrone wore a V-neck pull-over Argyle vest, glasses, and a bow tie. He looked like he was twelve. In the back seat lay the Fabroni's box. Floyd had loaned me a lime green Gremlin on top of which I'd fixed a generic "pizza" sign. Took us two days, stopping for the night in Richmond, where we stayed at the coloreds-only Lamplighter on the South Side.

We had breakfast at the Waffle Hut. Our waitress, a black beauty with hair out to here, looked out at the parking lot.

"That your Gremlin?" she said.

"Ahuh," I said.

"Looks like an Easter egg."

Fabroni's had a franchise in Greenville and that's where we picked up our pineapple, ham and bacon. It was only fifty-two miles to Baxter, short enough for the pizza to stay warm in its insulated bag. I'd cut my hair to the nub and wore a black watch cap pulled down to my ears and aviator shades. We cruised the cop shop slow around two, saw Billings's whip out front and that pig fucker Cummings through the plate glass window. How I'da loved to throw a brick through that window but that wasn't the way.

My way was better. I went around the block and parked in front of the Dykstra Funeral Home. I thought that was appropriate. I looked at young Tyrone. He was cool as the other side of the pillow, cool as Steve McQueen.

"You ready?" I said.

"Let's do it," he said, getting out of the car, opening the rear hatch and taking out the two boxes of pizza. The hot one was on

top. I'd rigged the bottom one with a detonator attached to the lid. Ham and pineapple was just what the pigs ordered.

Looking like a Catholic schoolboy working his way through college, Tyrone marched up the block holding the two pizza cartons on his head, whistling "People Get Ready."

I got back in the lime green Gremlin and followed him slowly to the corner, where I parked with a view of the cop shop across the street. Tyrone waited for the light to change next to an old honkey in a three-piece suit and hat carrying a briefcase—somebody's mouthpiece. Cars and trucks cruised Main Street as girls stared into shop windows. Marge's Women's Wear. Hobart Jewelry. Grodin Hardware. I kept the engine running. Found a station out of Columbia playing Sam Cooke. Watched Tyrone go through the cop shop doors.

My heart laced out a Pretty Purdie drum solo. I held my breath. I listened to Sam sing, "A Change Is Gonna Come." A few minutes later Tyrone reappeared, turned and waved to the pigs, crossed the street and strolled toward the car. You would have thought he'd just swallowed a canary. Got back in the car and stared straight ahead.

"Well?" I said.

"Tipped me five. Drive, Shred. Let's get the hell out of here."

I snapped to it, put the car in gear, pulled out onto Main and went in the opposite direction of the cop shop, heading out of town. We had gone two blocks when a massive crack split the air. I looked in the rearview at a column of smoke rising from the street as alarm bells rang and women screamed.

Josh went inside and dozed. The sound of a lawnmower through his open window roused him and he looked outside, where a lawn service had pulled up at the curb and a kid on a sit-down mower was working the yard. Josh's stomach rumbled but there was something he had to do first.

He got up, went into his office and online. He researched the bomb Global Resistance had detonated at the Pentagon in 1972. C4 with a detonator.

NEW CLIENT

A FLATBED TRUCK DELIVERED JOSH'S CHOP and Fig's Hawk Tuesday morning. The two bikes had been tightly bungeed to the frame and expertly backed down the ramp by a bike wrangler who looked like he belonged in the WWF. Josh tipped him a fifty. With his cracked ribs he wasn't sure how well he'd do on the seven-hundred-pound Road King.

Josh dropped four ibuprofen, put on goggles and threw a leg over the diminutive Hawk. He'd forgotten what it was like to ride a tiny, nimble machine. He enjoyed the run to University Hospital despite the constant throbbing in his ribs and his jaw. Leaving the bike on the east parking ramp, he crossed over to the main entrance and signed in. The pink mass of scar tissue on his jaw hardly drew a glance. Sunglasses hid his reconstructive eye surgery.

"I'm looking for Charlotte Newton," Josh said through his immobile jaw.

The receptionist consulted her computer. "I'm sorry, Miss Newton is in intensive care and cannot receive visitors."

Josh went up there anyway and found Lud Newton in the lounge area, unshaven and looking like he hadn't slept for days. Newton showed no surprise when Josh walked up to him.

"How is she?" Josh said.

Newton placed his head in his hands and sobbed silently. Josh didn't know what to do. For a minute he stewed in awkwardness, then sat next to Newton on the sofa and put his arm around the older man's shoulder. Newton sobbed until the sobs turned to dry heaves. A male orderly peeked in at them and left.

Finally Newton took out a well-used hankie and blew his nose, wiped his eyes. "I'm sorry. It's been rough. She's not responding. They're just waiting for me to give them permission to pull the plug."

A concrete slug settled in Josh's gut and cold fingers seized his heart. This couldn't be happening. Not again. He always killed the thing he loved. Somehow he held himself together.

A doctor appeared in a white coat holding a clipboard. "I'm sorry," he said, not looking them in the eye. That's when Josh lost it and it was Newton's turn to hold him.

Josh stayed with Newton while he signed various consent forms. The doctors let them both in to view the corpse. Fig looked like she was sleeping except she lacked that spark of vitality. Her absence was a black hole sucking in all joy. They left together and Josh offered to drive Newton home.

Newton was all but unrecognizable in his misery. To lose both children in such a short period, and in such unnatural ways. Neither spoke on the long ride back to Zebrawood. Josh pulled up under the porte cochere.

Josh cleared his throat and said like George Raft, "All I have is circumstantial evidence but I believe Stan's death, and those of many others, was caused by a directive from a professor here at the university."

"Who?"

"Jeff Wolfe."

Newton's grief transformed into slit-eyed hatred. "I knew it," he said to himself. "I always knew that self-involved phony wasn't content to rest on his past. I told the Alumni Foundation if they hired that piece of shit they'd never get another dime out of me. They hired him anyway. Fuck tradition. Fuck decency. Okay. What's the next step? Can I hire you to take out this guy?"

Josh got out of the car and followed Newton into the house. Newton went through the foyer to the big living/rec room overlooking the patio and filled two glasses with Glenmorangie. He gave one to Josh, who just stared at it.

"Oh," Newton said. "You need a straw." He rummaged in one of the bar drawers and handed Josh a soda straw, which Josh put in his drink, slipping the end between his lips.

"I ain't no killer," Josh said.

Newton tossed off his drink. "Fuck it. I'll do it myself."

Josh stared at him. "Don't be stupid. I'm not certain it was him. I still have some leads I need to track down. I think I've got enough to at least force the university to let him go."

Newton poured himself another drink and looked at Josh with fierce intensity. "What?"

"Sir, I'll know in a few days. And when I do I'll tell you. Just promise me you're not going to do anything stupid."

Newton took his second drink and waved Josh off. "No. No, I'm not a hothead. Never have been. But I'll tell you, if you can't figure out a way to take this guy down legally, I'll figure something else. I'm probably going to have a memorial service for family and friends this weekend. Maybe at the Unitarian Meeting House. She always loved that place."

Josh thought about how Fig and he were going to eat at the Frank Lloyd Wright restaurant in Spring Green. "Yes sir. Please let me know."

"What does Fig owe you for the investigation?"

Josh made a chopping motion. "Don't worry about it."

"Don't be silly. I don't expect you to work for free. How 'bout you're working for me now? I want to know everything there is to know about Wolfe."

"Give me a buck," Josh said.

Newton pulled out his ostrich-skin wallet and handed Josh a hundred. "That's for the first hour."

CHAPTER

66

FALLOUT

INSISTENT TAPPING WOKE JOSH WEDNESDAY morning. He threw on his jeans, padded through the silent house and peeked through the Venetian blinds. Katy Varner was there with her producer and cameraman, the WMAD News van parked at the curb. Katy saw the blinds move.

"I know you're in there, Mr. Pratt. It's Katy Varner of WMAD News! I'd just like to ask you a couple questions!"

Josh didn't know what to do. He wanted her to leave. He could feel the eyes of the neighborhood on him, hear their sighs of disgust. If he called the cops that would only make it worse. He opened the door a foot.

"Please go away, Miss Varner. I have no comment."

She actually stuck her sandaled foot in the door. Josh imagined the destruction he could wreak by slamming it.

"Mr. Pratt, two years ago your girlfriend died at the hands of Eugene Moon. Now your latest girlfriend has died as a result of injuries she received from Edward Martin. How do you feel about that?"

Josh didn't try to shut the door. He just turned his back and walked away. He went into his office, shut the door and went to the Wisconsin State Journal's web page.

VIOLENT TRAGEDY STALKS MADISON MAN by Alan Schneider, special to the State Journal.

Twice in two years violent felons have murdered Josh Pratt's girlfriends.

Two years ago, a felon named Eugene Moon killed his girlfriend Cass Rubio as well as prominent developer Nathan Munz and three hired security guards, at the Munz estate outside Janesville.

Last week another felon, named Edward Martin, killed Pratt's girlfriend Charlotte "Fig" Newton, the daughter of prominent developer Ludlow Newton. Both killings occurred during the course of Pratt's investigations.

Pratt makes no secret of his past as a member of the Bedouins Motorcycle Club, nor of his six-year stint in prison for assault, among other charges. Pratt credits Chaplain Frank Dorgan with turning him toward Christ, and was released without condition four years ago. Since then Pratt has worked as a private investigator.

Pratt was reminded of his violent past two weeks ago when four members of the Insane A**holes MC out of the Quad Cities were gunned down by Madison police as they threatened Pratt *in retaliation for a bar incident. Pratt had been working as a bouncer at Crazy Jack's in Dane County.*

Charlotte Newton was assaulted at a farm in Richland County when she and Pratt had arrived in connection with a case Pratt was working on. Martin, whose connection with the Insane A**holes remains unclear, followed them to extract revenge. There is some speculation Martin was related to one of the MC members gunned down on the far West Side. Earlier this week Ms. Newton succumbed to her injuries.

Pratt has not responded to our inquiries.

The fact that Schneider had written this story for the State Journal impressed Josh. He phoned Stoeckle and it went straight to voicemail.

"Where dat dossier, hoss?" he said and hung up.

The obituary appeared in Wednesday's edition.

Charlotte "Fig" Newton, 26, of Madison, passed away Tuesday at University Hospital from injuries. Born on June 3, 1990, to Ludlow C. Newton and Maureen Howe, Charlotte was the first of two children. Her younger brother, Stanley, died just one month ago, the victim of an apparent accidental drowning. Charlotte graduated with honors with a B.A. in business administration from the University of Wisconsin in 2011 and was working on her master's. An avid cyclist, motorcyclist and hiker, Charlotte was famous for her sunny disposition and kind heart.

A memorial service will be held this coming Friday at 1:00 p.m. at the Unitarian Meeting House in Madison. It should be noted that during the University Hospital expansion, Ludlow Newton, a noted developer, paid for the dismantling and reconstruction of the Frank Lloyd Wright house across the street at 912 University Bay Drive. The house now stands in Zebrawood in Dane County, a Newton Development.

Josh choked up. He leaned his elbows on the desk and wept into his hands. He heard a sound and turned. Katy Varner stood in the doorway to his office with her cameraman behind her. Josh surged from the chair knocking it down.

"GET OUT!" he yelled. Katy turned and collided with the camera. Josh hoped it gave her a black eye. She and the cameraman turned and hustled out of the house, sweeping the producer before them.

GARAGE

ON THURSDAY JOSH TOOK THE ROAD KING VIA the same winding route to the old Martin farm outside Richland Center. Yellow police tape stretched between the fence posts. Josh took it down and rode through. The ground was still damp from the rain as Josh rode between trees to the lonely farmhouse. He kicked his stand out on a rock and got off, removing his bolt cutters from the pillion. Police tape had scattered in the wind, bits and pieces of it clinging to the trees and the barbed wire.

A blue Chevy pick-up was also parked in the yard. "Miller Farms" was painted on the door in black block letters. The farmer was nowhere to be seen.

With the bolt cutters over his shoulder, Josh went into the barn, which smelled of damp, rot and horse manure. A bloody stain marked the spot where the Jesuit had died. Otherwise the barn remained as Josh had left it, with the fallen loft blocking access to the rear. The steamer trunk was still there, split down the middle. Josh knelt and pawed through its treasure. Mint copies of *Tear the Roof Off the Sucker, Take It to the Max* and *Stop Killing Me* sprawled in profusion. He gathered a half dozen copies of each and stuffed them in his saddlebags.

The trunk contained copies of Abbie Hoffman's *Steal This Book, The Autobiography of Malcolm X, The Population Bomb* and *Rules for Radicals.* There was also a photo album containing pictures of three small boys, about a year apart, from ages four to six. Pictures of the boys growing, posing in front of a suburban ranch house, in Little League uniforms, with their parents. As the photos got more recent, one of the boys began to distance himself with his posture and expression.

There was a group photo, identical to the one Josh had found in the Takeover office, of the Collective. And there were photos of a boy and a girl obviously head over heels in love with one another. The boy was Jeffrey Wolfe. The girl was Stacy Pembroke.

Josh got on his knees and reached way back into the depths of the trunk, past the folded sweatshirts. His hands closed on something flat and firm. He drew it out. It said "Diary" in gilt letters on black patent leather. Josh opened it up.

"I'm Stacy Pembroke and this is my diary."

He flipped through it.

Met the most wonderful guy! He is so smart and good-looking and even though he comes from money, his heart is in the right place. Jeffrey believes in revolution and the basic goodness of man, and that the only things holding us back are archaic institutions—capitalism, racism, sexual repression! We are going to a Grateful Dead concert next week!

Josh flipped ahead.

Since moving to the Collective Jeffrey has changed. He is no longer the fun-loving sensitive guy I met. When I mentioned commitment he accused me of clinging to my bourgeois values and said that perhaps I was not ready for a new world order. He made me so angry but in retrospect he may be right. When I suggested we go to counseling he laughed and walked out. He didn't return for three days.

Josh flipped ahead.

I'm pregnant! I can hardly believe it. I thought we were so careful but that one time, I was supposed to be safe, and we did it...I don't know how I'm going to tell Jeffrey. He is so commitment-phobic and he keeps harping on over population. He says it would be a crime to bring a child into the United States we know today.

Josh flipped ahead.

Jeffrey has been cold and distant all day. I think he knows.

That was the last entry.

Josh stuffed the diary and photo album in his saddlebags and walked behind the barn until he came to the garage. It remained sealed as it had been for decades. The vines covered the garage door so completely, Josh was unable to see its edges. He tore off voluminous vines to get to the padlock. His ribs screamed and his jaw ached.

It took him twenty minutes to nip through the case-hardened lock, stopping from time to time when the pain was too great, but at last it clanked to the ground. Gripping the corroded chrome handle, Josh twisted it vertical and lifted. Didn't budge. The hood had been frozen in place for forty years. He returned to the barn, took a spade off the wall and used that to lever the door up several inches. It took all his strength to pull it up, leaving his jaw and ribs throbbing. Once he cleared three feet he crawled inside and stood up.

Two dirt-covered windows along the left wall admitted faint light. He tried the switch on the wall, and to his amazement two bulbs mounted in bare sockets in the ceiling glowed on, revealing the shape of a tarp-covered car. Josh went around to the front and dragged the tarp off amid a fog of dust that got in his eyes, nose and mouth and left him coughing, jaw aching, grabbing his ribs every time he bent over. The tarp collapsed at his feet. At first he couldn't tell what he was looking at. An American car but that was about it. He used his hand to rub at the hood ornament, uncovering the familiar Cadillac logo surrounded by a chrome laurel wreath. He walked along the dark car's flank until he came to the trunk, which said FLEETWOOD ELDORADO in chrome script.

Josh pulled open the driver's door with a horrendous screech. The inside smelled of leather and dust, of sunny days and starry nights long gone cruising in a hallucinogenic cloud to the throb of Country Joe and the Fish. Josh slid behind the wheel and in the faint light saw an eight-track hanging from the dash. A plastic bin astraddle the center tunnel contained a half dozen tapes: Quicksilver Messenger Service, Jefferson Airplane, Jeff Buckley, The Doors, Big Brother & the Holding Company and the Dead's *Anthem of the Sun.*

He opened the glove compartment, found a faded envelope containing the car's registration. It was registered in '71 to Jeffrey Wolfe III. The professor's father, who had never, as far as Josh knew, reported it missing. He'd check on that.

The center console contained a hand-blown glass pipe and an ancient baggy of desiccated pot. Josh opened it and inhaled. There was no aroma. The keys were in the ignition. Josh turned them. Of course there was nothing.

Removing the keys, he got out, went to the rear and opened the trunk. A minute tendril of corruption tickled his nose, and he knew what he would find.

CHAPTER 68

THE HONORABLE

FOR OVER FORTY YEARS SHE'D LAIN WRAPPED in plastic in the Cadillac's trunk. Josh was aware he was disturbing a crime scene but the Pembrokes had a right to know. He slit the yellowed plastic with his pocketknife and looked at the desiccated corpse, blond hair still clinging to the ivory skull. A nylon cord was wrapped around her neck. Josh removed the gold amulet from around her neck, stuck it in his pocket and closed the trunk.

With a deep sense of weariness and sadness, he phoned Seth Pembroke. Voicemail. He left a message for Seth to call him. Josh called Calloway. Voicemail. With a heavy heart he got on his Road King and rode home. He felt his phone tingling in his pocket. When he got to his house, an institutional gray Malibu was sitting in the driveway. Josh pulled up next to it and kicked out the stand.

Roland Stoeckle got out of the sedan with his briefcase.

"How long have you been waiting?" Josh asked.

"I just got here."

Josh led the way into his house. It was unlocked. Ptarmigan was now one of the most patrolled streets in Madison. Josh went into the kitchen.

"Would you like coffee?" he said.

"Sure," Stoeckle said from the living room.

Josh put on coffee and returned to the living room. Stoeckle had opened his briefcase and set a fat manila envelope held shut with a tie on the coffee table. Josh sat on the sofa, picked it up, unwound the tie and withdrew a sheath of papers stamped "TOP SECRET" in red ink.

The first page said: "The Hon. Murray L. Fine, Associate Justice, United States Court of Appeals for the Ninth Circuit."

"I will stay here while you look at the document," Stoeckle said, "and then you will return it to me."

It began with Fine's birth date in 1948. Graduated U of W 1971 with a B.A. in political science and a law degree in 1974, obtained a master's at Harvard in 1977, admitted to the California Bar and joined the law firm of Beechum and Bingham in 1978, then became district attorney in San Francisco in 1982. Appointed to the Ninth Circuit by President Clinton in 1993.

As an undergrad he had belonged to Global Resistance, Students for a Democratic Society and Humans Off Planet, an "environmental activist group." He'd participated in the 1968 "Days of Rage" at the Democratic Convention in Chicago and had been active in party politics until his appointment to the Ninth. While attending the University of Wisconsin, he had been a member of the Collective along with notorious domestic terrorist turned academic Jeffrey Wolfe IV.

In 1998 Fine had taken a three-month course offered by the Department of Justice in conjunction with the FBI on cyber crime, covering darknet, hacking, phishing, smishing, vishing and the many permutations of this damp and fertile field of endeavor. On the bench he had sided with the majority 95 percent of the time, in favor of the snail darter, the delta smelt and the California skink.

Fine was married with two grown children, Alfred, a lawyer in D.C., and Meredith, director of the non-profit Americans for the Environment. "Judge Fine is among the most partisan jurists in the United States, a reliable vote for open borders, granting illegals driver's licenses and benefits, a carbon tax, implementing UN gun control guidelines, curtailing religious expression in public life, racial reparations, and against the 1st, 2nd and 4th Amendments."

Last year Judge Fine had reported taxable income as $546,000, including sale of stock, benefits from his blind trust with his old law firm Beechum and Bingham as trustee, and his salary. He gave $208 to charity, to Humans Off the Planet, and a donation to the Democratic Party.

Josh's phone vibrated in his pocket. It was Pembroke. Josh stood. "I'm sorry, I have to take this. I'll be right back."

Stoeckle was already poking at his tablet. "No problem."

Josh went out on the back deck. "Seth."

"What did you find?"

"Are you alone?" Josh said.

"Yes, I'm in my office."

Josh inhaled deeply and let it out. "I found your sister. She was in the trunk of an automobile that's been parked in a garage for over forty years."

Josh heard an inchoate grunt. He waited.

"How—"

"Seth, you don't need to hear this."

"Yes I do."

"She was strangled."

"Who did it?"

Josh's jaw and ribs throbbed. He sat down on a lawn chair. "I don't know for sure, but I think it was Wolfe."

"I knew it," Pembroke hissed. "All these years...I knew it!"

"I have to tell the police, Seth."

"I know. I'll be down there tomorrow. I'll call you."

When Josh hung up he saw that he'd had another call. Calloway. He called him back and told him what he'd found.

"Jay-ZEUS!" Calloway said. "Why don't you stay home? Just stay home! I'll notify Richland County. They're going to want to talk to you."

"Tell them I'll meet them at McKenna Boulevard." Josh did not want the cops coming to his house any more than they already had. He returned to the living room, where Stoeckle was casually reading his tablet. Josh sat and picked up the report.

"In 2001 Fine went on a fact-finding mission to Thailand,'" Josh read aloud, "where he engaged in sex with three underage boys."

"How is this guy still a federal judge?" Josh said with a note of exasperation.

Stoeckle looked up. "All that stuff in red ink falls under the Secrets Act. Why is he still a judge? Take a look at the current administration. They want him there."

"What if he were guilty of first-degree murder?"

"That would be something else. Do you have something to tell me?"

"No. Just thinking out loud."

"Are you done with that file? I really should be going."

Josh returned the file to Stoeckle, watched him go and rode to the West Side police station on McKenna Boulevard.

CHAPTER

69

SUSPICION

LEAVING HIS BIKE IN THE VISITORS' PARKING lot, Josh entered the chilled interior of the police station, stepped up to the counter and told the receptionist on duty, "I'm Josh Pratt. I just reported a body in Richland County."

"Oh you wait right here," the young lady told him. "They want to talk to you."

Shortly a squat, red-haired cop and a cop in plain clothes with his badge on his belt came out from behind the counter.

"Pratt, I'm Abe Nagel and this is Detective Sobol. Let's go."

They left through a side entrance. Nagel pushed a button and a Chrysler beeped and flashed. The two cops got in the front seat; Josh got in the back. It was 3:00 p.m.

It was four thirty by the time they turned to Miller farm, bypassing the house and the barn to go all the way back to the garage. There were four other vehicles in the yard: the Richland County Coroner's van, two county cars and a plain-Jane cruiser with Madison plates. Josh saw the tall figure of Calloway looming at the garage's entrance.

The three men exited the vehicle.

"Did you cut the bag?" Calloway said.

"Yeah."

"You know you're not supposed to fuck with a crime scene."

"It wasn't like I tampered with evidence. I just wanted to know who she is."

"Well do you?" Calloway said.

"Stacy Pembroke. She disappeared in 1972. She was Professor Wolfe's girlfriend."

Calloway shot him a look and headed for the sheriff, who gazed down into the open trunk as techs took photos. Josh watched them confer and then they both rounded on him.

The sheriff looked like a Mountie with his broad-brimmed hat and brush mustache. "Sheriff Ray Koenig," he said, sticking out a bear paw. "Let's sit in my office."

They sat in Koenig's cruiser beneath the shade of an elm tree, the rear door open with Josh's feet on the ground. The sheriff placed a small recording device on the front seat divider and turned it on. "Tell me how you found the body."

Josh told him how Fig had hired him, how it had led to Wolfe and his suspicions, but leaving out Judge Fine.

When he finished Sheriff Koenig said, "All right, the news organizations don't know about this yet and let's keep it that way. What about this Wolfe guy, Heinz? Sounds like he's got clout."

"That will dissipate in a New York minute if it turns out he murdered his girlfriend."

"I don't see a motive here," Koenig said, looking at Josh.

"She was pregnant," Josh said.

"How do you know?" Calloway said.

"It was in her diary," Josh said.

"Where's her diary?" Koenig said.

Josh cringed. "My place. I got it out of that busted steamer trunk. You guys had three weeks to search that barn and you missed it."

Koenig glared at him. "How is pregnancy a motive?" he said.

"Read the diary. She said he'd be furious. Wolfe has spoken often about sustainability and population control and loudly declared his intention to never sire a child. His wife feels the same way. Perhaps as a young man he wasn't ready to accept that responsibility."

"Huh," Koenig said.

"Are you questioning him?" Josh said.

"Are you willing to share with us what you've learned about him?" Calloway said.

"Sure." It was all public knowledge anyway. "So how long before you talk to Wolfe?"

Koenig looked at Calloway. "We'll probably turn this over to the Wisconsin Division of Criminal Investigation. Considering the politics they're least likely to fuck things up. I'll call them now."

Calloway excused himself.

"You suspect Wolfe in these college drownings?" Koenig said.

Josh shrugged. "I don't know. This guy's beaten the rap, he's at the top of his field, wined, dined, feted and honored. Why would he risk everything for some juvenile vendetta against, what? White privilege?"

Koenig shrugged. "You never can tell what people will do. I once knew a bank manager tried to smuggle a couple keys of coke into the country from Mexico."

They sat in silence.

"Very sorry to hear about your girlfriend," Koenig said. He stood. "Well, back to work."

CHAPTER 70

CONDOLENCES

CALLOWAY GAVE JOSH A RIDE BACK TO THE Mckenna station, where Josh retrieved his bike and headed for Dovetail in Middleton. He waited in the lobby for Kofsky to finish his meeting. As before, the cute young receptionist offered him video games and a Red Bull.

"We also have nine different types of water," she said.

Josh asked for a bottle of Finnish Glacier Melt and sat in the lobby reading an article in Wired about Harley's new electric motorcycle. It had 74 horsepower and 52 foot-pounds of torque. It weighed 570 pounds, had a top speed of 95 and a range of 80 miles. It was artfully styled. Josh found the whole thing repugnant, and set it aside as Kofsky emerged from the back wearing shorts and a blue Dovetail T-shirt.

"Let's go outside," Kofsky said, leading Josh to a side door that opened onto a patio with a picnic table. Kofsky sat on the tabletop. Josh gazed at the trees.

"What?"

"Judge Murray Fine sits on the Ninth Circuit Court of Appeals in San Francisco. He is allegedly involved in child rape in Thailand. I want film, if any, and I want you to see if he's using darknet to tell gangs to kill Whitey. And I want to see his college records."

"A federal judge? Are you nuts?"

Josh stared at him until Kofsky felt the weight, then said, "I'm not forgetting what's on that flash drive. The first step to committing a crime is to imagine it. I'm taking your word for the fact that you haven't taken that next step."

"Jesus! How long am I gonna have you hanging around my neck?"

"As long as I need you."

Kofsky sighed. "I'll phone you."

"Don't say anything over the phone. Just tell me to come over. Have you called Sandy since you got back?"

"What business is that of yours?" Kofsky said.

"She seems like a nice lady."

"She is a nice lady. I'm just...I don't know. Commitment-phobic I guess."

"Is it the sex thing?" Josh said. "You only get hard for children?"

Kofsky turned red. "I'm dealing with it."

"Sometimes you need help. Is there a priest or a rabbi you could talk to?"

Kofsky made a rictus. "Are you for real? You barge into my life threatening to splash my dirty little secrets all over and now you're Miss Lonely Hearts? Sorry to hear about your girlfriend, by the way."

"Yeah thanks," Josh said. He was already walking away.

LECTURE

THE KATHY L. FROMME LECTURE HALL IN THE Humanities Building was packed for Wolfe's lecture on "Corporations, the Kloch Brothers, and Dark Money in Politics." Wolfe looked out from the wings at the 350 eager young students who filled every seat and stood in the aisles and against the back wall, three deep. Since his appearance on *The View*, interest in his classes had soared and they were now providing closed-circuit television coverage in adjoining classrooms.

Wolfe primped in the mirror set backstage, smoothing his silver hair, making sure the arrow-point collars of his blue work shirt were outside his tweed jacket. He wore a hand-tooled leather, silver and turquoise belt given him by the Cherokee Nation in appreciation of his work on behalf of indigenous peoples. He wore hand-tooled cowboy boots from Jackson Hole. He wore Levi's blue jeans. He oozed Paco Rabanne.

He was supposed to start ten minutes ago; as with most of Wolfe's lectures, he had dragged ass, stopping to chat with colleagues, students and janitors, in the unspoken belief that he should always keep the audience waiting. It built anticipation. It reminded him of the time he'd gone to see Sly and the Family Stone at the Dane County Coliseum in 1970. Sly was two and a half hours late and rushed through a perfunctory forty-five-minute set. Most of the attendees were pissed off, but Wolfe had admired Sly's revolutionary spirit and refusal to cater to pop-culture, bourgeois instant gratification.

He walked to the podium, and immediately everyone in the room clapped. Some called out.

"You the man!"

"Wolfe! Wolfe! Wolfe"

Wolf howls.

Incoherent shrieking.

Wolfe smiled and held up his hands in a placating gesture, scanning the front row for nubile coeds. He and his wife had an open marriage, and it was no secret that Nedra was seeing the visiting Roberta G. Marshall-Stein Artist in Residence, New York sculptor Helena Root-Weedin. No biggie. Wolfe had never had much interest in Nedra sexually. Theirs was a political marriage bred of ambition and a seething malice toward the "fat cats"—the bankers, lobbyists, corporations, Republicans, independents, any and all who resisted their image of a perfect communist society. From each according to their abilities, to each according to their needs. By any means necessary. The end justifies the means.

He singled out a stacked little redhead who twisted this way and that displaying her assets. He caught her eye and winked at her. She did a mock shock with her hand and grinned lasciviously. Yes, she would do nicely.

"Hello and welcome to my speech about the Kloch suckers! I mean the Kloch brothers!"

The class hooted and howled, even those in the LGBT community.

"Who are the Kloch brothers? They are two billionaires who use their vast wealth to rewrite the rules of government to suit their ends. But the Kloch brothers are a mere synecdoche of a greater problem, the corrupting power of money—in particular, the ability of certain millionaires and large corporations to put their massive asses on the scale of democracy in ways that subvert the will of the people.

"The Supreme Court should never have ruled as it did in Citizens United, which would have brought the scales of political influence back into balance, in which 'We, the People,' not the one percent, determine the direction of the country.

"Charles and David Kloch, billionaire brothers, are the geniuses behind Americans for Prosperity. They claim to be for the little guy. But what the group really does is support extreme right-wing candidates who actively fight against the economic interests of workers and their families. The Kloch brothers have spent $45 million to buy control of Congress. That's the amount of money Americans for Prosperity spent in the 2010 elections. They helped Republicans control the

House with the most extreme group of conservatives elected in modern history. Every time I watch *Vikings* I think I'm looking at the Republican Congress!

"With this group firmly in control, every effort by the current administration to move legislation to revive the economy has been thwarted, and previous successes in health care and financial reform have come under unrelenting attack. The Kloch brothers are totally behind the stream of anti-regulation, anti-labor legislation passed by the Tea Party-drunk House. The Kloch brothers snap and the Republicans jump.

"Scott Walker won the governorship of Wisconsin and the ability to execute his attack on public workers there with $43,000 in direct contributions from the Kloch Industries political action committee and indirectly through the $1 million that the Kloch's PAC gave to the Republican Governors Association."

He spoke non-stop without notes for forty-five minutes. Hands shot up. Finally he finished. Standing O. A nerd in the third row waved his arms wildly. Wolfe pointed at him.

The nerd said, "Professor, how come you haven't mentioned the fact that Democratic fundraising outstrips that of the Republicans by at least 30 percent? Why isn't that dirty money?"

Other students booed and shouted at the nerd to shut up and sit down. Wolfe smiled. "Where'd you get that information, son? Fox News?"

Laughter, hooting.

"I think studies will show that most of that Democratic fundraising is done at the local level. Democrat contributions are like five dollars here, ten dollars there, whereas when the Kloch brothers give, we're talking six or seven figures."

"Where'd you get that information?" the nerd said. "MSNBC?"

Wolfe smiled. "If you see me after class I will show you the source of that information."

And learn your name.

Wolfe always entertained a few skeptics to illustrate his even-handedness. The cute redhead mimed writing her phone number in her palm, and Wolfe gave her a minute nod.

The bell rang; the class ended but most of the students remained, crowding the area in front of the stage to ask questions or just to make contact with the great man. Wolfe went to the edge of the stage and sat with his legs dangling. The redhead approached with her brunette wing woman.

"Hi," she said in that provocative way. "I really like your class."

"Thank you. What's your name?" Wolfe said, extending his hand and hiding her folded telephone number in his palm.

"Melanie," the redhead said.

Her friend looked over Melanie's shoulder to the edge of the stage with consternation. Wolfe followed her gaze. Two men, one tall, black, with a wandering eye, and one white and built like a fireplug, approached, both wearing off-the-rack suits and plain ties. They showed Wolfe their badges.

"Professor Wolfe? I'm Detective Calloway and this is Detective Berryman from the state Division of Criminal Investigation. Would you come with us please?"

CHAPTER

72

NEWSFLASH

KATY VARNER STOOD IN FRONT OF JEFFREY Wolfe's cubist dwelling in University Heights, just down the street from Frank Lloyd Wright's Airplane House and spoke to the camera. Make-up concealed the shiner she'd sustained running into her own camera.

"WMAD News has uncovered startling new developments in the case of UW drowning victim Stanley Newton, whose body was found by a jogger in Lake Mendota on the morning of June 5. Police are now questioning Professor Wolfe in relation to a body discovered at a farm in rural Richland County. The body was found by private investigator Joshua Pratt in the course of his investigation into Newton's death.

"Pratt's house was the scene of a wild gunfight on June 23 when police gunned down four members of the Quad Cities-based motorcycle gang the Insane—well, we can't say the next word but you all know it. Pratt had been dating Stan Newton's sister, Charlotte, who succumbed last week to injuries sustained in a savage attack at the rural Richland County location, where Pratt and Newton had gone pursuant to his investigation. Pratt killed their assailant, Edward Martin, in what the police say was a clear-cut case of self-defense. Stan Newton was Professor Wolfe's student in Wolfe's popular Politics in Multi-Cultural Societies class.

"Professor Wolfe has retained noted criminal defense attorney Jack McGinnis to represent him. Wolfe has declined comment."

She tapped her earpiece and looked away for a minute, then back to the camera. "Okay, we've just learned from the coroner's office that Stacy Pembroke, whose mummified body was found in rural Richland County, was pregnant. We will keep you posted on this bizarre case as it develops. This is Katy Varner for WMAD News."

Josh turned it off. He wondered how she'd learned that he'd been working for Fig. Probably Schneider. Newspeople were incestuous. Maybe Lud Newton had told her.

Josh wore his only suit, a gray two-piece he'd purchased for Danny Bloom's funeral. He only wore it at funerals. He wore a white dress shirt buttoned to the neck but no tie. He went out through the garage gazing forlornly at Fig's red Hawk GT, which rested on its center stand next to the basket case Harley.

He got on his Road King and rode toward the center of the city, peeling north off University Boulevard toward the Unitarian Meeting House, whose peaked roof resembled the prow of a ship. The parking lot was nearly full. Josh found a place near the rear door and entered, hearing Joni Mitchell's "Both Sides Now" over the PA system. Fig wasn't even born when that came out.

Josh found a seat near the back next to Avery Waldrop, who had been both Stan's and Fig's student advisor. Waldrop said sotto voce, "Sorry to see you under these circumstances. If there's anything I can do for you please tell me."

"Thanks," Josh said out of the side of his mouth. His jaw was still wired. It was fortunate that Waldrop sat to his right.

"What's Wolfe got to do with this?" Waldrop said.

"Don't know yet," Josh side-mouthed.

A young preacher with wavy hair wearing a black jacket over a gray turtleneck took the podium. "To know Fig Newton was to love her," he said. Josh tuned out, overwhelmed with a sense of grief and loss. He felt Waldrop's hand on his arm and realized he'd been crying. The preacher spoke for ten minutes and invited members of the congregation to share their memories. Josh couldn't take it. He got up and left. Waldrop followed him out.

"You okay?" he said, handing Josh a tissue.

Josh honked. "Yeah, I'll be okay. I just need time."

Seth Pembroke joined them. "Sorry I didn't get in touch sooner," he said. "I was delayed. Can we talk?"

Shamefaced because of the tears, Josh nevertheless looked Pembrokein the eye. "Come to my place. You have the address. I'll meet you there."

Newton joined them. "What's up?"

Josh introduced Newton and Pembroke. "Lud, why don't you join us?"

Josh looked up. The WMAD news van was there, Katy Varner standing with her arms crossed, the cameraman conspicuously holding his instrument at port arms to indicate he wasn't filming. Josh got on his hog and booked it.

CHAPTER 73

SURVIVORS

PEMBROKE ARRIVED FIVE MINUTES AFTER JOSH, parking his Lexus behind Josh's bike. Newton parked on the street. Josh held the door for them.

"Would you like some coffee?" he said.

"Screw the coffee," Newton said. "Got any Scotch?"

"Me too," Pembroke said.

Josh went into the kitchen, snagged a bottle of Jack and three glasses.

"This is what I got," he said.

They sat in the living room while Josh laid the whole case out for them from the night he met Fig.

"Are you saying this Judge Fine is involved?" Pembroke asked, incredulous.

"I don't know. I think so. He and Wolfe were pals back in the day. The question is, are these guys so crazy that they're willing to incite murder in the name of some bizarre concept of social justice? I think they are. Wolfe already tried bombing the Pentagon, and his bomb-making plans got at least two members of Global Resistance killed. 'Guilty as sin, free as a bird, God bless America.' That's what he said after getting off on account of the FBI's illegal tactics in investigating his crimes."

"This Fine character has been behind some of the worst decisions ever handed down," Newton said. "I have friends who had agribusiness in California and they say decisions by the Ninth killed them. They can't get water to irrigate because of some goddamn snail or something."

"Mr. Pratt," Pembroke said, "with all due respect I just can't see it. No federal judge is going to risk his reputation—his life!—on some harebrained scheme to kill college kids."

"Please call me Josh. It's not a harebrained scheme if it works, right? Wolfe's college rants are inflammatory. Fine's are sealed. What's the deal with that? I got a guy working on finding things like his master's thesis and whether the guy diddled kids in Thailand."

"Huh?" Pembroke said.

"Fine has already recognized pederasty as a legitimate form of sexual expression in Krilon v. Lemberg, which found that Krilon Software illegally terminated John Lemberg because he belonged to NAMBLA. Fine also upheld California's same-sex marriage law."

"Being for same-sex marriage isn't the same as supporting pederasty!" Pembroke said.

"I'm just sayin'," Josh said weakly. "Let's be realistic. These are two powerful, well-connected men. It may very well be that we will never bring them to justice."

"Oh yes we will," Newton said. "One way or another."

Josh kept his mouth shut. But he thought the same thing.

"That little motorcycle of Fig's, take it," Newton said. "I'll find the title and get it signed over."

Josh held up his hands. "That's not necessary..."

"What am I going to do with it?" Newton said.

"How are Mr. Schermerhorn and Squishburton?" Josh said.

"They're a comfort."

Josh was disappointed. He'd hoped to adopt those animals himself.

Pembroke stared at his hands. "How did it happen that men in high positions—educators and jurists—how is it we are even considering these outrageous acts?"

"You know, Seth," Newton said, "I've been asking myself that same question for the last thirty years. I feel that we're headed into a new Dark Ages. There are a lot of reasons. The breakdown of families. Government overreach. Thug culture. None of this is surprising. Plato predicted it. Cicero predicted it."

"The shit you see on regular television these days," Pembroke said. "When I was growing up it was unthinkable. Everybody drops the F-bomb. You can't tune in without seeing two queers sucking face."

"We sound like a couple of old farts bitching about kids these days," Newton said.

"We are," Pembroke agreed.

Josh bit his tongue. Prison had instilled in him a different understanding but he respected what these men had to say. His phone rang. It was Kofsky.

Josh stood. "Guys, I have to take this."

He went out the back door to the patio. "Pratt."

"Yeah, I found something. It's not something I can discuss over the phone. You want to meet me at the Laurel Tavern at six?"

"I'll be there."

Josh returned to his living room and sat. "Lud, what was Fig making? What was her product?"

"Center stands for Ducatis," Newton said.

THE LAUREL

THE LAUREL WAS A MONROE STREET INSTITUTION, the neighborhood bar and grill. Josh parked in back and went in the back door. Kofsky was waiting for him at the bar. They took a booth and ordered a burger, chicken soup, and beers.

"What if I got hold of Wolfe's hard drive?" Josh said.

"That'd work. How you gonna do that?"

Josh shrugged. He was no stranger to burglary, or robbery. He'd studied Wolfe's house from the street, noted the ADT warning signs. This from a man who claimed private property was the root of all evil. Before his incarceration Josh would have thought nothing of breaking into Wolfe's home. But after all he'd been through he'd changed, and now he had too much to lose. "Just thinking out loud. Where we at with the right honorable?"

"I broke into the Blackphone database," Kofsky said as soon as the waitress had gone.

"What's that?" Josh said.

"Blackphone is a company that makes a secure phone. It can't be tracked, it can't be eavesdropped and it leaves no record. Except we did it. That's what I couldn't tell you over the phone. As far as I know they've got some other company snooping on us and me telling you this violates the Patriot Act. Judge Fine is a subscriber."

"Yeah, so?" Josh said. "Spell it out for me."

"It means he can upload whatever he wants to the Internet—including darknet—and it can't be traced or snooped."

"Not even if we got hold of his phone?" Josh said.

Kofsky grinned. The waitress delivered their beers. Josh drank his through a straw. Kofsky downed half the glass. "Ah. That's another story. But how are we going to get hold of his phone?"

"Suppose I did," Josh said. "Could you take it apart and find out what he sent?"

"I think so."

"What about Thailand?" Josh said.

Kofsky looked around furtively, like a drug dealer. He leaned forward and spoke softly. "I'm in touch with a Thai guy who runs a whorehouse that runs boys. He says he has what I want but he wants five thousand for it."

"Can you verify that?" Josh said.

"The guy sent four seconds over my blackphone. Pretty sure it's what you want. He says it's got to be a money transfer deal to some bank in Dubai."

"Okay, let me get back to you on that."

The waitress delivered their dinners. A burger for Kofsky, chicken soup for Josh.

"I see your friend Wolfe's in the news," Kofsky said. "Do you think he really killed his girlfriend forty years ago?"

Josh shrugged. "We'll see."

OLD PALS

JEFFREY WOLFE STOOD AT THE BASE OF THE stairs at Dane County airport wearing wraparound shades, watching passengers arrive from San Francisco. He did not have long to wait. Judge Fine traveled first class and was among the first to disembark. Wolfe raised his arm when Fine appeared at the top of the stairs.

"Murray!" Wolfe boomed, embracing the taller man in a bear hug. They walked toward baggage claim amid a flurry of travelers.

"Congrats on the award," Wolfe said as they stood by the conveyor belt amid kids retrieving backpacks, young families grabbing strollers and businessmen snatching suitcases.

"It's a great honor," Fine said. "But you and I have a lot to talk about. What do the cops want?"

McGinnis had advised Wolfe not to discuss the case with anyone, but Fine was one of Wolfe's oldest friends and he was involved. "They found Stacy Pembroke's body. They think I killed her."

"Did you?"

"No. I have no idea how she ended up in that trunk."

"I was in San Francisco when that happened," Fine said. "Stacy was alive when I left."

Wolfe felt the weight of his own history crushing him. He had an overpowering urge to confess but his self-preservation was stronger. He hadn't come this far to throw it all away on something that happened forty years ago. Fine's bag shuttled forward. Fine grabbed it and they exited through the front doors across the street to the parking garage.

"Hope you can fit this in that tin can," Fine said when he saw the Boxster.

The bag barely fit in the little car's cramped trunk. As they drove through Madison, Fine expressed amazement at all the changes.

"Looks like an entirely different city. I can't believe the 602 and Headliners are gone."

"Progress," said Wolfe. "I'm on the City Planning Committee and I'm very proud of the way we've been able to reclaim so much of downtown for the public."

"How are the property taxes?" Fine said.

"They go up every year but that's part of the price you pay for civilization."

"Ain't that the truth."

Wolfe parked in his driveway and they got out. Fine looked at the house. "This wasn't here when we were undergrads."

"I had it built," Wolfe said. "I bought the old Tudor and tore it down. Come on in. Nedra's not here right now but she'll be back for dinner."

Fine retrieved his bag from the car. "How is Nedra?"

"Same as always," Wolfe said. "Busier than a tick on a dog. She's hosting her annual White Privilege seminar."

"Oh yes," Fine said. "I might drop in on that."

"She would love that."

Inside, Wolfe showed Fine to the guestroom on the second floor, with a wall of solid glass looking out on the tiny backyard garden. It was 4:00 p.m. They relocated to Wolfe's home office on the first floor, one glass wall and two walls covered with certificates, photos, degrees and honorariums. Wolfe with the President. Wolfe with the Secretary of State. Wolfe with the university President. Wolfe with Oprah. Awards from the Southern Poverty Law Center, Operation Push, the Rainbow Coalition and The Nation.

Wolfe opened a bottle of Macallan and set out two cut-glass snifters. "Smart coming in a day early," he said, pouring. "Otherwise we'd have news crews up the ass."

Fine and Wolfe clinked and sipped. "Have they been bothering you?" Fine said.

"Yeah, particularly this one bitch Katy Varner. I don't get it. I've helped her out on numerous occasions when they needed some kind of comment, and the first chance she gets she stabs me in the back."

"What do you mean?" Fine said.

Wolfe sank into his leather chair in exasperation. "These charges that I murdered Stacy are entirely spurious and no doubt generated by my many enemies, including but not limited to the Republicans, Posse Comitatus, Breitbart and the National Review."

Fine sipped. "Listen. I have some rather disturbing news."

Wolfe physically blanched, like a cur expecting to be struck. "What?"

"Several weeks ago I received a query from a private investigator named Josh Pratt wanting to know if I knew anything about these so-called Smiley Face Killings. Here. Take a look."

Fine reached inside his lightweight gray cotton jacket and removed a folded piece of foolscap and handed it to Wolfe. Wolfe opened it up.

Dear Judge Fine: I am a private investigator looking into the cause of death of Stan Newton, a UW athlete who was found drowned several weeks ago. Did you know there is a Murray Fine character in the Shred Husl books by Curtis Mack? Did you know Curtis Mack? Do you know Jeffrey Wolfe IV? Did Wolfe write the Shred Husl books under an assumed name?

"Shit!" Wolfe said, crumpling the paper into a ball and tossing it at his wastebasket. He missed.

"Now Pratt was hired to look into a student's death, right? And that student is the one you complained to me about, right? The one who always gave you shit in class?"

Wolfe seemed to shrink a little into his chair. "That's the guy."

Fine held up his glass and examined the hue. "Why not come clean about the whole Curtis Mack thing?" Fine said. "I don't see where it could do you any harm. Those books have become much sought-after cult classics."

"Y'know what'll happen if I do that?" Wolfe said. "They'll say that as a white man, I had no right to adopt that point of view. Fuck. I've said it myself a thousand times. It will expose me as being a big fat hypocrite."

"Hypocrisy is the price that vice pays to virtue," Fine said.

"Not gonna happen," Wolfe said. "None of this would have happened if that cunt hadn't hired that fucking thug to look into her brother's death. I had nothing to do with it! Fuck."

"Well let me see what I can do," Fine said. "I still have some suck around here. I'm sure we can get his investigator's license pulled at the very least."

"How?"

"There are a million ways. He could be stopped and they could find dope on him. We could easily justify a warrant to search his place. I understand he withheld evidence from the police for several days."

"What evidence?" Wolfe said.

"Stacy's diary."

Wolfe turned white. "She had a diary?"

Fine sipped his Scotch. "Didn't you know? They found it in a steamer trunk with several dozen of your novels."

"Don't say they're mine!" Wolfe snapped. "I didn't write them!"

"Jesus, Jeff. You don't really think you can keep the lid on that, do you?"

They heard the garage door open and a moment later the door to the kitchen. Minutes later Nedra found them. She was a plump doyenne with a gray Prince Val wearing a pale blue pantsuit.

"Murray!" she exclaimed, arms wide.

TOURIST

NEWTON HAD A CASHIER'S CHECK FOR FIVE grand messengered to Kofsky at Dovetail.

Josh met Kofsky at the Laurel, on a warm Thursday evening in July. They'd unwired his jaw the day before. Josh and Kofsky sat outside at the newly added terrace, which staked a claim to formerly public ground on the sidewalk.

"Sandy says hi," Kofsky said.

"So you two are back together?"

"Well..." Kofsky waggled his fingers. "I listened to what you said and thought about it. I know I'm fucked up. It's like any other addiction—like alcohol or cocaine. I want to change and I believe I have the power to change. So we're seeing a therapist."

"That's good," Josh said. "Is that good?"

Kofsky hesitantly nodded. "I think so. We actually had sex last night and I enjoyed it."

"Well there you go. Does she know about your kink?"

"Of course not."

"Keep on that path, brother."

"I transferred the funds," Kofsky said, "and he sent me the video. Are you ready to see this?"

Josh made a "gimme" motion and Kofsky handed him his tablet. The film was in grainy color shot from a ceiling cam and showed a naked Thai boy, who could have been anywhere from six to fifteen, sitting on the edge of a seedy bed in a seedy hotel room. The kid looked like Mickey from *The Little Rascals.*

A man entered the room wearing a green-and-red Hawaiian shirt, baggy shorts and sandals with socks. He sat on the bed turning partially to face the camera. It could have been Fine or any balding, middle-aged, pot-bellied sex tourist.

"Can you clean that up?" Josh said.

"Yeah, I will. I raced over here because I knew you wanted to see this."

The man put his hand on the kid's knee. Josh felt queasy. He'd seen the cons prey on stupid young men who ended up in the criminal justice system because of drugs or other petty crimes. How quickly they turned a sneer into a whimper. The man stood and unbuttoned his shirt. In that moment, for an instant, Josh saw that it was indeed the distinguished jurist. Fine removed everything but his socks and sandals, oddly enough, and when he sat, he took the boy's hand and placed it on his penis.

Josh closed the tablet and handed it back. "Can you send me this?"

"It's in your in-box," Kofsky said.

A couple walking by paused as the man did a double take. Tim wore his colors. "Chainsaw!"

Josh stood. "Hi, Tim. Tim, this is Aaron. Aaron, my man Tim."

Kofsky stood and stuck out his hand. "Hi. Who's your friend?"

"Rhonda," the woman said.

"Duuuude!" Tim said. "Glad to see you up and around! For a while there we didn't think you were gonna make it. In fact Bad Bob started taking odds. You cost me two hundred dollars."

"You bet I was gonna die?" Josh said.

"You didn't look too good! You try that reefer we brought?" Tim said.

"Someone did," Josh said.

"Shit. Somebody kuiped it?"

"'Fraid so," Josh said.

"Come on, Tim," Rhonda said, pulling on his arm. "We'll be late!"

"What's up?" Josh said.

"We're going to hear a Peruvian folk singer," Tim said, making a gagging motion with his finger.

"Come on!" Rhonda dragged him away. "It's a recital, not a mosh pit!"

"Later!" Josh shouted. He really should get together with the gang now that his no-contact order had been abrogated by the court.

"Okay listen," Josh said. "The university's hosting a party tomorrow night at Monona Terrace to give Judge Fine some kind of award."

"The Edward Ben Elson Distinguished Service Award," Kofsky said. "I did my homework."

"It's invitation only. I need you to get me on the guest list."

Kofsky snapped his fingers. "Is that all?"

"Me and one other."

"Who dat be?" Kofsky said.

"Carl Billings."

PROGRAM

THE UNIVERSITY OF WISCONSIN SCHOOL OF LAW
is proud to present an evening with the recipient of this
year's Edward Ben Elson Distinguished Jurist Award, the
Honorable Murray K. Fine of the U.S. Court of Appeals
for the Ninth Circuit.
This event will take place in the August Derleth Room
at 7:00 p.m. on July 9.

7:00 p.m.: Welcome by Dean Ambrose Watkins of the
UW School of Law. Introduction by the Honorable Helen
P. Voltz, Wisconsin State Supreme Court.
Presentation of Edward Ben Elson Distinguished
Service Award.

7:30 p.m.: Meet and greet.

8:00 p.m.: Dinner is served.

MENU
APPETIZERS

Char-grilled Arapaho County Asparagus marinated in Balsamic Vinegar and Olive Oil wrapped in Polenta, Smoked Junger River Coho Salmon, Baked Hummingbird Livers drizzled with Cider, Grilled Mushrooms with Wasabi.

SALAD

Door County Arugula tossed with Heritage Tomatoes, Yak Cheese, and Fair Trade Sunflower Seeds.

MAIN COURSE

Free-Range Clay-baked Whooping Crane, Hearts of Spanish Bayonet, Rice Pilaf.

DESSERT

Faculty-picked Fresh Mulberries in Crème Fraîche.

VEGAN MENU
APPETIZERS

Brandied Richland County Parsnips in an Apricot Reduction Sauce, Bitterroot, Cream of Rutabaga

SALAD

Swiss Chard, Bay Turnips, Tofu Cheese.

MAIN COURSE

Saffron Succotash in Aspic, Grilled Portabella Mushrooms marinated in cruelty-free Amontillado. Curried Kumquats in Raspberry Tofu.

9:00 p.m.: Dancing to the John Davis Blues Band.

CHAPTER

78

THE DISTINGUISHED JURIST

UNDERGRADS IN BADGER CRIMSON AND white greeted visitors beneath Monona Terrace on John Nolen Drive, holding doors and zipping cars to the Doty Street ramp, where the university had reserved two levels. Visitors took the elevator up to the August Derleth Room overlooking the bright blue Monona on the top level.

That's not how Josh arrived. He parked his car in Fleiss's lot and got out feeling awkward in his newly purchased black tux. He'd only worn a suit three times in his life—all for funerals and now this. Fleiss had fixed him up with Nedrebo's, who took the measurements and rented him the monkey outfit. Josh had a hard time wrapping his head around the fact that they rented the same suit out time after time, altering the fit for each new customer. And yet the tux looked brand new.

Women smiled at him as he walked up Wilson in the early-evening heat. He caught a vision of himself in a storefront and was startled, like a cat that sees its reflection in a mirror. He looked like an upscale thug. The opposite of slumming.

A steady stream of swells headed for the terrace, people who'd purchased tickets or who didn't want to pay for the valet parking. Josh joined the line at the door, showing his invitation and driver's license. Two Madison police officers stood nearby looking around.

Kofsky had no problem adding Josh and Billings to the guest list. Josh entered the cool building, went down the stone steps across the roomy vestibule to the August Derleth Room, their largest, overlooking Lake Monona. At least a hundred people were already inside, clustered into groups and standing in line at the bar. Josh stood in line, got a Capital lager draft and pushed a buck into the tip glass. He withdrew to the wall, willed himself invisible and watched. Wolfe and Fine entered together, Wolfe with Nedra on his arm. Wolfe wore a blue tuxedo, a white-and-blue shirt and a bolo tie with an enormous amethyst. Ever the rebel outlaw. Nedra wore an off-the-shoulder knit gown that did her no favors.

Glad-handers and sycophants buzzed them as a string quartet in one corner played Mozart. Shortly, the conversation stilled at the sound of a spoon striking a glass. A diminutive man with a balding pate and faux tortoiseshell-rimmed glasses stood by the windows clinking the glass. There was a squeal of feedback.

"My friends," he said into a portable mike when the room had quieted. "I am Dean Ambrose Watkins of the UW School of Law, and it is my great pleasure to welcome you to this auspicious occasion wherein we will honor one of our own, an alumnus of the class of '74 and one of the most significant and accomplished legal minds of our century. Here with us tonight to present the award is the Honorable Helen P. Voltz, chief justice of the Wisconsin State Supreme Court, a strong voice for feminism, climate justice, women's rights and the right to health."

Laughter and applause. Fine good-naturedly joined in.

The Hon. Voltz was a tiny bird-like woman in an ecru gown with an enormous collar. Watkins handed her the microphone.

"I have known Murray Fine since we were both grad students at Harvard under the famous Ken Adelman, who as you know went on to serve the Bush Administration as Solicitor General. Murray was a prankster. I remember when we both worked in the cafeteria, Murray would greet students by whispering out of the side of his mouth, 'Don't eat the chili.' They always wondered why no one liked the chili!"

Laughter and applause.

"Also, during winter, whenever he came across a car with a Nixon or NRA bumper sticker, he would scoop up frozen dog shit and deposit it in the back seat."

Whoops, applause and laughter.

Josh looked at the Hon. Fine, who at least had the decency to blush.

"It is with great pride and honor," Voltz continued, "that I present to Judge Murray K. Fine the Edward Ben Elson Distinguished Jurist Award! Come up here, Murray."

Amid enthusiastic applause a grinning Fine stood next to Voltz and accepted an oak plaque with the late Edward Ben Elson shown in bronze.

"My friends, from the bottom of my heart I thank you," the distinguished jurist said. "I knew Eddie Elson. Eddie was a friend of mine. Eddie always used to say, 'Fight the good fight, Murray! *Illegitimi non carborundum!* Don't let the bastards grind you down.' He was a tireless defender of the weak and disenfranchised, and whenever he saw some redneck bullying a hippie, Eddie would run up and smack that sucker in the face so hard he didn't know what hit him.

"I've tried to be like Eddie. As an assistant district attorney in San Francisco, I had the opportunity to steer law enforcement after the real criminals: corporate polluters, exclusionary trade and social organizations, and extremist religious leaders who abused their powers by targeting the weakest and most vulnerable among us. I have pledged my judicial career toward social justice, climate justice and gender justice, so it is with great pleasure that I accept this award from this great university that nurtured and schooled me.

"Go Badgers!"

An aide took the plaque from Fine, who went among the people to wild applause and backslapping. He was the center of quite a scrum for a minute until Ambrose and Voltz rushed forward as his Praetorian Guard, creating a perimeter that supplicants could enter only one by one.

Only Josh noticed "Carl Billings" heading for the exit.

Josh followed him.

THE PRESTIDIGITATOR

THEY RENDEZVOUSED ON THE TOP DECK overlooking the lake, where others gathered in the warm, still-light summer evening, sipping lattes, taking pictures or poking at their cell phones. The man who had been invited as Carl Billings stood at the rim with his elbows on the rail gazing out at the white sails flitting across Lake Monona.

Josh joined him.

Without looking, "Carl Billings," really Elliott Homolka, the prestidigitator Josh had met at Crazy Jack's, passed Josh the judge's cell phone. Josh stuck it inside his tux without looking at it.

"Thanks, Elliott. I owe you one."

"No prob," Elliott said. "I'm opening for Emperors of Wyoming at the High Noon Saloon next Friday. Come on by if you can."

"I'll do that."

As Josh turned to go, four uniformed Madison police officers entered the building.

Josh walked to his car, inhaling deeply of the early-evening air. He smelled the lake, grilled meat, beer, marijuana. The smell of Madison. The Committee City. An island of madness surrounded by reality. Four lakes, more flakes.

Only when he was in his car with the engine running did Josh remove the phone from his tux and look at it. It was a featureless, smooth black rectangle that reminded him of the slab in 2001: *A Space Odyssey*. He took out his own phone and called Kofsky.

"Got it," he said.

"You want to bring it over? I'm with Sandy."

"I'm downtown. I'll be there in fifteen."

Josh headed west on University, by UW Hospital, by the Unitarian Meeting House, by Shorewood and Performance Motorcycles until he came to the turn-off in Middleton. Josh parked his car in the Rusty Scupper's lot and went up the stairs, around the side of the condo to the lakeside, where Kofsky and Sandy were sitting on her patio over fading Weber coals, each clutching a Cuba Libre.

"Hi," Josh said.

Sandy meeped. Kofsky stood and held out his hand. Josh handed him the featureless rectangle.

"Want a drink?" Kofsky said.

"Sure."

Sandy got to her feet and hugged Josh. "I'll get it. Would you like a burger? We couldn't eat it all."

"I'd love a burger. With ketchup and pickles, please."

"How do you chew?" Kofsky said.

"I chew out of the right side of my mouth."

"How was the reception?" Kofsky said, poking at the phone.

"You could feel the love."

"This shit is encrypted," Kofsky said. "This might take a little while. Would you like me to e-mail you the results? What is it you're looking for?"

"I want all his e-mails."

Kofsky poked at the slab. "That's gonna be a shitload. This phone went operational fourteen months ago."

"That's what I need."

Sandy came out carrying a tray, which she set on a small table next to Josh's chair. Steve Earle played softly from a nearby unit. Josh added condiments and carefully chewed his burger on the right side of the mouth, enduring mild pain from the heavily industrialized left side.

Kofsky put the judge's phone in his jacket pocket. "I'll get on this tomorrow."

"You guys heard the Emperors of Wyoming?" Josh said.

"What's that?" Sandy said.

"It's Butch Vig's new band. You know—Garbage? He produced Nirvana and Foo Fighters?"

Blank stares.

"Well it's country rock," Josh said. "You'll like it. A friend of mine is opening. He's a magician."

"Oh I love magicians!" Sandy said. "Where?"

"High Noon Saloon next Friday. I'm going."

Sandy put her hand on Kofsky's. "Let's go!"

"Sure."

Josh's phone rang. It was Pembroke.

"Turn on the TV right now. They just arrested Wolfe."

CHAPTER 80

IT NEVER ENDS

KATY VARNER STOOD IN FRONT OF THE MAIN entrance to Monona Terrace in the horizontal rays of the fading light. Behind her stood pedestrians, tux- and gown-clad attendees, skateboarders and buskers.

"Wolfe's fingerprints have been on file since his arrest for sedition in 1973," she said into her camera. "Police will neither confirm nor deny that his prints were found on the plastic shroud in which local investigator Josh Pratt found the mummified body of UW undergrad Stacy Pembroke, who disappeared in the summer of '72.

"This case just keeps getting more bizarre. Pratt's house was the scene of a wild shoot-out on June 22 when four members of the Insane (beep) sought revenge for being ejected from a roadhouse where Pratt worked as a bouncer. Madison police gunned down all four. Two weeks later,

Pratt's girlfriend Charlotte Newton, who hired Pratt to investigate her brother's death, died at the hands of Edward Martin. Police are still looking for Martin's motive.

"This is Pratt's second girlfriend to die at the hands of a deranged killer. His previous girlfriend Cass Rubio died at the hands of serial killer Eugene Moon in an assault on the Richard Munz household outside Janesville two years ago.

"It is unknown at this time what part, if any, Professor Wolfe played in the death of Stan Newton, Charlotte Newton's brother."

Josh wanted to disappear into a black hole. He was a loner, a quiet man who shunned the spotlight, and now look: *Inside Edition, 20/20, Sixty Minutes* and numerous other crime/reality/news shows had contacted him seeking interviews. He cringed at the thought of these buzzards showing up on his doorstep, further inflaming his neighbors.

He just wanted to be left alone. That's all he'd ever wanted.

Josh stood.

"You hate this, don't you?" Kofsky said from the sofa, where he sat with his arm around Sandy.

"Yeah. Send me that stuff as soon as you can."

"I will."

Josh thanked Sandy for the dinner, let himself out, went down the steps to the Rusty Scupper parking lot, got in his car and booked it. He was home in fifteen minutes. As he let himself into the darkened, silent house he thought it would be kind of cool if he had a dog and realized he'd been subconsciously hoping to inherit Mr. Schermerhorn. And Squishburton, of course.

He scarfed three ibuprofens and flopped on the sofa with his book.

Tyrone and I high-fived and whooped the whole way back to New York. We were both so wired by the raid we drove straight through, taking turns at the wheel and arriving at my crib at nine thirty in the morning. Yolanda heard us and came out of my bedroom wearing my purple silk bathrobe and rubbing her eyes.

"What did you do?" she said.

"We blew that crackerbox to kingdom come!" I crowed. "Man, you should have seen it!"

"Man, it was redneck sausage!" the normally reticent Tyrone sang. "Where the TV?"

I grabbed the remote and turned on my big Sylvania color tube and flipped around until we came to Twelve News, which showed a Barbie doll with big hair at a desk, a still of Baxter's shattered pig box behind it.

"Authorities are still trying to find the source of the explosion that devastated Baxter, South Carolina's, police station yesterday afternoon, killing the chief and two deputies. They have not ruled out a gas leak, although there is some speculation that the explosion may have been an attack by domestic left-wing radicals such as the Weather Underground or Global Resistance."

I went into my den, grabbed a gram, took it out and chopped it up on a mirror on the coffee table. I hoovered a righteous line and offered some to Tyrone.

"No thanks," he said.

Yolanda wasn't so hesitant. I broke out the good rum and poured us each a couple fingers. Again Tyrone passed so I banged his glass. Tyrone gave a little salute, went down the long hall to the guest bedroom and closed the door. Me, I was too wired. I put on the O'Jays and Yolanda and I danced around the apartment singing. Even though I was on the top floor ain't nobody complain because there was nobody home beneath us.

We went into the bedroom and fell on my round waterbed with the purple sheets. When I get hard I can stay hard for hours. "Give it to me, baby," Yolanda purred and I gave it to her. After a while I must have zoned out because the next thing I know someone's banging on the front door and I'm thinking, ho shit, the pigs got a clue. I pulled my .38 from the night table stand, pulled on a pair of jockey shorts and padded down the hall to the front door. I seen that movie where they shoot the dude through the peephole so I stand by the side of the door.

"Who there?"

"It's P! Open up!"

I unlatched the door and let P in. He looked out of breath, red in the face and he was packing.

"Fuck's goin' on, P?" I said.

"It's the Jamaicans! They're bringing in some heavy hitters."

WOLVES AT THE DOOR

JOSH'S DOORBELL RANG SERIALLY. HE GOT UP, put on a pair of jockey shorts and padded down the hall to the front door. Katy Varner stood on the stoop with her cameraman and producer, and behind her at the curb were no less than three news vans.

Josh smiled. "Katy, I admire your perseverance."

Katy never broke character. "Mr. Pratt, what is your re-action to the arrest of Professor Jeffrey Wolfe for the murder of his girlfriend forty years ago?"

"I hope justice is done," Josh said.

A man in an expensive suit with very serious hair stepped to the stoop as his own cameraman jockeyed for position. "Mr. Pratt, Henry Wald from *60 Minutes*. I phoned about doing a profile. Could I have a minute of your time?"

"Boys, I'm not interested in a profile." Josh firmly shut

the door, found his phone and called Fleiss. It went straight to voicemail.

"Steve, there are news organizations camped out on my front line. What do I do?"

He hated it. He'd always been a reticent kid, one who hung at the back of the class hoping the teacher wouldn't call on him. Because of his old man's peripatetic nature, Josh had never gone out for team sports, indeed, hardly spoke throughout his adolescence. Now that he'd grown into a comfortable place in his life, he still shunned attention and desired nothing more than to ride his bike, make a living and get laid once in a while.

Fig had changed the equation. Now he had a gaping hole in his heart he doubted would ever be filled. She'd shown him what a happy relationship was like and in so doing had tilted his expectations. Previously, he'd never believed he'd find anyone who would love him for who he was, someone with whom he could live.

Cass Rubio had had her own demons that threatened to overwhelm her. So he did what he always did when events overwhelmed him. He turned off his phone, got on his bike and rode. He'd parked the bike in the garage, and turned it around before he opened the door, catching the news crews by surprise. They were comparing notes when he came out, thumbed the garage door shut behind him and took off heading west.

A couple made a half-hearted lurch toward their vans but it was too late. He was gone, baby, gone. He rode to Mount Horeb, to the little lake north of town, and parked by the side of the road. He walked around the lake and found a big, flat rock in the sun, lay down with his hand pulled over his eyes and wondered what to do.

By now his neighbors were ready to lynch him. If they succeeded in forming a neighborhood association, the first thing they'd do would be to vote him out. He had no intention of moving. This was the first and last home he'd ever owned. He'd never expected to own a home. He thought he'd die in prison.

Of course if someone offered him a million dollars...

Josh dozed. He dreamed he was chasing Fig on bikes through the Baraboo Hills. It was autumn, and gold flakes rushed at him in a river. Always, the taillight of her Hawk disappearing around the next bend whenever Josh thought he was closing the gap.

He heard laughter. Josh woke, disoriented. He realized where he was. He heard two kids, a boy and a girl, on the cusp of puberty, coming his way. Because he still lay flat against the sun-warmed rock, they didn't see him.

"If my father finds out he's going to kill us both!"

"I guess we'll just have to take that chance. Come on—I know a spot in the forest."

Josh lay flat until they passed. He didn't want to startle them. He checked his phone. He had a million messages. Fleiss had called, so he called Fleiss back.

"If you want to come and hang out at my place for a few days, they'll eventually get bored and go away."

"Thanks, man. I'll be over tonight."

"Whenever. You know where there's a key. Hey, did you hear?"

"Hear what?"

"They arrested Wolfe," Fleiss said. "Murder one."

"Yeah," Josh said. "Can't say I'm surprised."

"And Fine!"

"What about Fine?" Josh said.

"He cut short his visit and flew out of Madison last night."

ALERT THE MEDIA

WHEN JOSH ARRIVED HOME AROUND SIX, THE news vans were gone. Perhaps the neighbors had complained. Leaving his bike in the drive, he went inside and checked his e-mail. Kofsky had sent two files: one was a log of Fine online. The second was all Fine's e-mails. Josh started with sights visited, many of them on darknet. There was a line of asterisks where the domain name normally appeared.

There were the usual political sites. At least once a day Fine had checked in with prepubescentpoon, totswithtits, Asiaminor and rosebuds. Josh forced himself to look at their home pages. They were obscene, evil, untraceable.

Gang domains: Malabrusca—Spanish language, showing a graphic of a stylized revolutionary raising a rifle. Dylterio—looked like Helvetica font script with photographs of crucifixions, one a time-lapse job that showed the body rotting and being torn apart by vultures. Revolución—Spanish with pictures of beheaded Mexican policemen and soldiers.

Azatlan—*Fight the white power structure!* Link to a *Wisconsin State Journal* article noting Stan Newton's accidental death. A blurry photograph of Newton leaving the Brat Haus.

Josh clicked on "about us" and there was a photograph of a dozen Latino gangbangers standing outside Bandito's Bar & Grill, a Madison joint on South Park. Most of those pictured had bandannas over their faces and flashed gang signs.

A familiar page with Cyrillic script and a smiley face with crosses for eyes.

A fierce exultation crawled out of Josh's belly and clawed its way to his skull.

Got you!

The motherfucker ran back to San Fran like a little bitch. Josh didn't know whether to shit or go blind. The possibilities ranged from turning the phone over to the FBI to his cutting out Fine's heart with a Bowie knife. Josh couldn't just hand the Blackphone over to the cops. They'd want to know how he got it.

Fleiss would know.

Josh copied the Judge Fine video to a flash drive and stuck it in his pocket.

He started in on the e-mails but the phone would not let up. He called Fleiss.

"What?" the attorney said. Josh heard bar noise in the background—people talking, the Four Seasons.

"I'm heading over to your place. Can I transfer some files to your home computer?"

"It's not gonna eat up my hard drive, is it?"

"No," Josh said. "It's germane to my investigation."

"What investigation? Presumption of innocence aside, if he killed his girlfriend, what was stopping him from killing Newton?"

"I'm not so sure he's our guy," Josh said. "I'll tell you more when I get to your house."

"Okay. You know where the key is. Do me a favor. Don't transfer any files. Just leave 'em be."

"Okay."

His phone buzzed as soon as he hung up so he turned it off, packed a few things in a gym bag and rode to Fleiss's place on the West Side. Fleiss's '60s-modern home backed up onto a nature preserve and was in one of the quietest neighborhoods in the city. Josh parked on the front patio, a section of fitted stones studded with potted plants, plucked the key from under a pot and let himself in. Fleiss's Labradoodle, Boris, thrust his snout into Josh's crotch. Josh knelt to pet the dog.

"Good boy! Nice doggie!"

Josh went into the living room, tossed his overnighter on the sofa, went into the kitchen and pulled a beer from the fridge. He went out on the patio facing the nature preserve, Boris at his side, and settled into a recliner as the evening's first fireflies tentatively cleared their throats. He heard the sound of a ballgame through the trees—people cheering, dogs barking, the crack of a bat. Funny how sound traveled in the warm Wisconsin air. Mosquitoes drove him indoors.

As Josh stepped into the house, Fleiss's all-purpose woman Marcia Haynes came in through the garage entrance struggling with two bulging grocery bags. Josh rushed forward and took one.

"Thanks," she said. "Steve told me you're hiding out from the press."

"Yes, I hope it's only for a few days."

"Not a prob, Josh. You're always welcome."

Moments later they heard a car door slam, and Fleiss came in through the garage as the door rumbled down.

"Hey!" Fleiss said. "Turn on the news." Without waiting for anyone to respond, Fleiss cruised into the living room, grabbed the remote and turned on the big flat-screen TV over the fireplace. He clicked to a news channel where a talking head with helmet hair sat in front of a stock picture of Judge Fine.

"Fine was with Professor Wolfe when the police arrested him. Minutes later, Judge Fine was seen leaving the party in his honor and apparently went straight to the Dane County airport, where he booked the first available flight to San Francisco. Our West Coast affiliate WSFN met the judge when he de-planed."

The camera showed the judge wearing a beige three-piece suit—something Tom Wolfe might wear—heading toward the exit, pursued by an eager young man.

"Your Honor, why did you cut short your visit to Madison?"

Determined non-response, grim forward progress.

"Your Honor, would you comment on Professor Wolfe's arrest on murder charges?"

A functionary abruptly appeared, throwing hands up in front of the camera.

"We will continue to pursue this story until we get some answers," said helmet hair.

Josh pulled out the flash drive. "Got something I want you to see."

Fleiss stood and held out his hand. "Gimme." He plugged the flash drive into the game station appended to the television and ran the clip. Josh stood with his arms crossed, looking out the rear.

"My God," Marcia said. "Is that Judge Fine?"

The clip lasted twelve minutes and seemed to take forever. Marcia got up halfway through, went into the kitchen, and banged pots together. Fleiss, a hardened criminal defense attorney, watched the whole thing.

"Where'd you get it?" Fleiss said.

"It dropped into my lap. The question is, what do I do with it?"

"It may be inadmissible depending on how it was obtained, but if you just wanted to land Fine in hot water, you could send it to various media outlets and let them worry about it."

Josh nodded. "That's what I thought."

A MOMENT OF CLARITY

ON SATURDAY MORNING KOFSKY BOUNCED the video into orbit and back again several times before it finally arrived at CBS, NBC, ABC, CNN, Fox News, *The New York Times, The Washington Post,* Legal Insurrection, Drudge, *Inside Edition, 20/20, 60 Minutes*, TMZ, Move-On, Media Matters and *The Colbert Report.*

At first there was silence. An hour after the transmission, Kofsky said, "Go home and wait. No one wants to be the first to break this story, but once someone caves it's going to be all over the news. Trust me."

Josh arrived home at one to find his mail neatly piled on his coffee table courtesy of Louise Lowry. The newshounds were gone and his lawn needed mowing. He mowed his lawn, feeling the tug of his knitting ribs with every turn. When he finished he put the lawn mower away, went inside and showered. The doctor told him he could resume running six weeks after the operation. It had been only four and he was champing at the bit.

Josh left his phone in a dresser drawer, sat at his computer and went through the e-mails from Judge Fine's Blackphone. He began six months prior to Stan's death and worked his way forward. Kofsky had managed to pull the whole file before Fine discontinued the account. Most of Fine's e-mail pertained to legal matters, interspersed with friendly chitchat.

Wolfe: "I'll meet you at the airport. Need your advice."

Fine: "Oh?"

Wolfe: "DA may indict me for murder. It's a right-wing witch hunt inspired by this troglodyte governor! Remember Stacy?"

Fine: "Of course I remember Stacy! Whatever happened to her?"

Wolfe: "I don't know. They found a body."

Josh took a break at five and fixed himself a ham sandwich. He checked his phone. There were twelve calls, all from news organizations. He wondered if they paid. By six thirty his eyes were bleary and he needed a break. He cruised over to Whispering Pines and kicked out on the apron. The receptionist recognized him.

"Mr. Pratt. Mr. Beale is in the TV room."

"Thank you, ma'am."

Josh found Beale slumped in his wheelchair at the back of the room behind a dozen other retirees watching Shark Tank.

Beale's eyes were shut. Josh winked at the elderly woman who turned to look, and eased Beale's chair out of the room, down the corridor to the patio exit. At seven, it was still warm and light out. They got all the way to the koi pond before Beale woke.

"You again. Whaddaya want?"

"I want the truth, Mr. Beale."

"Can you get me another hit of windowpane? I might need a couple. Got some folks in here interested."

"Sure, I can do that, if you'll help me."

"Whaddaya want to know?"

Josh sat on the raised flat stone perimeter of the pond and faced Beale. "I found Stacy Pembroke's body stuffed in the trunk of a '68 Cadillac at the Collective's old farm."

There was a jolt of recognition in the old man's face. "No."

"Is it possible Wolfe killed her?"

Beale gazed skyward, a delta of grief emanating from the bridge of his nose. "We were all a little crazy back then. We were all capable of terrible things."

"So you think he might have done it?"

"He was a charismatic kid. We were all a little bit in his drift, even then. And there was a ruthlessness about him reflected in his writing."

"You lied to me about who wrote those books. Wolfe is Curtis Mack, isn't he?"

"He contacted me ten years ago. Some mutual friends told him I was down on my luck, and he offered me help."

"If you kept your mouth shut."

Beale looked away. The old revolutionary had traded his birthright for a nursing home. "He didn't want anyone to know. They would have questioned the books' legitimacy. He got a kick out of the fact he was putting one over on whoever read them, a lotta black people, who thought Curtis Mack was the real deal."

"How'd the car end up in the garage?"

Beale sighed. "Would you get me a cup of water?"

"Sure." Josh rose and went in the building. When he returned, Beale had wheeled himself to the edge of the patio, his eyes on distant trees. Josh handed him the water.

"What about Murray Fine?" Josh said. "Do you remember him?"

"Yeah. He was a little suck-up chasing around after Wolfe like that little mutt in the Warner Bros. cartoon."

"Did you know Wolfe was arrested yesterday?"

Beale shot him a startled look. "Seriously?"

"Yeah."

"Well, fuck." They sat in a companionable silence for a few minutes until Beale reached into his robe pocket and removed a crumpled tissue. He blew his nose. Tears ran down his eyes.

"You got to understand," Beale said. "We were going to save the world."

ROUGH JUSTICE

FED JUDGE KIDDIE SEX SAID THE 32-POINT headline in red ink beneath a flashing red-and-blue alarm icon. There was a link to the video. No story, just that link. While Josh watched, the website refreshed itself. The headline went to black with the sub-heading, PROSECUTORS TO QUESTION FEDERAL JUDGE.

Josh returned to wading through Fine's e-mails. It was past ten when he found it. The sender had no domain name or address.

Curtis: "Got one of those smug, self-entitled white boys heckling me."

Fine: "What's his name?"

Curtis: "Stan Newton. Natch he belongs to Delta Tau exclusive white boys' club. Shame if something happened to him."

Josh phoned Calloway.

"What?"

"What kind of phone was Wolfe carrying when you picked him up?"

"I'll have to get back to you on that."

"Is Azatlan a problem?"

"Yeah, they're a problem."

"Who owns it?"

"Shee-it. You don't know? Esteban Moreira. Listen—I'm in the middle of something."

"Okay thanks, Heinz."

Josh turned off his computer and sat in the dark, trying to map his progress since that night—had it been a mere six weeks?—when Fig entered his life. After a while he got up, went into his bedroom, took off his pants, put on a jockstrap with a steel cup and pulled his pants up. He put on a pair of blue-lensed Oakleys, pulled a watch cap down over his ears and rode to Bandito's on the South Side, a block off Park. By now it was dark. A half dozen choppers were lined up outside the stucco joint as Josh kicked out. Malo blasted through the open door.

Josh entered the dim interior, which smelled of beer and marijuana. The clientele was mostly Latino, with a couple of South Side blacks drinking companionably at the bar. Eyes scraped over Josh and moved on. He ordered a draft from a buxom Mexican bartender and sat at the bar scoping the joint through the mirror. He sat, he sipped, he watched.

There was a pool table at the back he couldn't see from the bar, so he rotated on his stool, half facing a big flat-screen TV hanging from the ceiling, showing a soccer match.

Josh looked at hands. Men and women wore multiple rings. A long, lean playa with tatted arms and neck wearing a black wife-beater lined up his shot beneath the green-shaded light hanging over the table. A brilliant red stone on his left pinkie gleamed.

The dude made his shot, missed, cursed, set down the cue and headed for the bar. The only open spot was between Josh and a line of cholos, and as the playa signaled the bartender Josh got a good look at the ring.

The playa returned to his game. Josh finished his beer, went outside, put on gloves, started his bike, rode around the block and parked in shade on the other side of the street a half block down. While he waited he checked the news orgs. Slate ran with, "Is this federal judge a sexual predator?" CBS: "Feds to investigate federal judge over allegations of child abuse."

Josh got off his bike and stretched. It was a quiet residential street save for Bandito's, lined with two- and three-story apartment blocks. By midnight most of the pedestrians had gone inside and lights winked out. Josh heard Spanish television through open windows. At one the lights went on in Bandito's. Closing time. A half dozen stragglers left, some getting on chops and exploding silence as they thumbed their starters.

Josh watched the playa leave, concerned he might get on a chop. But he didn't. He walked east toward the Dane County Coliseum. Josh followed him from the other side of the street. Someone had shot out the streetlights on a section of Garfield Street that fronted an empty lot overgrown with weeds. Josh padded silently across the street, ran up behind the playa, who at the last minute sensed his presence and half turned. But it was too late.

Josh wrapped his right arm around the man's neck, fitted his hand into the crook of his left elbow, kicked out the man's knee from behind and dragged him struggling into the empty lot. The cholo was strong and thrashed powerfully but couldn't break Josh's grip. Within seconds the cholo passed out from Josh's chokehold. Josh laid him in the weeds fifty feet from the cracked sidewalk and held up the man's left hand. University of Wisconsin Class of '15 and a Breitling watch. Josh took them off, stuck them in his pocket and dipped into the guy's hip pocket.

Felipe Echevarria. Half his tats were gang-related, including MS-13 and Le Eme. Josh smacked him lightly on the cheeks. The guy opened his eyes and lay there with a "what the fuck?" expression. Josh landed on his sternum with his knee and all the air went out. Josh pulled out his pocketknife and held the point against the man's jugular. He leaned in close.

"Where'd you get the ring and watch?" he hissed.

"Took it off a dead white boy," Echevarria spat, spasming to escape. Josh brained him with a rock, got up and kicked him in the ribs as hard as he could, which was pretty damned hard considering he still wore tape from his own broken ribs. Josh flipped Echevarria over, straddled him, got his arms around his neck and squeezed until there was nothing left.

HEAVENLY FATHER

Lud Newton stared at the ring and the watch on a coffee table in his den. He picked the watch up and turned it over in his hands as his eyes welled.

"I'm not going to ask you where you got this."

Josh sat mute.

"I'd like to pay you for your troubles."

"I have been more than sufficiently compensated," Josh said. "Should you see fit to recommend me to others I would appreciate it."

They stood. Gaining control of himself with a visible effort, Lud hugged Josh so hard Josh's ribs hurt. Josh left the house without looking back and rode home.

It was nine thirty Sunday morning. He rolled his bike into the garage and parked it next to the Hawk. He was tired but wired. He'd killed a man in cold blood and it had added weight to his soul. He went into the living room, got down on his knees and folded his hands.

"Heavenly Father, I killed a man. I beg for your forgiveness. All I can say in my defense is that I am but a sinner, a weak vessel for you to put your hopes in, and that I used to be a lot worse. I don't even know if it was the right thing. Time will tell. Anyhow, if you can find it in your heart to forgive me, I'll try to forgive myself."

After a while he got up. He looked at the line of mint-condition Curtis Mack novels on his fireplace mantel, picked up his phone and dialed a Milwaukee exchange.

"What the fuck you want?" said an irritated voice.

"Man, I'm sorry to bother you so early. This is Josh Pratt. You asked to borrow *Tear the Roof Off the Sucker* when I was done."

Jerell's attitude did a one-eighty. "My man, my man! Yes indeed I would like to borrow that book."

"Listen. You still giving away pups?"

"Why, yes I am. Why do you ask?"

A LOOK AT: NOT FADE AWAY
BIKER #3

MIKE BARON DRAWS YOU IN AND DOESN'T LET YOU GO WITH THE THIRD BOOK OF THE INTOXICATING BIKER SERIES.

Reformed motorcycle hoodlum Josh Pratt has had some curious cases, but this is the first time he's been asked to find a missing song. After the late, great Wes Magnum wrote "Marissa,'" his band Cretacious rose from small-town Wisconsin to storm the world's stages.

Marissa Yeager claims Wes wrote the song about her and gave it to her. But she's never been able to prove her claim and now an insurance company is using it as a jingle. Marissa hires Josh to prove she owns the song.

Josh sets out to prove the impossible, embarking on a journey that will lead from the drug-fueled clubs of Hollywood to a tragic encounter with a ninja clan, and finally to a shattering discovery that will set the world of rock on its ass.

"Mike Baron scores big with this story!"

COMING IN AUGUST FROM MIKE BARON AND WOLFPACK PUBLISHING.

ABOUT THE AUTHOR

MIKE BARON IS THE CREATOR OF NEXUS (WITH ARTIST Steve Rude) and Badger two of the longest lasting independent superhero comics. Nexus is about a cosmic avenger 500 years in the future. Badger, about a multiple personality one of whom is a costumed crime fighter. First/Devils Due is publishing all new Badger stories. Baron has won two Eisners and an Inkpot award and written The Punisher, Flash, Deadman and Star Wars among many other titles.

Baron has published ten novels that span a variety of topics. They have satanic rock bands, biker zombies, spontaneous human combustion, ghosts, and overall hard-boiled crimes.

Mike Baron has written for The Boston Phoenix, Boston Globe, Oui, Fusion, Creem, Isthmus, Front Page Mag, and Ellery Queen's Mystery Magazine.

Find more great titles by Mike Baron and Wolfpack Publishing, here: https://wolfpackpublishing.com/mike-baron/

CPSIA information can be obtained
at www.ICGtesting.com
Printed in the USA
LVHW091317070420
652496LV00001B/378